About the Author

Stephen is a theatre director and writer. Mainly directing musicals and pantomimes, he has worked extensively in the UK and the USA. Twenty of his pantomime scripts have been published, and productions have been seen across the country including the West End. Also in Europe, Australia and New Zealand. His involvement with musicals includes collaborating on the writing of four original shows and the directing of over 180 musical productions. "Final Curtain" is Stephen's first novel.

Final Curtain

Stephen Duckham

Final Curtain

Olympia Publishers
London

www.olympiapublishers.com
OLYMPIA PAPERBACK EDITION

A CIP catalogue record for this title is
available from the British Library.

ISBN: 978-1-80074-490-5

This is a work of fiction.
Names, characters, places and incidents originate from the writer's
imagination. Any resemblance to actual persons, living or dead, is
purely coincidental.

First Published in 2022

Olympia Publishers
Tallis House
2 Tallis Street
London
EC4Y 0AB

Printed in Great Britain

Dedication

For Hilary, Hayley and David,
With love

Acknowledgements

Embarking on the writing of a first novel can be a daunting experience. The process has been, at times, frustrating, uplifting and ultimately a rewarding adventure. I am indebted to the good friends and colleagues who have encouraged me to continue and finally complete the project, by reading, correcting and suggesting. They are Dave Crossfield, Graham Parsons, Philip Reynolds and last but by no means least, Ann Renard. An act of fate brought Ann and I together after she published her first book, and her help and advice has been invaluable. Our meeting proved to be a rewarding and happy one.

ACT ONE

SCENE ONE
TUESDAY, DECEMBER 21ST 1999
(MORNING)

The whole scene was filled with an air of mystery and suppressed anticipation. On first viewing it gave the appearance of being rather gloomy, until a faint shaft of blue light illuminated what looked as though it might be the side of a large rock. The rock had a narrow ridge along which a tall, imposing figure of a man moved through the shadows; his right hand stretched out in front of him. In his hand something glinted in what little light there was. Suddenly it flashed out into the semi-darkness and was gone. The figure cautiously moved on a few more paces and then seemed to stumble.

"Aagh! Shit!"

"Now what?"

"Trevor, I can't see a bloody thing. It's far too dark."

From the gaping void stretching out in front of the limping figure, another expletive was being uttered. Then a loud, dictatorial voice, with rather sarcastic undertones, called out, "Gavin, *dearest*, it's supposed to be dark. It's for the maximum effect. Now try it again."

"I can't. I think I've broken my toe."

"God give me strength. Lights!"

A stark white light suddenly lit up the scene, shattering the darkness. Trevor Curtis-Smyth, director of the King's

Theatre, Seahaven, strode manfully down the centre aisle of the theatre's stalls. The 'y' of Smyth was his own affectation, his father's name was Smith, and he had tagged on 'Curtis' which was his mother's maiden name. He was a man in his mid-forties, about medium height with a slight paunch and a slowly receding hairline, which he desperately tried to cover up by combing everything he still had forward.

Carl, one of the dancing boys in the company with razor-sharp wit, was once heard to say, "If he pirouettes it'll look like a beard on the back of his head."

Looking very harassed, with beads of perspiration starting to break out on his already troubled brow, Trevor clung to the orchestra rail and called up to the stage. "And what about your lamp? It's been flashing away like Blackpool illuminations ever since you came on."

"There's something wrong with it. I think a wire has come loose."

"Why didn't you get stage management to have a look at it?"

"I was too busy with the quick costume change you wanted me to make." The actor took a step-down stage to emphasise his point by showing the overlong cloak he was wearing. The move further aggravating his now throbbing toe. "Oww!"

"What is the matter with you?"

"It really hurts," whimpered Gavin. "I don't think I can put any weight on it."

"Oh, for goodness' sake. Is there a stretcher handy? Abanazar wishes to be conveyed aloft to his dressing room like Cleopatra!"

"There's no need to be sarcastic, Trevor. I couldn't see a

bloody thing up there. I stubbed it against that rock piece."

The offending piece of scenery was the entrance to the magic cave. The King's Theatre Company was in the last stages of rehearsal for the annual pantomime, "Aladdin", and Gavin Embry was playing the role of the wicked uncle.

A good-looking man of about twenty-seven with bright blue eyes and a mass of fine auburn hair, Gavin had achieved reasonable success playing a variety of parts on stage and television since leaving drama school six years ago. However, the role of Abanazar in this production, he considered totally unsuitable and was doing it as a favour to his agent — and the fact that there was nothing else on offer.

Gavin had always loved acting, and this continued during his teenage years at Brampton Boarding School for Boys, a large, austere building in the Gothic Revival style. Originally built in the late eighteenth century, it had been added to over the next one hundred and fifty years, so there were also traces of Victorian, Edwardian and even a little Art Deco.

The only post war additions had been partial central heating and a new kitchen. But in the mid nineteen eighties, with the arrival of a new, young, forward-thinking headmaster, things had started to change.

Gavin was also new to the school. At fourteen his parents decided it would be the making of him. They were not sure how to handle his predilection for anything theatrical and his devotion to the musical movies of the 1940s and '50s.

His father, a partner in a firm of chartered accountants, had hoped Gavin would follow in his footsteps and take up a similar profession. When told by his son, "I would really like to be an actor when I've finished school," his face drained and he immediately began to make plans to remove him from the local grammar school and send him to Brampton.

Strings had to be pulled as normally, to secure a place, one's name had to be put down at birth, but Mr Embry was not without influence and after a few phone calls everything was organised.

"No son of mine is going to get mixed up with that poncy crowd of no hopers," he said to his wife, after leaving Gavin in the care of his new Housemaster.

"I do hope he will be all right, Arthur," said Mrs Embry, anxiously, as they drove out of the school gates. "He's never been away from home before."

"It'll be the making of him."

Gavin hated the first few days of his new school, but then fate took a hand. Coming down to breakfast one morning he saw a brightly coloured poster on the school notice board.

There will be a production of the musical 'Oliver!' at the end of term. All those interested in taking part or helping backstage please report to the hall during lunch break.

Gavin couldn't believe his eyes. He never thought for one minute that this mausoleum of a school would ever do a musical. That lunchtime he was first in line and auditioned successfully, securing the part of Sowerberry, the undertaker. Rehearsals during the autumn term went well and Gavin began enjoying his time at the school.

Then, a week before opening night disaster struck. Sean Ryan, a handsome thirteen-year-old playing the part of *Nancy*, tripped on the long Victorian skirt he was wearing and broke his collar bone. An emergency meeting of the cast was held to decide who could replace him at such a late hour. Gavin, who knew the whole show by heart, volunteered if someone could take on his much smaller role. One of the boys in the chorus said he would and Gavin was elevated to leading lady. He knew his parents would be horrified, but as his father was away on a business trip, they wouldn't be coming for him until the last day of term, and by that time the show would be over.

The production was a great hit and played for three nights to packed houses. Gavin was the saviour of the show and got a special mention by the headmaster in his last night speech. As he stepped forward to acknowledge the applause, Gavin spotted in the third row a red face surrounding two steely blue eyes about to burst out of their sockets. Father's business trip had ended a day earlier and he had caught his sons' "performance".

Luckily by the time Gavin had washed and changed, the headmaster had intercepted Mr and Mrs Embry and was singing their son's praises. Embry could say nothing as congratulations were lavished on Gavin. Over the festive holidays the production was never mentioned in the Embry household.

Maurice Casey was almost a year older than Gavin. He stood a good six inches taller and was already showing signs of obesity due to the constant delivery of food parcels sent by his parents.

"They're on a world cruise," he informed Gavin. "They have been for the past two years."

Maurice and Gavin became the best of friends during rehearsals of 'Oliver!' and the next term became even closer.

One-night Gavin heard a strange sound emanating from the bed opposite. He raised his head and peered across the room. A sliver of moonlight through the large window lit up part of Maurice's bed and Gavin could make out the sheets rising and falling in a rhythmic motion. The sounds were now defined as moans and Gavin thought his friend must be in a great deal of stomach pain! Slowly he climbed out of bed and tiptoed across to find out what the matter was. Maurice lay there with the sheets pulled up under his chin and his eyes closed. Suddenly Maurice's eyes opened and he stared up at Gavin.

"Are you all right?" whispered his concerned friend.

"What?"

"Only I thought you might want me to call the nurse."

"She won't do what I want doing," came the reply.

"What do you want doing?" enquired Gavin, innocently.

A smile crept across Maurice's face as he slowly pulled back the bed sheets. Gavin's eyes grew bigger as he looked down on his friend's naked body.

"Hop in. I'll show you."

Gavin, still in shock, lay next to his friend.

"What do I do now?" he asked.

Maurice took his hand and in that moment all of the puzzled thoughts and secret longings Gavin had harboured, suddenly disappeared.

The next day he wrote to his father saying how much he was enjoying his second term and how he would be forever grateful to him for sending him to Brampton.

By now other members of the company had sauntered onto the stage to see what was going on. Laura Parkin, an overdeveloped eighteen-year-old, who had recently left her home in Llanelli and joined the company as works experience in wardrobe, moved quickly to Gavin's side.

"I'll have a look at it for you, Gavin," she said in a soft Welsh accent. "I did first aid in the Brownies." And before he could reply she had yanked off his boot and was removing his sock.

"Be careful!" said Gavin, trying to balance on one leg whilst clinging to another precarious piece of scenery.

"It's all right", said Laura, inspecting the toe. "You may get a bit of bruising, or the toenail might turn black, but it's not broken. There's no permanent damage." She fluttered her heavily mascaraed eyelashes at him as she clung a little too eagerly to his leg.

"Thank you, Laura, our own Florence Nightingale." hissed Trevor through clenched teeth. "Now if we could get on with the technical rehearsal. I don't have to remind you all that we open in two days' time. At this rate the first night audience will be arriving before we've had the final dress." And with that he turned abruptly and walked up the aisle to his place half way back in the stalls.

"It's all right for him," muttered Gavin, as he pulled on his sock and boot. "Trying to be arty farty with the lighting while we're all in danger of breaking our necks."

"Do you want to come to my dressing room and put some ice on it, darling? I've got a cooler full." The offer was made by Aladdin, alias principal boy Beverly Dufayne.

"Better not. Don't want to get his lordship's temper up any more. Besides, I think the ice could be put to better use in a 'G and T' later."

"Splendid idea," smiled Beverly. "Just tap on my door. It's open house you know."

It was always open house in Beverly's dressing room. The Christmas pantomime was one of her favourite productions and this year, as she had for a number of years, she was yet again donning the tights and tunic to play the eponymous hero.

"Come along people, let's get going." Trevor was

clutching his script, madly turning the pages to find a suitable place to pick up the action. "Take it from your entrance again Gavin and this time for God's sake mind the rock!"

The lights returned to the dim effect before the toe incident and Gavin prepared to enter on the *"rock piece"* again. This time all went well as he avoided the scenic obstacles, but just as he turned to call on Beverly the temperamental lantern in his hand burst into life shining straight into his eyes.

"Follow me, dear nephew—" The speech was never finished as, blinded by the light, he missed his footing and plunged into darkness behind the shaky rostrum, landing with a thud. As the working light came back on for a second time, members of the company were seen huddled on the rock piece looking down into the murky depths.

After a few seconds of total silence *Florence Nightingale* moved down to the front of the stage and, squinting out into the auditorium, pronounced, "Gavin's had a bit of a fall. I think he's unconscious."

A groan was then heard, not from the stricken actor, but from the director who was now slumped over the seats.

***

Seahaven is a coastal town in East Sussex. A mixture of old Victorian, Edwardian and more modern-day styles of buildings, with hotels and guest houses commanding prime positions on the Esplanade. Various other amenities are found dotted along the sea front including cafes, restaurants and gift shops offering everything for a seaside holiday from sticks of rock to blow-up water wings. On the corner of the Promenade stands a large, imposing building, the façade of which contained a banner advertising the forthcoming attraction of the annual pantomime.

The King's Theatre is the only building to house live entertainment in Seahaven. Built in 1910 to commemorate King George the Fifth's succession to the British Throne, it stands on the corner of the Promenade and Northbrook Road. The façade, foyer and auditorium are still part of the original building. The stage and backstage area had been rebuilt after suffering a direct hit from one of Hitler's bombers, shedding its load whilst returning from a raid on London in 1940. Throughout the fifties and sixties, it continued to pull in the crowds with a regular fare of pantomimes, drama, local dancing shows and one-night stands. An annual Summer Show provided entertainment for the hordes of seaside trippers and once a year the Seahaven Amateur Operatic Society proudly presented their musical offering.

During the early seventies the tourist industry took a turn for the worst as more and more people found the delights of Spain and Greece a little more appealing than Seahaven's fish and chip stalls, amusement arcades and rusting fun fair at the end of the pier.

The King's Theatre began to experience more and more "dark" periods until finally the council leased it to a cinema chain. It managed to keep going until a new multiplex opened on the outskirts of the town in the late eighties. Reduced to showing the seedier type of film to an audience of leering, raincoated gentlemen and a few randy schoolboys who managed to pry open the fire exit doors and get a free viewing, it was in danger of closing for good.

Enter Trevor Curtis-Smyth, a second-rate director who

had formed a touring company in the early seventies. His productions mainly consisted of second-rate farces and thrillers mounted on a shoe-string. For some time, he had been on the lookout for a small theatre from where he could start his tours and also provide a base for himself and his mother, the actress Delphina Curtis. Having come into a legacy left by his ninety-six-year-old grandmother, Trevor bought the lease of the King's from the cinema chain for a very reasonable sum.

"I hope you know what you're doing," warned his solicitor as contracts were exchanged.

Luckily the structure and most of the interior was sound, the council and the cinema chain having been forced to bring it up to regulation health and safety standards during their ownership. With a generous lottery grant and a small amount from the Arts Council, the King's Theatre, returned to its former glory, reopening its doors in the mid-nineties. Trevor decided to mount a spectacular first production using local talent. That way he would get maximum coverage in the press and on radio and TV. Also, local talent wouldn't require paying and all the performers would sell plenty of ticket to families and friends thereby ensuring a healthy return at the box office.

As well as the Operatic Society, Seahaven also boasted two dancing schools, a Women's Institute choir and the New Age Drama Club. There was no shortage of willing helpers who wanted to be part of the King's return to *legitimate theatre!* On the first of April Nineteen Ninety-six with Trevor at the helm, sixty-five people of all ages, shapes and sizes presented "Seahaven Remembered". It was an entertainment charting the history of the town starting with an account of a few brave souls who single handily tried to repel the Norman Invasion. Some sceptics thought opening on April 1st a little unwise, but regardless of the standard everyone seemed to enjoy the show and after a week's run Trevor announced from the stage that the King's Theatre was back in business.

***

Efficient was the best way to describe Amelia Fothergill. Accomplished and capable were just as good, but efficient summed her up neatly. As neatly in fact as her appearance. Always immaculate, Amelia prided herself in taking infinite care of how she looked as well as how she lived and worked. At first this could be construed as independent and slightly aloof, but Amelia was neither of those things.

As an only child, her upbringing had been strict under the watchful eye of her parents. With her father, a solicitor, and mother, a teacher, Amelia's early years had been regimented and organised. At school, this initially left her rather shy and retiring. But the sudden premature death of her father propelled her to being a more responsible person, as her mother crumpled under the loss of her husband and began to rely on Amelia more and more.

On completion of her schooling, where she achieved excellent results in her A-level exams, Amelia took a secretarial and business course at a local college. She had been expected to continue on to university, but her mother had never recovered from the loss of her husband, and so Amelia continued help around the home whilst furthering her education.

Although making a number of friends at college, she had a very limited social life. Unable to really relax in groups, she rarely mixed with people and was never seen in the company of a man — or even a woman friend for that matter. It was odd then that her big passion was with the most social of recreational pursuits.

The theatre.

Amelia loved the theatre. From drama to musicals to pantomime, the excitement of sitting in an auditorium waiting for the house-lights to dim never ceased to thrill her.

This was partly due to her grandfather, who had lived and worked in Seahaven. He was employed as Front of House Manager at the King's Theatre.

During school holidays, Amelia and her parents would take a trip from their Midlands town to visit her grandfather for a few days by the sea. On many occasions, Grandfather would often sneak the star-struck youngster in to the back of the stalls to watch a performance. Amelia harboured a secret yearning to be on the stage, but her shy reserved nature had always kept her from taking part in school plays. Amelia was a closeted performer.

"I could see you up there on that stage, little one," her grandfather would say as she applauded enthusiastically at a performance. This made her cheeks turn red with embarrassment in the darkened auditorium at the thought of doing such an extrovert thing.

By the time Amelia began work as a secretary in a large textile firm, her mother had been forced to give up teaching on health grounds. This meant Amelia was the breadwinner, and any further social life was out of the question. Excelling at her job, after a number of years she was promoted to personal secretary and assistant to one of the managers. Proving more than capable in that position, her boss encouraged Amelia to think about applying for his job as he was about to retire and emigrate permanently to his holiday home abroad. The idea appealed to her and she would have followed his suggestion had it not been for a catastrophic change of circumstances.

Returning home from work one evening, Amelia found her mother slumped between the living-room door and a large settee. She had suffered a stroke sometime during the day and was unable to raise the alarm. By the time she was found and the ambulance called, there was little life left in her. She was rushed to hospital with Amelia by her side, but slipped quietly away during the night.

For the next two weeks Amelia was kept busy taking care of all the arrangements. Her extended family consisted of two cousins and an aged aunt, her father's sister, who lived over a hundred miles away. Apart from attending the funeral, their involvement was non-existent. Her boss was kind and told Amelia to take whatever time off she needed.

It was after the funeral when those few who had attended had finally left, that Amelia sat quietly with a cup of tea and let the events of the past weeks wash over her. Then suddenly a thought came into her mind.

For the first time in her life, she was free.

Immediately she chastised herself for allowing such a thought to enter her head. But slowly, as she sat pouring a second cup, she realised that it was true. From as far back as she could remember, her life had been governed by what her parents had wanted or needed her to do. Now she was on her own. She could lead her life as *she* wanted to. Her thirty-eighth birthday was fast approaching and if she didn't break the bonds that had tied her from birth, she never would.

Within minutes Amelia's mind was made up. A new century was approaching, so a complete change was needed.

A fresh start in life, with new doors opening for her.

Once all of her mother's affairs had been dealt with, Amelia announced to her employer and other members of staff at her place of work that she would be leaving in three months' time. She felt it only fair to continue to work until her replacement had been found; a job her boss knew would be a challenge. The substantial family house was put on the market and sold within a couple of weeks.

On her many visits to Seahaven, Amelia had often noticed an attractive house set in a mews, just off the sea front. It was a detached property with a small garden at the front which continued down one side of the house to a manageable patio, lawn and flower beds at the rear.

Whilst searching for available properties in the town, Amelia was delighted to find the house was up for sale. The present owners were moving to a retirement village, so as Amelia was a cash buyer; there was no chain. Her offer was accepted and the purchase went through in a matter of weeks. The next task was to find a job.

A street away from the King's Theatre was a whole new development, part of which was the new council offices. This smart, six-story building had been completed earlier that year and a number of new departments had been created to consolidate all the council business. When she had decided on a life-changing move, Amelia had registered with an agency primarily handling appointments in the secretarial and business sector. She was delighted when a number of positions in the new council offices became available and immediately submitted her CV. With her qualifications, experience and a glowing reference from her previous employer, Amelia soon secured a job as personal secretary to the head of the planning department.

Her move to the seaside town and her new career breathed new life into Amelia, and for the first time in her life she began to enjoy herself and make new friends. She also made frequent visits to the King's Theatre.

SCENE 2
TUESDAY, DECEMBER 21ST 1999
(AFTERNOON)

The dark blue curtain with faded gold trim along the bottom slowly descended, cutting off the transformation scene. Act one of *Aladdin* had finally ground to a close. It had been fraught with difficulties; Gavin's altercation with various pieces of scenery aside. The actor playing the emperor had an impressive headdress for his first entrance which was far too big and kept slipping over one eye every time he spoke.

"It makes him look like Norman Wisdom rather than the Emperor of China," grumbled Trevor as Patti Lynton, the wardrobe mistress, rushed backstage to try and fix it.

There had also been problems in the Twankey laundry scene with the trick washing machine that had completely disintegrated when the character of Wishee Washee was thrown into it. And to cap everything the trap producing the Genie of the lamp stopped half way up making him look like one of Snow White's dwarfs rather than a *Magnificent Being* capable of granting any wish.

Stan, the stage manager, appeared through the centre of the house curtain. "Shall we press on with Act Two, Trevor?"

The harassed director looked at his watch. It was five forty-five and they had been going since ten that morning. "No. Give them an hour break. We'll start again at seven." Stan turned to go. "Oh, by the way, how's Gavin?"

"He'll live," said Stan turning back. "It was only a two-foot rostrum so he didn't fall far. Going to have a nasty bruise though, in a rather delicate place."

"Serves him right, the clumsy queen."

Stan disappeared through the curtain to relate the director's wishes to the rest of the company.

In his dressing room, Gavin stood before the mirror, the bottom of his costume around his ankles and his body twisted so as to get a look at his right buttock.

"I shall be black and blue by morning," he muttered to himself.

"Don't worry, you won't have time to show it to anybody tonight."

"Beverly. I wish you'd knock before barging in to my dressing room," said Gavin, quickly retrieving his costume.

"Oh please, I've seen it all before — and bigger. Anyway, I thought you might be in desperate need of one of these." She held out two large glasses of gin and tonic.

"Am I just," said Gavin sitting gingerly on his chair and taking one of the glasses. "I can't believe I'm doing this crappy production. Terrible script, tacky costumes and a set that is a death trap! I'm going to talk to my agent. Equity has got to do something about all this."

At that moment the loudspeaker above the door crackled and burst into life.

"Everyone, take an hour break. Act two at seven, prompt."

"Oh God, we're going to be here until midnight," said Beverly.

"I hope not. I wanted to get to the Crown before last orders. I feel adventure in the air tonight."

"Darling, the only adventure you're going to get is if the Magic Carpet scene works. That is if you manage to stay on it."

"Bitch!" he called after her as she left his room to replenish her glass. Outside in the corridor various members of the company were milling around, talking and generally wondering if the show would ever go on. Beverly knew better. She smiled to herself as she entered her dressing room. Having been in a number of Trevor Curtis-Smyths' productions over the years, she knew what to expect.

Forty-five going on thirty best described Beverly Dufayne. An elegant woman with a fabulous figure and a mass of perfectly coiffured blonde hair. At least it was blonde this month. It had gone through so many changes that the only clue to the original colour was her school photographs. She was married to Greg Westcott, an entrepreneur in used car sales. He owned two large garages, one on the outskirts of the town, the other next to the railway station and was more than able to keep Beverly in the life style to which she had very quickly become accustomed.

At seventeen, as Beverly Potts, she had won the "Miss Seahaven" beauty contest and, as part of her award, been given the chance to appear in the King's Theatre summer show, "Seahaven Follies". With this first foray she quickly acquired a taste for show business, changed her name to Dufayne (which she had picked up from an American movie magazine) and headed off for the bright lights of London. As she boarded the train at Seahaven station her mother's words were still ringing in her ears.

"No good will come of this, my girl. You don't know what you're getting yourself into."

After arriving at Victoria station, she checked into the cheapest place she could find — the YWCA in Charing Cross, which provided her with a cramped, basic room containing the minimum of furniture. The bathroom and toilet were down the hall and she soon learned that if you were late up in the morning all you got was a cold shower.

Every week she would scour the audition notices in "The Stage" and was soon joining the hordes of hopefuls at the numerous "cattle calls" for the latest musical or provincial tours. After three months and twenty-four rejections later, she was beginning to think that mother was right. Then, as she was leaving her twenty-fifth audition after hearing the now all too familiar phrase, "we'll let you know", one of the shows backers approached her and handed her his card. He was a very unattractive, short and vastly overweight man of about fifty who always seemed to have too much saliva in his mouth when speaking.

"Shorry you weren't shucshessful," he spluttered. "But you might be intereshted in coming to work at my place." Beverly looked at the card.

"The Blue Parrot". Gentleman's Club. Proprietor Percival Peake.

The job was as one of the "hostesses" who were employed to look after the male customers. She thanked him saying, "I really am waiting for the right part to come along. It is my ambition to be an actress!"

"Ambishun is all right, my dear, but you've still got to pay the rent."

"I'll think about it," she added politely and hurried away before another stream of saliva poured out of his mouth. One week and one more rejection later, she did call him and was

31

offered a job.

The Blue Parrot was a dark, seedy establishment in Soho. For six months her ambition started to become a reality in as much as she had to "act" the interested hostess nightly. She also quickly found out that there was extra money to be earned if you were so inclined.

Finally, disillusioned with the bright lights, she returned home slightly older, slightly wiser and vastly pregnant. Mrs Potts with, "I told you so" written all over her face, packed her off to Aunt Flo, a hospital sister in Brighton who could "take care of everything".

For the next three months, Beverly was confined to her aunt's spare room in a terraced house not far from the hospital. After what seemed a lifetime, she woke early one morning with agonising pains shooting through her body. Her aunt immediately knew it was time to get her to the hospital, where she went through a torturous labour.

Finally, after much cajoling from a sympathetic nurse, Beverly finally gave birth, only to have the infant quickly taken away. In a semi-conscious state, she pleaded with her aunt to let her see the child at least once, but the grave expression on the hospital sister's face said it all. The baby hadn't survived, she was told, and her aunt was sparing her more pain.

After a short convalescence, Beverly returned to Seahaven where, three years later whilst working as a dentist's receptionist, she met Greg Westcott who finally gave her the life she craved.

Greg and Trevor Smith had been at school together in London and always kept in touch. He had even invested in some of Trevor's early touring productions. Beverly was introduced to Trevor at a New Year's Eve party shortly after she and Greg were married. Trevor was short of a soubrette for his forthcoming tour of *"The Desert Song"* and to secure Greg's investment, offered her the part. She continued working in Curtis-Smyth productions on and off for the next few years and was delighted when Trevor took on the lease of the King's Theatre. This meant she could live at home with her husband and do the odd show on her doorstep. Now established as a "celebrity" of Seahaven, often opening fetes and judging baby shows, Beverly Dufayne appears in the odd role whenever Trevor is stuck and always performs principal boy in the pantomime. Very few Curtis-Smyth productions reach the stage without some hiatus, but Beverly knew how to ride every storm with a smile, an encouraging word and a large gin and tonic.

***

Russell Craddick opened the bottom right-hand draw of his desk and lifted out a glass and a half bottle of malt whisky he kept there for special occasions. He poured himself a generous measure and raised the tumbler in his right hand.

"To the future," he said to himself in a toast and crossed to the other side of his office. There, laid out on a small table, was a large ground plan of his vision. A new high-rise luxury holiday apartment block with seafront park and recreation area for Seahaven. Just what the town needed to attract the extra visitors who were so vital to the economy. He stared at the plan and then took another sip of malt.

In his early sixties, with a portly appearance and a shock of white hair, Russell had little time for anyone who couldn't further his ambitions. To say that he had climbed the ladder of success within the council by less than fair means was an understatement.

Since his appointment as head of town planning, he had been looking at numerous ways to revitalise the town centre; and in doing so line his own pockets. And there it was stretching out before him. His dream, his idea and his way of making a killing. Russell was so engrossed in the plans that, at first, he didn't hear the soft tone of his intercom. A second tone brought him out of his reverie and he moved quickly back to his desk.

"Yes?" he snapped abruptly.

"Mr Stone is here and would like a moment of your time if it is convenient," said the voice of Russell Craddick's recently appointed secretary.

"Of course, Miss Fothergill. Send him in, send him in." Russell reached into the bottom desk drawer for a second glass as the heavy oak panelled door to his office opened and Barrie Stone walked in.

"How's tricks, Russell?" grinned Barrie.

"Just in time for a quick celebratory drink, my boy"

"Then it's all gone through? The council has agreed the project?"

"All signed and sealed," said Russell, handing over another generous tumbler of malt. "Just a few minor formalities and the sale of the land will be ready to go through."

"It's a pleasure doing business with you Russell, as always. I'll see to it that the usual *arrangement* will be forthcoming as soon as building starts." And in one gulp he swallowed half the whisky.

Stone was a tall, gaunt looking man of forty-seven. He had inherited his father's building firm when the old man, whilst visiting one of his own building sites, suffered a direct hit from a loose piece of scaffolding. He never regained consciousness and the family business passed to the son and heir.

Many people thought it was divine retribution that Stone senior departed this earth the way he did. Bits had been falling off his buildings for years, so this seemed a fitting way to go.

Russell had met Old Man Stone some years before when a contract for a council estate had run into difficulties and the builder had taken the job over. An expert at cutting corners, he brought the project in under budget much to Russell's great relief. During the ensuing years Russell managed to put a number of other deals the builder's way to the mutual and financial benefit of both parties. After Stone's sudden demise it looked as though Russell's off shore pension fund was going to dry up, until a quick phone call from Barrie assured him that it would be "business as usual"!

"It's going to make us a fortune," beamed Russell. "And that's the only thing standing in our way." Russell crossed to his window and pointed. "That monstrosity! That relic of a bygone age."

"The old theatre?" said Barrie gulping down the remainder of his drink and joining him at the window.

"Yes. Curtis-Smyth, or whatever his fancy name is, is in there now rehearsing the Pantomime. And a right *pantomime* it will be. Talk about tacky."

"So, what's going to happen? We need all that land for the recreation area and road access."

"And have it you shall," said Russell turning to face him

with a broad grin on his face. "The lease runs out at the end of March and the Council has agreed to its demolition. I shall be sending the minimum ninety days' notice informing Mr Curtis-Smyth that it won't be renewed."

"I suppose we could use the old factory grounds." Barrie was pointing in the other direction to a group of ramshackle buildings that at one time were home to a thriving fish paste business. When the fishing industry on that part of the coast went into decline, so did fish paste and so the business collapsed. The deserted factory soon became a haunt for courting couples and teenagers experimenting with banned substances and, in no time, fell into disrepair.

"No," said Russell, shaking his head. "It would cost a lot more to re-route the road that way. Besides I've got future plans for you to add another block on that sight. No, it's got to be that old fleapit. I can hear the bulldozers revving up even now. The theatre is going to be demolished."

***

After a brief musical introduction, the curtain rose on a scene depicting the Emperor's Garden. The chorus ensemble, which consisted of four girls and two boys, executed an opening dance in front of a set that bore a remarkable resemblance to the Seahaven Operatic Society's version of "The Mikado" eight months previous. Trevor had kept the scenery in return for a reduction in rent knowing that it would come in useful for the pantomime — albeit that "Aladdin" is laid in China, not Japan.

"We'll tart it up a bit with some Chinese lanterns," he told Stan. "No one will notice."

After the dance the scene proceeded with very few mishaps, then just as Trevor started to relax a little, disaster struck.

The scene was the flying carpets. It was supposed to be quite a simple effect. A couple of moving platforms on casters with rods attached so as to be operated by stagehands in the wings. Gavin and Claire Stevens — the Princess — were on one and Beverly with *"Mother and Brother"* on the other. It started smoothly enough until the sword fight between Abanazar and Aladdin. When Trevor called out for Gavin to "put some life into it," the frustrated actor turned round with such force to take a swipe at Beverly, causing his carpet to swerve to one side. This in turn pulled the stagehand operating it forward and he crashed into the prop girl, waiting patiently for the scene change.

An assortment of Chinese props flew into the air. The poor girl tried to catch them like a demented juggler as they landed with a tremendous clatter all over the stage. In trying to regain control of the wayward carpet, the stagehand pulled the rod back with such force that it sent Gavin headlong into the path of the second carpet. Luckily, he managed to jump onto Beverly's carpet before it ran him down. Landing on his knees with a thud, he thought the only thing to do was stay there and try to keep the fight going.

The carpet was now being propelled backwards and forwards across the stage while Gavin was madly waving his sword about, missing every thrust and parry that Beverly made. But the weight of four on the flimsily constructed platform was too much and with a loud crack the whole thing broke into two pieces flinging the traumatised actors into a heap. The music that had underscored the whole debacle screeched to a stop, and for a moment there was total silence.

"Well, I don't know what the kiddies are going to make of that scene." The words were uttered in a loud Wagnerian manner from someone in the shadows at the back of the stalls. Those who were able, turned to look at where the voice was coming from.

"Mother, what the bloody hell are you doing here?" said Trevor, his face already drained of any colour.

"I've come to see if my little boy wants any help. And not before time by the looks of things."

Delphina Curtis was an actress who had learned her trade with the likes of post war impresarios and playwrights such as Terence Rattigan and Noel Coward. Just after her eighteenth birthday in 1949, she met and married assistant stage manager Frank Smith whilst appearing in a tour of *"Hay Fever"*. Everything was fine for a couple of years until Delphina announced that Smith junior was on his way. Fatherhood was the last thing Frank wanted. Before the arrival of his son, Frank had found comfort in the arms of a chorus girl and the marriage was over before the boy's first birthday.

Delphina continued acting all over the country with young Trevor in tow. He grew up with the smell of greasepaint and the roar of the stage manager telling him to, "Move it son, we've got a scene change coming up," as he stood in the wings watching his mother in a variety of ingenue roles. In 1967 Delphina decided to take the plunge and try Broadway. A new musical was announced called *"How Ernest"*, an adaptation of that quintessential British classic *"The Importance of Being Earnest"*. Trevor begged her to take him with her, but New York was no place for a fourteen-year-old boy. So, while mother headed for the Great White Way, junior was deposited

38

with Grandmother Curtis who lived with them in a small house in Hampstead.

"I'll write every week," Delphina promised her son. "And telephone when I can afford to."

Life wasn't as bad as Trevor had first thought it would be. Grandmother Curtis doted on her only grandchild and supplemented his meagre pocket money which enabled him to take fortnightly trips to see a West End matinee.

Delphina's Broadway debut was short lived as, fraught with problems, *"How Ernest"* was withdrawn during previews. She next tried her hand in a featured role Off Broadway, in what was billed as *"a hysterical musical revue"* called *"Like It A Lot"*. Well, the New York critics didn't like it and Delphina was heading for home three weeks later.

Once settled back at the family house in Hampstead, she managed to keep a steady income with various jobs on stage and TV. In 1969, Delphina landed a role in a new play and managed to get Trevor, who was more than ready to leave school, a none-speaking part at the end of the first act. Until that point in his short life, Trevor had just been an enthusiastic "theatre goer". But with the bright stage lights shining in his eyes and the sound of laughter and applause coming across the footlight he knew that theatre was definitely in his blood and before long had made up his mind that it was the only profession for him.

After a few years of bit parts and brief television appearances, Trevor told his mother that what he really wanted to do was direct. Delphina had long held the desire to play *St Joan* in George Bernard Shaw's masterpiece, but no management had been willing to mount a production.

"Why don't we do it ourselves?" he asked his mother. "I'll

direct and we'll get all your old friends to be in it. It'll be a hoot." Delphina was a shrewd businesswoman as well as an ambitious actress. She knew the pitfalls of doing such a revered role but Trevor's idea was too much of a temptation to resist.

After entertaining a few of her "gentlemen friends" and persuading them to back her own production, she went out on a tour of all the major provincial towns and finally came into Haymarket Theatre in London. The critics were sharpening their pencils before the first night curtain rose. Headlines in the next morning's papers became collector's items.

"A production that has to be seen to be believed." blasted The Times.

"Playing with Fire!" the Guardian told its readers.

"The Maid of Orleans ain't so hot!" reported the Daily Mail.

Of course, curiosity got the better of most theatregoers and business was very brisk at the box office, prompting Delphina to thumb her nose at the critics. When the production closed it actually turned in a profit — albeit a mere one hundred and fifty pounds. Nevertheless, the mother and son team decided that they had learned a lot from the mistakes of this production and that it wouldn't be long before they'd be on the road again. And so, the Curtis-Smyth Production Company was born that eventually led him to Seahaven.

"It's about time you got someone in who knows how to build sets," pronounced Delphina as she inched her way along the row to sit next to her harassed son.

"Mother, I've got enough on my plate without you telling me what I already know."

"Why don't you send the cast home and let the stage staff

work on the scenery. They all look worn out and with a good night's rest they'll be much fresher in the morning."

"It's not a bad idea, boss," said Stan, who had looked at the broken platform and come up the aisle to report his findings. "It's only a couple of strengtheners that have given way under the weight. We can have it fixed in no time, ready to go again in the morning."

Trevor lifted his head out of his hands and looked at his stage manager and then at his mother. Delphina was right, of course. She invariably was, but it always stuck in her son's throat to admit it.

"I suppose it's the only thing I can do," he sighed. "All right everybody. Listen up." He got up from his seat and moved down to the orchestra rail. "I'm going to break the company now. We'll start again promptly at ten tomorrow morning. All have a good night's rest." This announcement seemed to perk the cast up and very soon they were vacating the building.

"Come on darling, let's go home and have a night-cap," said Delphina as her son plodded wearily back up the aisle.

"Wait for me at the stage door, will you? I'm going to the office to collect my things."

"Don't worry. It'll be fine."

"I hope you're right."

"Aren't I always?" And with a peck on the cheek, she left him and made her way to the stage where the stagehands had started work repairing the set.

***

"I'm going to call it a day, Miss Fothergill," said Russell, glancing up at the large clock on the wall of his secretary's office. Amelia Fothergill stopped work at her computer keyboard, slipped her silver framed glasses off her nose letting them hang on the chain around her neck and looked at her boss.

"Very good Mr Craddick. I've just got these letters to finish."

Her expression never changed. Russell often thought she couldn't have possessed an emotional bone in her body. She never smiled, she never laughed and, as far as he knew, she never cried. But she did carry out her duties exceptionally well. He couldn't have wished for a more efficient secretary. She had only been with him for eighteen months, but in that time, she had revolutionised his office. After a succession of incompetent school leavers and menopausal middle-aged women, her arrival was like manna from Heaven. She may not have had a sense of humour, but she knew how to run an office.

Russell, pulling on his overcoat and reaching for his gloves, moved towards the outer door.

"Oh, Mr Craddick, you won't forget I have a dentist's appointment first thing tomorrow morning?"

"That's fine, Miss Fothergill. Just leave those letters on my desk and I'll see to them when I come in."

"Thank you, Mr Craddick. Good night."

"Good night, Miss Fothergill." Russell opened the door and made his way out of the building towards his car.

Amelia quickly finished the letters and, placing them in the leather-bound folder, entered Russell's office and crossed to his desk. She placed the folder in the centre and straightened up some pens and paper clips he had left lying around. As she moved back towards the door, she noticed the drawing on the small table.

During her short time in the job, numerous plans, tenders and prospective developments had arrived at the office. Usually, she took scant notice of them, but this one made her stop and take a closer look. There, clearly marked, was Northbrook Road. It ran from in front of the council offices down towards the sea front, where it joined the Promenade. The new development took up all the land on the right corner, but something was wrong.

Where was the King's Theatre?

She looked closely again at the plan. Her finger traced the various buildings. There was the derelict factory, there was the furniture warehouse and petrol station near the top of the road, but no theatre.

Russell should have been there to witness the look on Amelia's face. A flicker of emotion flared in her cheeks and her colour drained slightly.

"Surely, they're not going to demolish the King's?" she said to herself and looked out of the window into the dark night that had descended. In the distance she could make out the lights of the Promenade and the shape of the theatre. "They can't!"

Her mind started to race. What was going on? She knew that a new development to revitalise that part of the sea front had been in progress for some time, but not that it meant demolishing the King's. Craddick can't pull the theatre down. He just can't. Who wants another apartment block?

That old building was part of the heritage of the town. They can't destroy it. Since her childhood, and more since her move to Seahaven, the King's had come to mean a great deal to Amelia.

She looked back at his large mahogany desk that

contained three drawers — two on the right-hand side and one large one on the left. The top right contained the usual stationery, diary and various unimportant papers, the bottom his bottle of malt. Her hands slowly moved to the left-hand drawer. She closed her grip around the handle and pulled. It was locked. She stood looking at it for a moment and thinking fast. Spare keys. Every door, desk and cabinet in the building had to have a spare key in case of emergency and they were kept in the security office on the ground floor. They had to be signed for and requesting them at this time of night would be highly suspicious. But she had to get into that drawer. She was sure the answers were in there. Quickly she moved across the office and went out into the corridor. It was empty. Everyone had gone home as very few council workers stayed beyond the allotted finishing time. Normally Amelia despised their lack of commitment to the job, but at this moment she was glad of it.

Shutting the outer door and the office door, she returned to her bosses' desk. Her actions over the next few minutes were so out of character. Had she taken leave of her senses? Both hands reached down and lifted her plain grey skirt to above her knees. A second later she lowered herself onto the floor and lay on her back under the desk. It was an old desk and she hoped that there was a gap between the underside of the desktop and the drawer compartment. Her hands moved along the side of the drawer and around to the back. Slowly she inched them up and — yes — there was a gap. Quite a large one in fact.

By now she was straining to reach inside the drawer with her right hand, her left one against the side of the desk for support. Her wrist was beginning to hurt as she scraped it on the back panel. Bit by bit she felt around until her fingers touched what seemed like a file. Using her fingertips, she slowly pulled the file back until she could get a good grasp of it. Perspiring profusely (a thing her calm composure never allowed her to do) she carefully eased it out of the drawer. For a moment she sat staring at it in her lap. Even in the shadow of the desk she could make out the lettering on the front. "New Promenade Apartments". She shifted her position from beneath the desk and stood up shaking her right arm, which was now scratched and throbbing with pain.

As the blood started pumping through her veins again, she laid the file on the desk and slowly opened it. There before her was the whole story. Demolition orders and a draft letter to the theatre informing them that the lease would not be renewed. An agreement to sell the land to Stone for redevelopment in conjunction with a company she'd never heard of called Delancey Holdings.

Amelia just stared at the paperwork. Surely there must be a way to stop this from happening. What could she do? No way could she let on she knew about the plans. That would mean her immediate dismissal. Her mind was racing. What had her grandfather told her? "It's one of the few theatres left that bore *his* original designs." Whose? She was so wrapped up in her thoughts that she almost failed to hear the outer door open. With a startled look she instinctively grabbed the file and dived back under the desk.

The office door opened and Russell Craddick stood there catching his breath. He had driven halfway home before realising he had left his mobile phone on his desk. Striding across to the room he snatched up the article and thrust it into his pocket.

"Bloody thing," he muttered and turned to leave.

It was only then that he noticed the lights were still on. "That's odd," he thought. "Not like Miss Fothergill to leave lights blazing away." He looked back at his desk and noticed the leather folder containing his letters. He walked around the desk and opened the folder.

The figure hiding below drew a large, almost audible breath and held it. If he sits down, Amelia thought to herself, "I'm sunk."

Russell turned a few of the letters over and instinctively took out his pen to sign them. In doing so he caught sight of his watch and realised he was late for dinner, and there was a particularly good film on television that he wanted to see. The morning would be soon enough for the unimportant correspondence. He closed the folder and went to put the pen away, but seeming to have a will of its own it fell from his hand and landed on the floor about four inches away from Amelia's left foot. Russell tutted as he bent down to retrieve it. His hand groped around and just as he was about to lower his head to see where it was Amelia jabbed at it with her foot. It spun around and came to rest by Russell's thumb and forefinger. Grasping it firmly he stood up, placed it back in his pocket and crossed the room thinking again to himself how strange it was that his secretary had left the lights on in both offices.

"Must have rushed off in a hurry for a 'hot date'," he thought to himself, as he flicked off the switch and plunged the office into darkness. Knowing full well there would never be a "hot date" for the frigid Miss Fothergill, he smiled to himself as he switched off her office light. He was still smiling as he closed the outer door, not noticing that her coat was still on the stand in the corner.

Back in the office Amelia was more than frigid. She was

frozen to the spot. Her pristine white blouse now had two large perspiration marks under the arms and rivulets of the same moisture were running down her face. For what seemed like an eternity she sat huddled up in her cell.

Taking a deep breath, she pulled herself together and carefully eased the file back into the drawer. Crawling out from her hiding place, she stood up and was bathed in a beam of moonlight flooding through the window. She looked again at the old building in the distance.

"Nobody's going to pull you down if I can help it," she said out loud to herself and moved back into her own office. Gathering her coat and bag as she pulled the outer door shut, locking it as she left.

Outside in the cold night air she was aware for the first time of the preparation on her face. Wiping the moisture with a tissue from her bag, she got into her Vauxhall Corsa and, still shaking, started the drive home. The thoughts of her discovery continually pounding in her head.

***

"Elaine? It's Amelia. Could I ask a favour of you?"

"Of course, my dear, but I am about to close up for the night."

Elaine Horton was the local librarian and self-proclaimed historian of the East Sussex town. She also ran a literary group attached to the library, and Amelia, always a keen reader, had joined, not only to further her appreciation of literature, but hopefully to make new friends. She and Elaine, who had been recently widowed, had hit it off straight away with their mutual affection for the works of the great playwrights.

The phone call from her friend came through just as Elaine was registering the last borrower's three books.

"Yes, I'm sorry to call you so late", whispered Amelia, automatically observing the library's rules. "But I've only just arrived home myself. I need some information about the King's Theatre."

"The King's?"

"Yes. If you've got time in the morning, could you see what you have on it?"

"No problem," a delighted Elaine replied. She relished the chance to once again delve into the archives, having become something of an authority on the town whilst doing research for *Seahaven Remembered*. "Drop by on your way to the office and I'll show you what I've got."

The next morning Amelia woke bright and early and, after taking her customary shower and breakfast of tea and lightly boiled egg, she made another phone call to her dentist.

"I'm so sorry to cancel at the last minute," she croaked almost inaudibly into the mouthpiece. "But I seem to have got this dreadful throat. I can hardly speak!" To the best of her knowledge, she had never knowingly told a lie before, but she felt this one was justified, which made her sound all the more convincing. "I feel it would be very inconsiderate of me to pass anything on to the dentist," she continued.

"That's very thoughtful of you, Miss Fothergill," said the receptionist, altering her computer records.

"I'll reschedule your check up for the same time next week. Will that be all right?"

"Perfectly."

"Thank you for calling, and I hope you are feeling better soon."

Amelia replaced the receiver, put on her coat and left her house. She drove straight to the library and parked in a thirty-minute free zone.

"I've found this book on the designer, Wilfred Latchman," said the librarian, pulling out a large volume from beneath the counter.

Wilfred Latchman. That was the name of the person my grandfather used to speak of, thought Amelia.

"It's got a picture of the theatre when it was opened in nineteen-ten," continued Elaine, turning the pages and stopping at a sepia print of the King's Theatre looking resplendent.

"It's hardly changed," said Amelia, gazing at the picture.

"The front part is intact, but the rear suffered damage in the war."

"May I borrow this, Elaine?"

"Well, it is only a reference book," the librarian leaned forward across the counter and whispered conspiratorially. "But seeing as it's you."

"Thank you. I'll take great care of it."

"What's this all about?" enquired her friend, taking two P D James thrillers and running them under the scanner for a woman who was taking far too much interest in their conversation.

"I'll explain everything to you later," said Amelia, glaring at the woman who left looking very guilty. "I have to get to the office, but I'm sure I shall be needing your help in the near future."

"You know where to find me," said Elaine, turning to the next borrower. Amelia put the volume in her bag and left for the council building.

Once in the office she put her bag under her desk and switched on the computer. Russell Craddick, who had already been in for an hour, opened his door.

"Everything all right at the dentist?" he enquired.

"I'm afraid I have to go again next week — for a filling." Her second lie that morning!

SCENE THREE
WEDNESDAY, DECEMBER 22ND

The full company was in by 9.25 a.m. and getting into their second act costumes. Stan and his crew had worked well into the night fixing the broken carpet.

"It works like a dream," he told Trevor, the minute he saw the director appear in the wings.

"As long as the 'dream' doesn't turn into a nightmare again like yesterday." Trevor sipped his second coffee of the morning. "Is everyone in?"

"Yes. Gavin was the last to arrive a couple of minutes ago."

"Limping?"

"Not that I noticed. But he was yawning a lot."

"Been out on the razzle last night no doubt," retorted Trevor. "I don't suppose his toe gave him any bother once he'd got a few drinks inside him."

In his dressing room, Gavin was in a very different mood to when he had left the theatre the night before. Smiling to himself as he started to get into costume — his thoughts were not focused on the impending rehearsal, but on what had happened once the cast had been dismissed following the mounting problems of the previous day.

On hearing the company had been given the rest of the evening off, he had quickly removed his make-up, taken a shower in the rather antiquated bathroom next to his dressing room, then headed off to The Crown, a very "friendly" bar he had been told about by an acquaintance of his who had been in Seahaven the previous season.

"You do get a bit of passing trade," his friend had informed him. "The odd lorry driver on their way to Dover, but not many of the locals. Too close to home for comfort."

Gavin had always enjoyed the excitement of exploring new pastures. Whenever he was working away from his home in London, his first task was to find out "where the boys were".

An icy blast of wind greeted him as he left the theatre. Pulling the collar of his coat up around his neck, he took out his car keys.

"Don't stay out too late." Beverly was just manoeuvring her car out of one of the few spaces at the side of the building. "Remember your beauty sleep."

"Who needs it? Besides, I told you I feel adventure in the air tonight."

"Have fun." She laughed, turning the steering wheel and speeding off down Northbrook Road.

Gavin opened his car door, quickly climbed in and turned the ignition. It took four attempts to start the car.

"I must get it serviced," he muttered to himself and pushed the gear lever into first. As he drove along the road, he noticed a few other members of the cast battling against the wind. "I should offer them a lift," he thought to himself. "But they're not going where I'm going." And with that he pushed a CD into the player set in the dashboard. Ethel Merman was belting out a song from one of his favourite musicals — *Gypsy*.

Gavin launched into a duet with her and, at the top of his voice, continued to the end of the number. By the time he had completed all three strippers' verses in *"You Gotta Get a Gimmick"*, he was turning into the car park of The Crown.

His watch showed nine forty-five as he entered the lounge bar. The Crown was an old pub and thankfully had kept the Old-World charm about it. Individual tables were dotted around the room and there were a few stools at the bar. An open fire was roaring away in the grate and gave an immediate feeling of "bonhomie".

"Good evening. G and T, is it?" asked Ricky, the young barman with bleached blonde hair and at least three ear piercings through each lobe.

"You've got a good memory." Gavin smiled, quite pleased at being recognised.

"Never forget a pretty face, dear," giggled Ricky as he held a glass under the optic. "Now let me get this right. You're at the flea pit, aren't you?"

"The what?"

"Sorry, I mean the King's."

"Yes, I'm doing pantomime there."

"I thought I remembered you from last time. You were in here with some friends." Ricky put the glass of gin in front of Gavin and reached for a bottle of tonic.

"Oh yes, a couple of weeks ago." He had found the pub on arriving at Seahaven and gone there with the two dancing boys, Carl and Alex. They had since paired off, so he was free to go back for a second time and not have to be a taxi service at the end of the night.

"All in?" enquired Ricky, holding up the bottle of tonic.

"No. Don't want to kill it." Ricky poured half of the tonic into the glass and picked up a five-pound note Gavin had placed on the bar.

Watching Ricky move away to get the change, Gavin lifted the glass to his lips and took a long slow sip. Glancing around the lounge he eyed up the rest of the clientele. At a table over in the far corner two men were deep in conversation. Another bespectacled man with a bushy red beard sat at a table on his own reading the local evening newspaper and at the end of the bar, perched on a stool, was an older man, also drinking gin and tonic. He wore a beige sweater that looked a size too small and light coloured, slightly flared trousers at least two sizes too small. As his eyes met Gavin's, he raised his glass in a knowing salute. Gavin half smiled back politely and then noticed the man's hair. It was obviously a toupee that had slipped to one side obscuring the top of his ear. Gavin drew a quick breath of surprise and in doing so, gulped a mouthful of gin that made him cough.

"Steady dear," said Ricky, as he returned with the change. Gavin pocketed the coins and turned to look at the other side of the room. "Bit of a slow night tonight," continued Ricky. "The cold weather's keeping them all tucked up at home."

"I didn't think there'd be time to get here, but we finished early. Slight problem with the scenery."

"Oh dear. What's the matter with it?"

"It's a pile of crap," said Gavin, recalling the events of the day.

"Me and my friends have got tickets for Boxing night," said Ricky, enthusiastically. "We always look forward to the pantomime. We love screaming out *'He's behind you'* like a load of schoolgirls. We just send the whole thing up and have a real good laugh."

"At our expense," thought Gavin.

Over the next twenty minutes a few more customers came

in. One of them wore a thick black jacket with leather patches on the shoulders and arms. When he took it off all that remained covering his muscular torso was a short-sleeved T-shirt.

"One of the itinerant lorry drivers," thought Gavin, and wondered how on earth anyone could wear so little in this freezing weather. The lorry driver took scant notice of the other drinkers as he picked up his pint of bitter and started to play on a video machine situated next to the log fire.

Gavin finished his drink and wondered if he should have another or call it a day. The air of adventure that he had hoped for was fast fading when, at that moment, the door opened and in walked a handsome man of about thirty. He moved towards the bar, nodding at the two men in the corner and took out his wallet.

"Well hello stranger," gushed Ricky, as he moved to serve him. Some of the others glanced at the newcomer, including the lorry driver who seemed mildly interested.

"Hello Ricky. A pint of lager please." Ricky started to pull the pint never taking his eyes off the new arrival who, like Gavin, was casting the same cursory glance around the room. He too caught sight of the offending toupee on the man at the end of the bar and turned away smiling to himself.

"Not bad. Not bad at all," thought Gavin, and decided he would stay for another.

"There you are, dear," said Ricky, placing the pint of lager in front of his customer.

Gavin watched as the man picked up the glass and took a long drink. He noticed the long, well-manicured fingers firmly holding the glass. A mass of immaculately cut dark wavy hair perfectly complimented the features of his smooth face.

"This is better than 'not bad', it's got very good possibilities," Gavin told himself. He was staring hard at the man who was now sitting at a table with his back to the bar watching the flames of the fire licking around the thick logs.

"I take it you'll be wanting another one?" Ricky said to Gavin, with a very knowing tone in his voice.

"What?" said Gavin turning to the barman.

"Same again, or does something else take your fancy?" The tone was still there.

"Same again, please," said Gavin, ignoring Ricky's pointed remark.

This was stupid. Normally in his own local pub, if a new face came in, Gavin would be straight over and start chatting. Here, he was looking at the new face and didn't know what to do. He felt a strange sensation begin to creep over him. He desperately wanted to look across the room again, but had lost his nerve. Was it that Ricky had noticed he'd been staring at the man ever since he came in? So what? Wasn't everyone there for the same thing? If there were more people around, he would feel better about going over and talking. Here, with only a handful in the pub, if he made a move and was rejected everyone would be watching. That kind of an audience he didn't want!

Finally, as he picked up his second drink, he turned quickly and looked across in the man's direction. Were his eyes deceiving him? Had this Adonis been looking at him and had now turned away, slightly embarrassed at being caught out? This "cat and mouse" game was something Gavin swore to himself he would never play. If you want something, then go and get it. So why couldn't he?

The man got up from his table and walked over to the two

in the corner and exchanged pleasantries with them.

"Very cute, isn't he?" whispered Ricky, with devilment in his eyes. "Everyone's mad for him, but he's never seen with anyone from around here. Would you like me to introduce you?"

"That won't be necessary," Gavin said sharply.

"Please yourself," said Ricky with a toss of his head, and moved away to take some glasses out of the dishwasher.

"I can do without him doing his *Dolly Levi*, matchmaking act thought Gavin as the man turned to walk back to the bar.

Was that another glance in his direction? Was he looking to see if he was looking at him? Oh, this is stupid. Why didn't he just go over and say "hello"? What harm would it do? These thoughts were racing around in Gavin's head until finally he swallowed the last of his gin and prepared to throw caution to the wind.

At that point the lorry driver glanced up from the video machine and stared at Gavin, then turned his attention to the man. Putting down his glass, he crossed the room and headed for the Gents.

"Interesting." Ricky whispered rather loudly to the man with the toupee.

"Now what do I do," thought Gavin, as he observed Ricky watching him. Should I go and speak before the lorry driver comes back? I can't have another gin or I'll be over the limit.

He was in a state of turmoil and felt that everyone in the pub was reading his mind. Why was he letting such an opportunity slip by? For a full thirty seconds Gavin stared across at the man, then looked at the door of the Gents. The lorry driver returned and crossed to stand next to him at the bar.

"Can I buy you another?" said the driver, nodding towards Gavin's empty glass.

"No, thank you," replied Gavin, rather too quickly.

The lorry driver shrugged and ordered for himself.

"See you again soon." The new face was crossing towards the door as he called to Ricky.

"Do hope so, dear," came the reply. And with that the man opened the door and disappeared into the night.

"Shit!" said Gavin under his breath. "Shit, shit, shit. You idiot. You stupid idiot." His adventure had disintegrated before his eyes. He was still admonishing himself when Ricky leaned across the bar and whispered, "Sure I can't tempt you to something else?"

"No thanks," said Gavin, smiling bravely. "I'd better be off. Early morning call." And he made his way to the door, avoiding any knowing looks from the other customers.

Outside the wind had dropped and a frosty blanket covered the car windscreen. Gavin opened the car door and reached inside for his scraper. The frost wasn't too thick and he quickly cleared the windscreen.

"Damn!" he said out loud as the car refused to start on the first turn. He tried again and again, but still, it wouldn't fire and he could hear the battery slowly starting to die. "Great. The perfect end to a perfect fucking evening." He hit the steering wheel with an angry gesture knowing full well that if the car had been serviced this wouldn't be happening. Furiously pulling the keys out of the ignition, he opened the car door.

"Can I be of any assistance?"

Gavin gasped. Standing there smiling at him was the face with the immaculate wavy hair and smooth features.

"I— I, the battery seems to have died on me."

"I've got some jump leads in my car, but it's too cold a night to be fiddling with engines. Can I offer you a lift and we can come back in the morning and get yours going?"

Gavin's head was swimming around. Was this really happening? Did he hear him right? *"We"* can come back in the morning. What were the implications behind the comment?

"That's very kind," he stammered. "But I couldn't put you to any bother."

"It's no bother I assure you." He smiled a warm smile and added, "I'm Robert Andrews by the way."

"Gavin Embry."

"My place is only a mile from here. The central heating is full on and it will take two minutes to make coffee; unless you prefer something stronger."

Gavin was still staring at him, trying to take it all in as he got into Robert's Audi.

"I was waiting for you to come out," Robert said, as he started to reverse.

"Really?"

"Yes, I was trying to pluck up enough courage to speak to you at the bar, but couldn't find the words. And then that chap in the white T-shirt…"

"Yes. I noticed."

"I don't know what I would have done if your car had started." He flashed another smile at Gavin who was now beginning to make a little more sense of the recent events.

As they drove out of the car park, Gavin looked at his abandoned vehicle and smiled to himself. What a stroke of luck he hadn't had it serviced.

The sudden announcement of "Act Two beginners",

brought Gavin out of his reverie and back to the reality of the day ahead. But throughout the rehearsal, a certain person wouldn't be far from his thoughts.

***

Act two went surprisingly smoothly.

"I told you a good night's rest would pep them up," said Delphina, who had insisted that she attend the last day's rehearsal.

As the production was opening with a school's matinee the next day, dress rehearsal was scheduled for four o'clock that afternoon. The company broke for lunch at one after a lengthy note session from Trevor and Aubrey Clarke, the choreographer, who had missed the trials and tribulations of the last two days because of a head cold.

"I need the dancers back at three," he croaked, still rather sore from the illness. "We need to tidy up the final dance. You looked like geriatric Tiller Girls!"

"Oh good," Gavin whispered to Beverly. "That gives us a couple of hours off."

He scurried off to his dressing room leaving Beverly thinking, what a very different person he was from the accident-prone grouch she had performed with yesterday. Half an hour later, whilst leaving the theatre to enjoy a quick lunch with her husband, she noticed Gavin climbing into a car driven by a handsome man with black wavy hair.

"The old devil," she remarked to her husband. "He must have had quite an adventure last night."

"What do you mean?"

"I'll bet Abanazar's been rubbing more than his lamp."

***

In her rush to keep her appointment at the library, Amelia hadn't had time to prepare her customary lunch box of a rye bread ham sandwich and an apple. She decided to break with tradition and see what the council employees' dining room had to offer.

"I'm off to lunch, Mr Craddick, unless there is anything more you need," she said having just finished taking a letter to the local scout headquarters, refusing them permission to build a new recreation hut at the far end of Seahaven Park.

"No, that's all for this morning."

Her statement came as a surprise to Russell, who always thought she spent the lunch hour at her desk.

"I'm having a working lunch with Jim Hyton from transport. A few things we need to sort out." Amelia noticed he was looking at the plan of the new development.

"I'll see you later this afternoon," she added, closing her shorthand pad.

"Yes, I should be back around three."

In the dining room Amelia decided to have a bowl of French onion soup and a wholemeal roll as well as an apple. After paying for her food, she took her tray to a table in the far corner and sat looking back across the dining room. She was surprised at the number of people devouring platefuls of carbs in the middle of the day. "How can they ever hope to have a balanced diet?" she thought to herself when suddenly a voice came from the next table.

"Hello Amelia. We don't often see you down here." The speaker was Jane Tilbury, secretary to Jim Hyton, her bosses' lunch partner.

"I was in a rush this morning — dental appointment." Another lie. She was getting rather good at it. "No time to prepare my lunch."

"I see our two boys are dining at the Castle Arms. Nice for some."

"Yes."

"I've no idea what they're up to, have you?"

"No, I haven't." Not really a lie, but she had a pretty good idea.

"Oh well, we'll know soon enough I expect." And with that Jane turned back to chat to the other council workers at her table. Amelia quickly finished her soup and returned to the privacy of her office.

She took the library book from her bag and placed it on her desk. Taking a bite out of the apple, she opened the volume and started turning the pages. It was fascinating to read the history of the designer, Wilfred Latchman and of the other theatres he had been responsible for over the late Victorian and Edwardian period. Looking again at the picture of the King's Theatre, she resolved to do everything she could to try and save the building. Finishing lunch early she turned to her computer and quickly typed up the letters from the morning's dictation.

By two o'clock with all of her work for the day completed, Amelia sat thinking about the King's Theatre demolition plans. After quite some time of sitting perfectly still, pondering on the problem, she picked up the telephone and dialled a number for the second time in two days.

"Seahaven library, how may I help you?"

"Elaine, it's Amelia."

"Oh hello. How are you getting on with the book on Latchman?"

"Very interesting, but I need some more information. I don't know whether you can help me."

"I'll do my best. What is it you want to know?"

"Whom does one approach to get a preservation order on a particular building?" said Amelia slowly.

Elaine's curiosity was instantly aroused. "What building?"

Slightly reluctantly, Amelia told her friend a little of her discovery, swearing her to secrecy.

"Come round to my house for dinner tonight," Elaine insisted. "You can tell me everything then and I'll bring all the information you need."

Over a delightful dish of Mediterranean quiche and salad, Amelia related the events of her office espionage activities from the previous evening.

"I don't believe it," said her friend. "It's like something out of James Bond."

"Not an experience I wish to live through again, I assure you," said Amelia, shuddering at the thought of what she had gone through.

"Well, our information department told me you first have to get in touch with English Heritage, but there is a lot of red tape and it can take some time." Elaine produced a piece of paper with a phone number and address and read it out to Amelia.

"Time is what we haven't got. Craddick intends to serve notice on Mr Curtis-Smyth any day now telling him that the lease will not be renewed."

"You mean he doesn't know yet?"

"I'm sure he doesn't. Craddick doesn't want anything to stand in the way of this project, so he's giving the minimum amount of notice. Ninety days."

"But that's appalling. All those people out of a job in the New Year."

"And no more King's Theatre."

"Amelia, if you want to start a campaign to save the theatre, count me in."

"Thank you, Elaine, but I'm not sure where to start."

"Give English Heritage a ring," said Elaine, as she began to clear the dinner table.

***

Except for a few lighting cues and a moment when the band got completely lost in one of the musical numbers, the dress rehearsal went surprisingly well. Aubrey Clarke had re-choreographed some of the final dance and it looked a little better, although, as Delphina pointed out to Trevor, it still had the resemblance of the elephant ballet in "Fantasia"!

Following another note session and the customary "thank you" from the production team, the company finally clambered out of their costumes and removed their make-up around eight o'clock.

"We thought of having a quick one at The Crown," said Carl, popping his head around Gavin's dressing room door.

"Do you want to join us?" added Alex, the other male member of the chorus.

"I think I'll give it a miss if you don't mind." Gavin flopped back in his chair and ran his hand through his hair giving the impression of a very weary soul. "These last few days have been so hectic. I think I need an early night."

"OK, but you never know, 'Mr Right' may be there waiting for you," teased Carl.

"I very much doubt it."

"See you tomorrow," said Alex, closing the door.

"Have fun," shouted Gavin. As he turned to look at his reflection in the mirror, he said reassuringly to himself, "Mr Right won't be at The Crown. He's waiting at a very nice apartment overlooking the Marina."

Trevor's office was situated behind the box office in the foyer. He had not been there all day and the morning mail was still waiting for him. Next to the pile of letters on his desk Mrs Nesbit, the box office manageress, had left an up-to-date account of the takings in advance bookings.

"Not bad at all," he said, showing his mother the figures. "The last week is a bit thin, but that's when the schools go back. Hopefully word of mouth might pull them in."

"In my day," his mother reflected, "we used to play twice a day from just before Christmas right into March. I remember playing Coventry with Arthur Askey. He bounced on to the stage one night and shouted to the audience 'Come on, where's your Christmas spirit?' It was the week before Easter!"

"Yes, but mother, that was before videos and home computer games," moaned Trevor. "Now we're lucky to get a month's run." He picked up the mail and turned to the door. "Come on, I'll look at these when we get home."

Back in the auditorium, Stan was going through a few last-minute adjustments to the scenery.

"Goodnight Gov'nor," he called, bashing a few loose nails with as much vigour as he possessed first thing in the morning.

"Goodnight Stan. Don't stay too late."

"That man's a treasure," said Delphina, completely forgetting that the day before she had commented on his lack of ability to build sets. As they made their way to the stage door, they saw Patti Lynton in the wardrobe attending to an ample brassiere.

"Just adding a bit to the tits, old love." The booming voice belonged to Max Pendleton who was wearing the false boobs as part of his Widow Twankey character. "The bigger the pair, the bigger the laughs," he added as Patti stuffed in another handful of cotton wool.

"You know this means I'll have to let out your finale dress," she said, through a mouthful of pins. Patti had done more alterations to Max's costumes than any other member of the cast.

"And it will look wonderful. Just like all the others." Max leaned in to her with a flattering smile and gave her a pinch.

"You can cut that out," she said, gritting her teeth. "I'm not one of the chorus girls you can use your charms on."

"Who can be bothered with chorus girls when an artiste like yourself is available."

"I am not available, as my six foot four, fifteen stone husband will tell you."

"I'll wait for you in the car," Delphina said to her son. She knew Max of old; and all his familiar dialogue.

"Goodnight, old love," Max called to her, as she disappeared through the stage door. "She's still in good shape you know Trevor, even after all these years."

"Max, I've been meaning to talk to you about the last front cloth scene…"

"Ah the one where I give my famous rendition of 'Dreaming'," interrupted Max.

"Er, yes. That's the one."

"Knocks them in the aisles every time, you know. Did I tell you the time when I sang it at the Royal Variety? Stopped the show it did."

"Yes Max, you did tell me. But do you really think it's right for pantomime?"

Max was mid-way removing his bra. "Of course it's right. All my fans expect me to sing it."

Trevor thought that the odd half dozen pensioners from the *Cosy Nook Retirement Home* would hardly cause a riot if they were deprived of his rather tired rendition.

"But all four verses?" said Trevor, wearily.

"Well, I suppose I could cut it to three."

"How about just a couple of choruses? After all, Willie is waiting to do the song sheet with you."

Willie Waters was playing the part of Wishee Washee and had been secured by Trevor after making a big hit on a children's television show.

"Willie Waters," sneered Max. "What a silly name."

"But the kids love him. Pantomime is for kids, you know," chimed in Patti, pleased to be able to have a dig at Max.

"And while we're on the subject of Mr Waters, would you please ask him not to hit me so hard with that ruddy balloon of his."

"But Max, that's his trade mark," Trevor reminded him.

"And 'Dreaming' is mine, but I'm reduced to two sodding choruses!"

If you listened to all of Maximillian Pendleton's theatrical anecdotes, you could be forgiven for thinking that he had been around since the time of Thespis. The catalogue of performers he had shared the stage, dressing rooms, digs and occasionally a bed with, ran into hundreds. The longevity of his career meant he must have started performing — in every sense of the word — at a very early age.

Most green rooms up and down the country had been the setting for his fanciful recounting of times with many great theatrical personalities. His stories and swaggering charm had a winning way with many a young actress, hopeful of gaining as much experience as possible. If she was pretty, with a good figure and a large bust, her education would be rapid. Max liked big busts.

He started as a singer in the early fifties when he was just eighteen. A lucky break gave him a chart hit with the song "Dreaming" — something he had been trading on ever since. When the age of the crooner gave way to Rock and Roll, he moved, via a couple of undistinguished musicals, into the world of straight theatre.

"Had a wonderful time at Stratford with Johnny and Larry," he would say, and then launch into numerous tales of the two great actors, so well documented that any seasoned performer knew them by heart. No doubt he had been at Stratford and the Old Vic, even the National and Barbican, but his programme biography never actually said in what roles. Eventually his reputation caught up with him and offers of work became rather sparse; which finally led him to work for Trevor.

"Casting him as pantomime Dame will kill him off," Delphina had exclaimed, when Trevor told her what he had done.

"I had no option. No one else was available, and he flatly refused the emperor as it's a none singing role."

"So now we'll have to listen to him bleating out that awful

'Dreaming' every night."

Trevor had directed the scenes with Max so that the other performers did most of the business. When the company first ran the laundry scene containing a slap stick routine, he got so out of breath that Beverly remarked, "We'll be carrying him through every performance."

"To his coffin, with a bit of luck!" retorted the agile TV star, Willie Waters.

Max had insisted on his "hit" song going in somewhere, so finally Trevor relented and let him do it at the end of the show.

"Just as a filler while Willie is changing," he was told.

The scene was never rehearsed until the first run through and by that time Max had worked out with the Musical Director an entire act with a possible encore.

"We'll be here all bloody night," Aubrey Clarke groaned to Trevor. "You've got to cut it."

Trevor knew that he would have a hard time with Max if the entire song was cut, so there in the wardrobe he tried for a compromise.

"You know what you're always telling the youngsters — 'Leave 'em wanting more'."

"All right. But if they start cheering, I insist on another chorus." And with that he flung his bra over his shoulder and trudged off to his dressing room.

***

Marina Towers, a very desirable residence overlooking the bay and of course the Marina, was an address that Trevor would have liked to have been able to call home. Unfortunately, the five-story block of luxury apartments was way out of the price range for a theatrical producer who lurched from one production to another, showing an occasional meagre profit. In the three years since he took over the King's, the accounts had barely managed to keep out of the red; bills usually being paid on the final demand. No, Trevor had to be content with his small, two-bedroom apartment in Castle Hill Mews, another five-story block further up the road almost behind Marina Towers. At least from his lounge window on the fifth floor he could see part of the bay and the apartment did have a small balcony from where he could sit and watch the world go by on lazy summer evenings.

Delphina had arrived from London a few days earlier to spend the Christmas holiday with her only offspring. Having made herself very much at home in the spare room she had taken it upon herself to turn up at rehearsals and tell everyone (Trevor included) what they were doing wrong.

"They're very nice." Delphina was admiring Marina Towers as Trevor pulled up at traffic lights outside the luxury block.

"And a nice price, too," he retorted.

"Your place is all right. Just what's needed for a bachelor pad."

"Yes, plenty big enough for one," he said, pointedly.

"Don't worry. I'm only staying over the holiday. You don't have to put up with me any longer than necessary."

"I didn't mean…"

"I know what you meant. After a couple of weeks down here I'll be champing at the bit to get back to London."

A sharp horn blast from the car behind indicated to Trevor that the lights had turned green. With a slight jump, he crunched the gears into first, turned the corner and drove up to his apartment block. Once inside the apartment, Delphina threw off her voluminous fake fur coat and headed straight for the drinks' cabinet. She poured herself a large whisky and reclined on the sofa. "Are you having one?" she asked.

"In a moment. I must look at this mail." He had moved to a small writing desk left to him by his grandmother and switched on the reading light. Most of the mail was bills and circulars except a buff envelope with a council crest stamped on the front. Trevor picked up a silver handled paper knife and slit open the correspondence. For a full minute he read and reread the letter.

"Is everything all right?" asked his mother.

"I think I'm going to need that drink." Trevor slowly turned to look at her, the letter shaking in his hand.

"What on earth's the matter? You're as white as Banquo's Ghost."

"They're closing us down."

"What?"

"Those bastards at the council are closing us down. They're not renewing the lease."

Delphina put down her whisky and rose from the sofa. "But they can't. You're running a business there. You've got productions pencilled in 'til Easter."

"Ninety days. They've given us until the end of March."

Delphina took the letter from Trevor's still shaking hand. "But this is monstrous. Surely there's something that can be done. They can't just close you down."

"It's always been a short-term lease arrangement," said Trevor, pouring himself an even larger whisky than his mother's. "It says here that the whole area is being redeveloped."

"You must go and see them. Tell them you'll fight them

all the way."

"What with?" bemoaned Trevor, and flopped down on the sofa. "To fight the council, we'd need the very best solicitor, and that costs money. Money, we don't have. Anyway, they have a perfect right to not renew. I was warned that they could invoke a ninety-day closure if they ever wanted to. I just never thought it would happen. Not once we were up and running."

"I'm going to give Bernie Lovelace a call," said Delphina, picking up the phone.

"I don't think the local Equity rep will be able to help. He can't suggest we strike. That would be playing right into their hands."

Delphina slowly replaced the receiver and crossed the room to sit in a chair facing her despondent son. Usually, she would have taken control of any seemingly impossible situation, but this news had even stopped her in her tracks.

"You'll think of something," she said, trying to sound optimistic. "Have a good night's sleep and things will seem clearer in the morning." Trevor looked at her. The last thing he needed to hear was that well-worn cliché.

"Really mother."

"I'm sorry dear, but what else is there to say?"

"Nothing. They've got me by the short and curlies. Their timing couldn't be more perfect. They know I'm opening tomorrow and the Council offices will be closed for Christmas and New Year. I can do nothing for a week or more."

They both sat silently for a few moments, then Delphina stood and picked up both glasses. "Have another drink, you look as though you could—" Her voice trailed away as she decided not to finish another cliché.

SCENE FOUR
THURSDAY, DECEMBER 23RD

The morning sun slowly began to break through the clouds and shine down on the seaside town. The overnight frost sparkled away on the hedgerows and windows, heralding the forthcoming festive season like some giant Christmas card. In a detached house on the secluded and rather select Sycamore Grove estate tucked away behind the cliff top golf course, Beverly lay in a bubble filled bath with her eyes closed.

She had been awakened from an unusually good night's sleep by the touch of her husband's hand on her back. Turning to face him she felt his lips brush her ear lobe and then descend onto her mouth. Responding to his advances they made love quite passionately, almost as though they were indulging in the act for the first time.

"Mm, panto openings must be some sort of an aphrodisiac," Greg said to his wife, as they lay entwined in each other's arms.

"You are going to be late for work," giggled Beverly, as his hands began to caress her body in anticipation of a repeat performance.

"That's all right. I know the boss."

When they finally left the bedroom, Greg took a long shower whilst Beverly busied herself in the kitchen preparing a light breakfast.

"Will everything go all right, do you think?" he asked, taking the top off his boiled egg.

"Who knows? We ironed out most of the problems yesterday, but Trevor skimps on so many things, anything could happen."

"I don't know why you put yourself through all the hassle. You don't need the money. The business is doing better than ever. Why don't you just relax and enjoy life?"

Beverly looked at him. She adored her husband and knew that he would do anything for her, but sitting around being just a housewife was not her idea of enjoying life.

"I'd be bored rotten in a month, you know I would." She poured him a second cup of coffee. "Besides, I could never become one of the Townswomen's Guild or Local Residence set. God, can you just see me baking cakes and entertaining the neighbours to afternoon tea?" She took a bite out of a piece of toast. "Life upon the wicked stage may be fraught with dodgy scenery, temperamental actors and a director who doesn't seem to know one end of a script from another, but there's nothing to beat the thrill of being up there. The excitement — the applause."

"It sounds like some masochistic pleasure to me," Greg said, standing and kissing his wife on her forehead. "Anyway, my darling, have a wonderful opening. Break whatever you need to — if someone doesn't break it first."

"Don't mock," she scolded. "We need all the luck we can get."

After he had left the house, Beverly drew her bath and indulged herself in a long soak. Lying there in the warmth, she went through her lines and began to feel quite confident about her performance. After all, most of the "business" in the show, she and her fellow actors had worked out together. This was the *norm* with a Trevor Curtis-Smyth production. He had never been a strong director, just a very good manager of people — some would say *"con artist"!*

Lost in thoughts of excitement and trepidation about the imminent opening, Beverly slowly reached for the sponge when the phone rang. Putting out a soapy hand she picked up the cordless receiver and pressed the switch.

"Hello darling," a very theatrical voice boomed into her ear. "Just to wish you lots and lots of luck, not that you'll need it — or will you?" The caller laughed inanely. It was Aurelia Dumont, another of Trevor's Troupe from the earlier touring days.

"Hello Aurelia," Beverly responded wearily. She knew that Aurelia would require all the gossip and a blow-by-blow account of everything that had happened during the rehearsal period. "I'm just having a long soak in the bath before heading off to the theatre. We have a school's matinee this afternoon."

"Won't keep you then, darling. Just wanted to let you know Reggie and I are thinking about you."

Aurelia and Reggie Dumont had been an old Variety double act for as long as anyone could remember. When bookings in that type of entertainment began to dry up, they started playing character roles and cameo parts for Trevor. Now retired, because of Reggie's *health problems* — the rather debilitating condition of not being able to remember lines due to excessive imbibing of whisky — they reside in a bijou maisonette just outside Brighton, where they regaled the neighbours with endless theatrical anecdotes.

"How is Reggie?" asked Beverly, immediately regretting the question, as Aurelia launched into a detailed scenario of all his ailments.

"Just take more water with it," Beverly murmured under her breath.

After another ten minutes of probing questions digging for information, Aurelia finally said, "Well I mustn't keep you. I'm sure you have a million things to do."

"Yes," said Beverly, feeling the bath water already starting to cool off.

"We'll be down to see your little show. Sometime after Christmas."

"Pop round afterwards." Another thing Beverly immediately regretted saying.

"Of course, darling. Can't wait to see everyone. Are you still having your usual 'open house' on Christmas morning?"

"Oh yes." Beverly cursed herself for making her third slip up during the conversation.

"We'll see you then. Hugs and kisses, darling." And she was gone.

Quickly getting out of the bath, Beverly dried herself and dressed in a warm trouser suit. The theatre had very little heat at the best of times and the last thing she wanted was to catch a chill. After writing a batch of "Good Luck" cards, indulging herself with a couple of chocolate biscuits and a cup of tea, she finally left for the King's at about mid-day.

***

Trevor's day was not going at all well. For a start he had a disturbed night's sleep, his thoughts constantly returning to the contents of the letter. He got up just after seven o'clock and read it again. How could the council take away his livelihood without any consultation?

Delphina was dead to the world when he looked in on her. Not a care in her head, he thought to himself. That and four or five large whiskies made sure she always had an undisturbed night's sleep.

Over two cups of black coffee, Trevor tried to work out a plan of action. He decided not to say anything to the company, especially as it was the day of the opening. No need upsetting them before the show. He decided to phone Mister Russell Craddick and try to arrange a meeting as soon as possible. If a compromise could be worked out then the fewer people who knew about the situation the better. He didn't want the local rag getting wind of the plans and splashing adverse publicity all over the front pages.

Flicking on the television set he tried to concentrate on the morning news, but thinking his problems were far more world shattering than wars, famine or the state of the economy, gave it up as a bad job and switched off. Finally, with his watch showing nine o'clock, he picked up the phone and dialled.

"Mr. Craddick's office. Amelia Fothergill speaking. How may I help you?"

"Is he available?"

"I'm afraid he won't be in today."

What a surprise, thought Trevor, assuming the Councillor had anticipated his call and made himself scarce. "When can I speak to him?"

"I'm afraid it won't be until after the holidays now."

"Is there no one else I can speak to? It really is imperative that I talk to someone in planning."

"If you'd like to tell me what it is in connection with, I may be able to help."

"To whom am I speaking?"

"Amelia Fothergill, Mr Craddick's personal secretary."

She's probably in on it — more than likely typed the letter, Trevor thought. "I think I'd better speak to Mr Craddick himself," he said. "I'll try again in the New Year."

"Whom shall I say called?" she enquired.

Trevor pondered for a second wondering whether to divulge his name or not. What the Hell.

"Trevor Curtis-Smyth."

Amelia slowly replaced the receiver and removed her glasses. Trevor Curtis-Smyth. Wasn't that the name above all the productions at the King's? Why was he ringing up so urgently? Does he already know about the plans for the King's? It was only late yesterday afternoon that Craddick had informed her he would be leaving early for the holiday. So that was his little game. Inform Curtis-Smyth about his intentions and then not be available for the next ten days. Of all the low down, dirty tricks. Amelia now knew that she must take action, even if it meant her position of employment would be in jeopardy. Her hand was still on the telephone receiver. Slowly she lifted it and dialled the London number her friend had given her the night before.

***

By one o'clock the King's was a hive of activity. The excitement surrounding the opening of a new production was already pervading the air. Max Pendleton was hovering in the doorway of his dressing room wearing his now vastly enlarged false boobs and very little else.

"What about these lovelies?" he asked Carl and Alex as

they made their way to the green room for a quick snack before changing.

"Not really our scene, love," said Carl.

"Why don't you drive over to Portsmouth?" suggested Alex. "I hear the fleet's in."

"Sarcastic buggers," Max called after them as they disappeared down the corridor. "I don't know what the profession's coming to. Never had their sort in my day."

"Oh yes you did, darling. You just never realised." Beverly had opened the door to her room and was laughing at Max's put down. "Remember that tour of *The Shifting Heart*?"

"When I shared a dressing room with Warren Scott."

"Yes. And he always had tea and sandwiches ready before every performance."

"Yes," said Max slowly, wondering what was coming next.

"Well, he and his partner Raymond are living happily in Eastbourne and have been for the last twenty years."

"Good God. I hadn't the slightest idea."

"Don't worry. He never fancied you." Beverly was still laughing as Max move back to his dressing table, wondering whether or not that was a compliment.

Trevor was sitting in his office when Delphina arrived.

"You might have woken me," she snapped. "You know I wanted to be here for the opening. I had to wait ages for a taxi. It is nearly Christmas, after all."

"Sorry mother, but I needed to be on my own."

His mother softened when she saw the worn countenance on his face. "Have you done anything yet?"

"I tried ringing this Craddick chap, but he's away for the

holiday."

"Typical council worker. Never around when you want them. It's an absolute disgrace the way they waste our rates."

"It's not called rates any more. It's council tax."

"It's daylight robbery. Swanning off on holidays when they should be here telling us why they want to close us down." Delphina was now in full flight and Trevor felt that any minute she would launch into her Lady Bracknell act.

"All right mother, there's enough drama around here without you giving us your entire repertoire."

Slightly deflated, Delphina sat down. "Well, what's your plan of action?"

"At the moment I'm only concerned with getting this blasted panto on. I'm not going to say anything to anyone until after the New Year. I don't want the thought of closure to dampen down their spirits and start affecting the production. And that means I don't want you gossiping to *anybody* about this!"

"Darling! How can you say such a thing? You know I'm the soul of discretion."

"You'd better be. You and I are the only ones who know about the council's plans and that's the way I want it to stay for the time being." Trevor fixed his mother with a warning stare. She was just about to retort when there was a knock at the door. Mrs Nesbit popped her head around.

"Will it be all right to open the house? We've had clearance from stage management."

"Yes, of course Mrs Nesbit. I'll be right out," replied Trevor, welcoming the intrusion.

"I'm going to do my 'break a leg' bit backstage," said Delphina, rising from her chair.

As she passed him Trevor whispered in her ear, "Remember what I've told you." She flashed a condescending smile at him and disappeared through the pass door.

Backstage was a zoo. The wheel of a rickshaw used for Max's first entrance had come away from its rather flimsy axle and Stan was hammering away with force to get it back to working order. Ordinarily the noise of the banging would have carried into the auditorium, but it was drowned out by the hordes of youngsters shouting at each other and squabbling over sweets and crisps.

"I hate these school's matinees." Gavin was standing in the wings resplendent in his Abanazar costume. "I shall barely get my first line out before they start screaming their heads off and yelling abuse at me."

"But that's what they are supposed to do," said wardrobe girl Laura Parker, with a giggle. "Aren't you excited Gavin? I am. This is my first show. Oooh, I'm tingling all over." She was holding on to Gavin's arm showing, what he thought, was an unhealthy interest in him.

"Some of the braiding on my turban has come unstitched. You couldn't be a dear and fix it for me, could you?" He took off his headdress and handed it to her.

"Of course, Gavin. Must have you looking your best," she cooed, and dashed off to find her sewing kit.

"Heartbreaker," said Beverly, who had observed the scene of unrequited love. "Do you want me to put her right before it goes any further?"

"There's nothing to put right, thank you very much," came the sharp reply.

"You don't want your new friend getting jealous of a schoolgirl crush," she teased.

"I don't know what you are talking about."

"Oh, come on. Isn't it about time you told your Auntie Beverly what you've been up to?"

"Later," smirked Gavin. "Let's get this fiasco over with first."

"It'll be fine. Those kids are hell bent on having a good time. I just hope they've all been disarmed before taking their seats!"

Gavin laughed. "You know, I don't think this *engagement* will turn out to be so bad after all."

Trevor made his obligatory rounds of the dressing rooms trying to keep a brave face on and wishing everyone to "break a leg". Those who knew him well may have detected a slightly downbeat manner in his call to arms as they prepared to do battle with the hoards sitting out front.

"Are you all right, old love?" enquired Max. "You look a bit peaky. Not sickening for something, are you?"

"Just a few first night nerves."

"Nerves? From an old pro like you," laughed Max, digging Trevor in the ribs. "You've got nothing to worry about. The kids, and the mums and dads'll love us. Especially when I get 'em up on stage at the end for the song sheet."

"Yes," said Trevor, hoping Max had remembered he was only doing two choruses of his "famous" number. "Have a good show Max," he said with a nod, and moved to the pass door ready to make his way to the back of the stalls.

The house was packed. As Trevor glanced around, he noticed Delphina sitting in a stage box looking for all the world as though she were guest of honour at a Royal Command Performance. The majority of the audience was under fourteen and the noise was deafening. Trevor noticed they were all gorging themselves on sweets and chocolate bars, so the confectionery counter must be doing a brisk trade.

Staring at the bold designs of the proscenium arch and the delicate motifs on the auditorium doors, the only thought constantly in Trevor's head was, *"How could they think of closing this building?"* Still lost in thought on what could be a bleak future, a great roar brought him back to the present. The house lights had dimmed and the four-piece band in the pit had struck up the overture.

Backstage, Stan had requested beginners to stand by and the flies ready themselves to raise the house tabs. As Gavin took his place on stage for the first scene, he forced himself to think only of his performance and not let his thoughts wander over the events of the last couple of days — idyllic though they were.

Dramatic chords from the orchestra pit heralded the cue for the house tabs to rise accompanied by a role of thunder over the sound system. The character of Abanazar was revealed and caused such a barrage of "boos" and rather too much abusive language to emanate from the predominantly young audience, that Gavin was brought back to the reality of the moment very quickly.

"I am Abanazar, the most powerful man on earth," he pronounced in his deepest and gruffest voice.

"You look like a right poof to me!" shouted an acne ridden fourteen-year-old from the front row, to the mass approval of his friends in the adjoining seats. But being totally professional and remembering all that he had learned from actors playing villains in previous pantomimes, Gavin continued with his first speech ending with a cue to bring on the Fairy of the Ring. This drew rapturous applause and wolf whistles and momentarily took the attention away from Gavin.

Through the rest of the scene the audience quietened down while the plot began to unfold. As he finished the scene with a swirl of his cloak and walked towards the wings, the abuse started again and a half-eaten apple hit him on the right shoulder causing his voice to rise at least an octave.

"Keep the character butch, darling," said Beverly, who had witnessed the incident from off stage.

"Fucking little bastards. They should all be drowned at birth."

"They're enjoying themselves, old love." Max had also watched the scene as he prepared for his first entrance on the rickety rickshaw. "I'll have 'em under control in no time when I get on."

"It's always the same on the first matinee," added Beverly. "Wait 'til they start calling me a lesbian when I have a love scene with the Princess."

"I don't know whether I can stand another four weeks of this," moaned Gavin, and moved away towards his dressing room.

From the back of the stalls Trevor watched the rest of the act unfold in a catalogue of heart stopping moments. Max had indeed got their attention on his first entrance. Not because of his acting, but because the other wheel on the rickshaw decided to vacate its place on the axle, pitching Max over the side so that he ended in an undignified heap centre stage. When he finally managed to struggle to his feet, his oversized bust was at a very peculiar angle, which prompted another stream of salacious remarks from the front row. Max took a little time to regain his composure and seemed almost relieved when Willie Waters bounced on stage to whoops of delight from his army of fans. Straight away he got their attention and for a time an air of calm descended on the auditorium. This was shattered however when Beverly's duet with Claire Stevens, who was playing the Princess, began. True to form the catcalls and lurid insinuations were hurled at the pair, quite unnerving Miss Stevens.

"Ignore them and keep smiling," Beverly whispered through clenched teeth during a musical interlude. "They'll soon get fed up." She was quite right and at the end of the number an appreciative round of applause broke out.

The rest of the act staggered along with a few hairy moments during some of the scene changes and lighting cues that blacked the stage out at the most inappropriate times. Trevor was beginning to fear the worst as the transformation scene drew nearer, but to his (and the company's) surprise the whole sequence went very smoothly. Gavin negotiated the "rock" without a hitch and the Genie appeared from the trap at precisely the right moment. The curtain fell to cheers and a big round of applause. Trevor managed a feeble smile as he saw Delphina heading towards him across the foyer.

"It's going very well, darling," she said, elbowing a couple of youngsters out of her way.

"We do have another act to get through. And there were a lot of mistakes."

"This crowd won't have noticed." Delphina waved a hand indicating the swarms of children surrounding the confectionery counter. "All they want to do is gorge themselves and have a giggle with their mates. They've not an ounce of appreciation for artistic merit."

Trevor had witnessed very little artistic merit in the production so far, but the more pressing problem of the theatre's future still weighed heavily on his shoulders. Delphina chatted to a few of the adults who had recognised her before treating herself to a coffee and an ice-cream tub and making her way back to the box. The bell rang for the commencement of the second act and Trevor moved back into the stalls taking up his place behind the back row.

The second act started off positively. Even the flying carpets worked as Stan had predicted, but disaster was lurking in the shape of Max and his "famous" song. The kids heckled his oversized bust so much when he arrived on stage that he was forced to cut short his song and the scene was yet again saved by the appearance of Willie Waters. He started the song sheet sequence while Max did a quick change. Complaining bitterly to anyone who was in earshot, he almost missed his next entrance.

Willie made some jokey comment when Max finally arrived back on stage and left him to introduce the six children who were now waiting to help sing the song.

"Widow Twankey wants to know all your names," he said, holding a microphone in front of the first little girl.

"I'm Tiffany."

"And how old are you?"

"Nine," she said, sniffing loudly.

"And are you here with your mummy?" Max enquired.

"No, she's run off with the bastard from the corner shop!" A sympathetic tut went around the auditorium as Tiffany related the family secret. Max quickly moved on to the next child.

Various other pieces of information were extracted from the rest of the children including one boy who didn't know where he lived, didn't know what school he was at and couldn't care less whether Aladdin had got the lamp back safely or not. Arriving at the last child, Max fixed the boy with a hard look and wondered what sordid detail the youngster was about to expose.

"And what's your name, son?"

"I ain't tellin' yer," said the rather dishevelled ten-year-old.

"Oh dear, why not?" sighed Max.

"'Cos I don't wanna." came the reply.

"But you are going to help me sing the song, aren't you?"

"No, I ain't," the boy said, turning his back on Max.

"But that's why you were chosen from all the boys and girls out there to come up and help sing the song."

"I ain't singin' no bleedin' song."

At the back of the auditorium, Trevor was now gripping the back of a seat so hard his fingernails were digging into the fabric.

"Leave it Max, leave it," he muttered under his breath. Something was going to happen. He could feel it. "Just sing the song and get the bloody scene over with."

On stage Max tried one last time to get the boy to respond. "Well," he said with a forced smile. "If you don't want to tell me your name and you don't want to sing the song, what do you want to do?"

The young boy looked straight into Max's eyes. "I wanna fuck the fairy!"

Max felt his knees begin to buckle as the boy's words echoed around the theatre. A great roar erupted and pandemonium began to break out. At the back of the auditorium, Trevor slumped against the back wall.

On stage, the boy was now laughing at the reaction he was

getting and accompanying it with a number of very suggestive hip thrusts and finger gestures. Max staggered towards the wings, and for the third time in the performance Willie Waters saved the situation by entering with bags of sweets for each of the song sheet participants. Finally, as the children left the stage, Trevor saw Tiffany throw up over the boy with acne in the front row. Not able to take any more, the director fled the auditorium.

***

"Doesn't it look lovely, Russell? Just like a Christmas card." Hazel Craddick was gazing out of the car window at the fresh covering of snow lying like a white sheet over the Somerset Hills.

"Very nice," said Russell, sounding much less impressed than his wife. "Not very pleasant to drive in though. All this slush and muck on the road."

"We don't see much snow where we are. It makes a nice change."

"If you say so." Russell much preferred the warm summer days when he could take the odd afternoon off from the office to play a round of golf. Winter had never been his favourite time of year. He detested snow and had done ever since he was at school. For some reason he had always been the target for the other boys' snowballs, never having the guts to fight back.

Hazel was Russell's second wife. His first one had walked out on him after hearing about one too many liaisons with junior office staff. Hazel had also been married before and, after giving birth to a son, been tragically widowed. She and Russell had been introduced by a mutual friend, and finding themselves both in a similar situation, continued seeing each other and eventually married. Lisa was born a year later and Russell went back to bedding any willing female; so far without Hazel finding out.

The Craddicks' had left home early that morning to spend the holidays with their daughter, who lived with her husband Tim and their two children, just outside Shepton Mallet in Somerset. Normally the family would gather at their parents' home in Seahaven, but this year Lisa, who had just given birth to her second child, thought it best for them to act as hosts. This suited Russell who wanted to be as far away as possible from Seahaven, Council business and telephones for the next ten days.

After piling Christmas presents into the boot of the car, they had set out to cover the hundred and twenty or so miles, stopping off at Salisbury for lunch. It was late afternoon and already dark when Russell swung the car into the drive and sounded the horn to announce their arrival.

The modern, two-story house stood in its own grounds and boasted five bedrooms (three of them en-suite) and a split-level lounge with dining room and open plan kitchen. It had been designed by the Craddick's son-in-law, Tim Mordent, a partner in the successful architect's firm of Dudley and Mordent of Bath. Russell had tried to cultivate Tim as a willing participant in one of his shady deals, but realised early on that he was as straight as they come and would never enter into anything that wasn't done "by the book". At a dinner party given by Russell, Tim had been introduced to Lisa and a year later they were married.

"One scheme that seems to have back fired on me," Russell had whispered to Barrie Stone on the day of the wedding. Now he had to watch every word he uttered when talking to Tim about any of the Council projects.

Tim opened the front door and stood waving at the in-laws with his four-year-old son in his arms.

"Grandma," shouted the youngster.

"Hello Jamie. Hello my precious," cooed Hazel, as she got out of the car and hurried towards her grandson. Russell swore quietly to himself as he was left to bring in the luggage and Christmas gifts.

"Let me give you a hand, Russell," Tim offered, as his mother-in-law took charge of his son.

"You'd think we were stopping for six months by the amount she's packed."

"Never been one to go anywhere unprepared, has Hazel," laughed Tim, as he athletically picked up two cases and headed for the house. "Can you manage the rest?"

"Yes." Russell wearily gathered up an armful of packages and followed Tim into the warmth of the house.

Hazel was already in the spacious lounge and holding her new granddaughter.

"She's got your nose, Lisa," said Hazel, in between making baby noises at the bundle in her arms.

"But definitely Tim's eyes," replied Lisa. "Hello Daddy."

Russell had appeared in the doorway after depositing the Christmas presents in a utility cupboard out of the way of prying little fingers. "Hello my dear. How are you feeling?"

"Fine. Having babies seems to agree with me."

"Are you thinking of a third?" enquired her mother, eagerly.

"Hazel." Russell quietly admonished his wife.

"We've got our hands full with these two," said Tim,

joining his wife after putting the cases in the guestroom.

"How's my handsome step-brother?" enquired Lisa. "I'm sorry he couldn't join us this Christmas."

"He has some business meeting next week in London," her mother replied. "So he's staying there with friends over the holiday."

"Christmas won't be the same without your uncle and his corny jokes," laughed Tim, as he playfully tickled his son.

"Left all the kids parcels with us," said Russell. "Thinks we're a delivery service."

"Now Russell." Hazel shot him a disapproving look. She knew her son and his stepfather didn't always see eye to eye, and any chance Russell had to make a sniping remark about her precious offspring, he took.

"Granddad, look!" yelled Jamie, who had rushed up to Russell and was beating him with a brightly coloured balloon almost as big as himself.

"My, what a wonderful balloon. Where did you get it?"

"From the Fairy Godmother!" squealed Jamie, with delight.

"What Fairy Godmother?" asked his grandfather.

"We took him to the pantomime in Bath yesterday afternoon and he rushed up onto the stage at the end of the performance to help sing the community song," beamed Lisa, who was very proud of her son.

"That was his prize," added Tim.

"And sweets, Daddy."

"That's right. A big bag of sweets." Tim lifted Jamie onto his shoulders and his son now started beating Russell about the head.

"Hey, that'll do young man," said Russell, trying to make

light of the moment and retreating to the safety of an armchair.

"Next year we'll have to take him to the pantomime at the King's," said Lisa. "They do still have one, don't they?"

Not for much longer, mused Russell to himself as his daughter handed him a much-needed Scotch.

***

"Bloody little brats!" Max was stomping up and down the Green Room, his ample bosoms bouncing haphazardly in front of him. Gavin was sitting on a long couch on the far side of the room, drinking a cup of tea and thinking to himself how ludicrous Max looked in dame's underwear, full make-up and no wig.

"I thought you would *'have 'em under control in no time',*" he said, repeating Max's off-stage comments.

"And I don't need any of your smart-arsed remarks," fumed Max. "This is all Trevor's fault. He should never let so many of those little bastards in unsupervised."

"Those little bastards help to pay your wages." The words rattled out like bullets from a machine-gun. Everyone in the green room turned to see Trevor standing in the doorway, his face looking like thunder. "The first rule of pantomime is to keep control of the audience, especially the younger ones. All you seemed to be doing up there was making vulgar and suggestive comments about those oversized tits of yours whilst trying to plug an ancient song that failed to sustain more than two weeks in the top ten, fifty years ago!"

Max was momentarily stunned by Trevor's tirade against his performance. His bottom jaw just seemed to hang loose while a number of guttural sounds struggled to get out.

"It was the most shameful exhibition of amateurism that has ever been my misfortune to witness," continued Trevor.

"Act one seemed to go all right," chirped in Beverly, who has just arrived and caught the last part of Trevor's dressing down.

"But act two was a fiasco. In an hour or so we have the dubious pleasure of performing to the second house, and if there isn't a marked improvement you will all be back in first thing tomorrow morning for further rehearsals." A dull mutter went round the room as Trevor turned to go and came face to face with Willie Waters.

"Hello gov'nor," he said, in his cheeky chappie, cockney sort of way.

"Willie, you gave an admirable performance in what was otherwise a lamentable afternoon in the theatre." And with that he walked away to seek the solitude of his office.

Max finally regained his power of speech. "In all my years in the business I've never been so insulted." he stated grandly, trying to cover his obvious embarrassment.

"Oh Max, you must have been," suggested Beverly, with a wry grin on her face that sent other members of the company into fits of giggles. Max turned on his heels and disappeared into his room, banging the door with so much force that the hinges nearly came away from the well-worn frame.

"Old Max is not a 'appy bunny!" said the jovial Willie.

"It's his own fault," said Gavin, crossing to the tea urn and replenishing his cup. "Another old stager grossly overacting."

Claire Stevens had also witnessed the scene from her room and, pulling on a dressing gown to cover her under garments, she joined the others.

"I agree with Gavin," she said. "He's done nothing but

make suggestive comments about my bust ever since we started rehearsals."

"Oh, Max is all right," said Beverly, feeling she ought to defend the old actor whom she had known for a number of years. "He's the same in every company. It doesn't mean anything."

"Well, if he continues sidling up to me in the wings, I shall report him for sexual harassment," said Claire, as Gavin handed her a cup of tea.

"That should be interesting. His boobs are bigger than yours," quipped Carl, and the whole room broke up into laughter. The tension was relieved for a time and everyone agreed that they should all watch their step during the evening performance. No one wanted to be called in for rehearsal on Christmas Eve, especially as they only had a matinee performance.

"What's everyone doing for Christmas?" asked Beverly.

Most of the company were fairly local or lived around London, so they were making quick visits home before returning on Boxing Day for two performances.

"Well in that case, how about New Year's Eve at my place?"

"What about Greg? Won't he mind?" said Willie.

"He'll do what I tell him," Beverly replied. "Besides, he needs no excuse for a party. By then Max will have come round and I'll get Trevor and Delphina along as well." Everyone thought this a great idea and it did wonders to boost the company morale.

The evening's performance went much better with a very appreciative audience consisting of all ages. Even Max seemed happier as his first entrance was greeted with a round of applause and his "song" went down exceptionally well.

"It'll be all right now," said Delphina, as she and Trevor drove home after the performance. "Just a few teething troubles, that's all this afternoon was."

Trevor remained silent for most of the journey. His mind kept leaping from the question of the future of the theatre to the problems that led him to his outburst backstage. Before leaving the theatre, he had sent a message to the company via Stan that tomorrow's call would be for just the one performance. Thinking to make his peace with Max, he knocked on the Dame's dressing room door, but discovered that he had left the theatre as soon as he had got his makeup off.

"I'll have to catch him tomorrow before the show," he said to Beverly. "I don't want there to be any bad feeling between us. We go back too many years."

She reassured him that Max was much better after the warm audience reaction and told him not to worry about it.

He turned the car onto Marina Drive and once more looked up with envy at Marina Towers. The lights at the corner of his road were on red, and as he slowed to a stop, he noticed a man get out of a parked car in front of the luxury block and walk quickly up to the main door.

"Good God," he exclaimed.

"What's the matter?" said Delphina.

"I'm sure that's Gavin Embry."

"Where?"

"Up there, by the door." By now the man was disappearing inside having been buzzed in.

"Living in Marina Towers? I don't think so. Not on the wage you're paying him." Delphina laughed and turned to notice that the lights had turned green. "Come on, get me home. I need a whisky."

***

"I'm going to spend the day with my sister in Putney." Gavin was answering Robert's question as to what he was doing for Christmas Day. "What about you?"

"I'll be in Windsor with Daniel, an old friend of mine."

"Old friend?"

"Actually, we were an item some years ago."

"Oh." Gavin looked a little crestfallen.

"Don't worry. His partner will be there to make sure we don't get up to anything," said Robert quickly.

"Oh, I didn't mean…" Gavin blushed ashamedly.

"Only known me two days and already getting jealous."

"No, that's not what…"

Robert burst out laughing. "I'm only kidding." Then he added tenderly, "It's very flattering to have someone care so much."

"These last two days have meant such a lot to me. Not least keeping me sane during that debacle at the theatre."

"I hope when the run ends it won't mean that we end too."

Gavin just sat there staring at his newfound companion. The events of the past two days were still a jumble in his head. To think that Seahaven, this God forsaken hole, was where he had found someone he could possibly get serious over. But he knew so little about Robert. Had he always lived in the town? Where was the rest of his family? Was he being serious over their relationship, or was it another fling while the show was in town? So many questions, and Gavin was afraid to ask them in case he shattered this idyllic feeling that had overtaken him at a period when his personal life was at an all-time low.

Gavin had taken the pantomime job when a projected TV series that he had been offered was put on hold because the "star" had been hospitalised with a hiatus hernia and would be out of action for six months. It was late in the year and all the other Christmas productions were fully cast. Seahaven was not a number one date and Gavin had urged his agent to try and find something else, but to no avail. It was Abanazar or nothing. At least being on the South coast he wasn't too far from London; and Brighton was only fifteen miles away. Near enough to make a quick dash in search of "adventure" in what little time he had off. Little did he think that "adventure" would be a stone's throw from where he was lodging.

With all these thoughts whirling around in his mind, Gavin was suddenly brought back to the moment by Robert calling his name.

"Gavin."

"Sorry, I was miles away."

"What were you thinking about?"

"Nothing. No, that's not true," Gavin admitted. "I know we only met each other a few days, but there's so much I want to know about you. We've not talked much, have we?"

"Other things took preference," said Robert, with a broad grin on his face.

"Oh, you mean the pantomime," said Gavin, feigning innocence.

"You know what I mean." Robert swung his legs over the arm of the couch and lowered his head onto Gavin's lap.

"Well, you know I dress up in ridiculous clothes and put makeup on my face for a living, but what do you do?"

"Nothing so glamorous," replied Robert. "I'm an investment broker for the London finance company of Brindley and Hammond. We have an office here, also in Brighton and Chichester. I handle a number of high-profile accounts at all these branches."

"You must handle them pretty well to be able to live here," said Gavin, eyeing the tasteful surroundings of Robert's apartment with a certain amount of envy. "My little four roomed flat in Walthamstow would just about fit into this lounge."

Robert laughed. "That's why I bought down here. London prices are a joke. I was lucky though. I had just moved down here from head office and was looking for somewhere to buy. These apartments were just nearing completion when the last housing slump hit. They couldn't give them away."

"A good investment by a good investor."

"I'll say. They've almost doubled in price and with so many businesses moving out of London, very sought after."

"So, do you think I ought to trust you to invest the very generous salary Mr Trevor Curtis-Smyth is paying me to perform this crap for the next three weeks?"

"You know what they say, 'look after the pennies and the pounds will look after themselves'," quoted Robert.

"Pennies is right," said Gavin. "After paying the rent in London and food and lodgings down here, pennies are about all I have left."

"Well, there is a way of saving a little more during your stay. Why don't you move in here?"

Gavin stared down at the face looking up at him. "I couldn't."

"Why not?"

"Well — we've only just met and…"

"And you've spent most of the last two days here anyway."

"I know, and it's been wonderful but—" His sentence was cut short as Robert's arm reached around his neck and pulled his head down. Their lips met.

"It's settled then. You move in tomorrow."

"My God you are persuasive. Do you have this effect on all your clients?"

"Only the handsome ones."

SCENE FIVE
FRIDAY, DECEMBER 24TH

"The Olde Fob Watch" is a tastefully decorated tearoom on Seahaven's main Promenade. At eleven o'clock on Christmas Eve morning it was heaving with last minute shoppers desperate for liquid refreshment before once more assaulting the various department stores in search of that one elusive present. At a corner table sat two ladies partaking of tea and lightly buttered scones. They were deep in conversation and speaking in hushed tones.

"So, you managed to get through?"

"I did," said Amelia, glancing round to make sure no one was close enough to hear them. "Not that I gleaned much information. I only spoke to an assistant in the office. The main man, is a Mr Hapgood, but he's away in Yorkshire until December 28th."

"Couldn't the assistant tell you anything?" enquired Elaine.

"Only that the name Wilfred Latchman was known to them. The assistant remembered that some years ago, a concert hall in Harrogate, designed by Latchman, had a preservation order placed on it after a developer tried to have it demolished."

"That's a start," said her friend.

"It's so frustrating having to wait over the holiday period.

I'm sure Mr Curtis-Smyth knows about the plans. He phoned the office yesterday morning wanting to speak to Craddick."

"Did you tell him what you knew?"

"Of course not." Amelia's voice rose slightly and she immediately checked it. "I have to get all my facts straight, otherwise I could do a lot of harm to the theatre, not to mention myself."

Elaine finished her second scone and leaned across the table conspiratorially. "My cousin is assistant editor at the Seahaven Courier. When you think the time is right, let me know and I'll get him to write an article."

"Oh, that would be splendid," said Amelia. "We'll need all the help we can get. Another cup?"

"No thanks Amelia, I ought to be making a move. There's still a mountain of things to do before tomorrow."

Both living on their own, Amelia and Elaine had agreed to spend Christmas Day together.

"My brother and his wife are joining us for Boxing Day lunch, and you'd never believe what a fussy eater she is." said Elaine, rolling her eyes. "I'll see you tomorrow."

"Looking forward to it. I'll be there in plenty of time to give you a hand with the preparations," said Amelia, rising from the table.

The two friends picked up their bags and started to make their way across the crowded tearoom, only to be pushed against the wall as two more weary shoppers threw themselves into the vacated chairs.

***

Friday's matinee was the best performance yet.

"I'm so pleased it went well," said Claire Stevens. "I heard that someone from the Seahaven Courier was in to review the production."

"You don't want to take much notice of what that rag says," Beverly quipped sarcastically. "They usually send the gardening correspondent or if we're really lucky the person who compiles 'Births, Marriages and Deaths'." A gale of laughter went up from the rest of the company. They were all assembled in "The Dog and Trumpet" across the road from the stage door, for a Christmas drink before setting off to their various destinations to celebrate the festive season.

"Well, I hope they say something nice and at least mention who's in the show," said Max. "I can't be doing with these parochial reviewers who tell the story and say how clever we are to remember all those lines."

"I'm sure you'll get a mention Max, if only about the size of your boobs," said Willie Waters, which caused another burst of laughter to erupt from the company. Max bristled, but Willie quickly continued. "Only joking me old mate. The audience really loved you this afternoon. That song of yours went down a treat." He turned and rolled his eyes at some other members of the cast, who stifled a giggle.

"I always knew it would. Told the governor so," retorted Max, knocking back his second whisky. "Anyone for any more?"

Most of the company declined and thought about setting off. Goodbyes and compliments of the season were exchanged in a mass of hugs and kisses. Left finishing their drinks were Carl, Alex and Gavin. Beverly joined them.

"One whole day off. Are you boys going up to Town tonight?"

"Too right we are." Carl rubbed his hands together in tremendous anticipation. "There's a big Christmas Eve party on at *Heaven* and an ex of mine who's in *'Phantom of the Opera'* has got tickets."

"We'll be dancing the night away long after Santa has done his rounds." chirped in Alex, with an impromptu choreographic arm movement.

"Where do you get all your energy from?" queried Beverly. "I just fancy a quiet night with a G & T after what we've been through."

"You ought to come with us, you'd love it. All the boys would make such a fuss of you."

"Thank you for the compliment, Carl, but my days of all-night clubbing are a dim and distant memory. I'm an old married woman now."

"Oh, the times I've said that," quipped Alex. "But then I find myself free and single again and I'm back on the town."

"What about you, Gavin? Are you going to London?" Beverly was looking straight at Gavin.

"Yes, to my sisters."

"On your own?" she added enquiringly. She still hadn't managed to find out who his mystery companion was from a couple of nights ago.

"I'm going with a friend," he said, looking down at his drink. Carl and Alex were agog with interest.

"Oh?"

"Come on tell us more," they pleaded.

"This wouldn't be a certain dark-haired gentleman whose car I saw you getting into after dress rehearsal?"

Gavin was still looking down as Beverly continued to probe, but a smile had spread across his face.

"You dark horse." exclaimed Carl.

Alex added in a mock Scarlett O'Hara accent, "I do declare. Got himself a beau and wasn't going to let on."

"I was going to tell you. It's all happened so fast, what with rehearsals and the opening."

"Excuses, excuses," they cried. "Come on, give us the gory details — and make it fast. We've got a train to catch."

Gavin knew they would not let him go until they had heard the whole story, so he related a slightly abridged account of his meeting with Robert. The two boys hung on every word. Beverly just sat smiling. Her thoughts, as Gavin related his tale, were of the numerous affairs she had heard about that start during the run of a show. All too soon the show ended, and so did the relationships. Gavin sounded so elated as he spoke, she hoped his ending would be a happy one.

"It's like something out of Mills and Boon," said Carl, feigning a swoon as Gavin brought them up to date.

"When are we going to meet him?"

"Is he coming to pick you up here?" The questions started to come thick and fast until Beverly drew their attention to the time.

"Shit, we'll miss the London express," yelped Carl.

"To be continued," demanded Alex, wagging a finger at Gavin. "Have a lovely Christmas."

"See you the day after." More hugs and kisses and off into the night they fled. Beverly thought she may illicit more information from Gavin when, right on cue, in walked her husband.

"Ah, there you are," said Greg swaying slightly as he crossed to the table. He had been out with his staff for a Christmas drink and sensibly left his car at the office. "Got a taxi outside if you're ready for home."

"My lord and master calls and I must away." Beverly rose from the table while Gavin and Greg exchanged "hellos" and seasonal pleasantries.

"See you at the New Year's Eve party my wife thinks I know nothing about," said Greg, gathering Beverly in his arms and giving her a big kiss to the amusement of the other customers.

"You will come, won't you — and bring a friend," said Beverly, pointedly.

Outside, Greg's taxi was waiting, and as Beverly climbed in, she noticed another car pull into the car park. She recognised the driver and then saw Gavin heading for the open passenger door.

SCENE SIX
CHRISTMAS DAY

The small tree standing on the corner table in the lounge at Castle Hill Mews looked every bit as festive as the one in Seahaven town centre. The tiny lights twinkled on and off in steady, rhythmic intervals and the decorations, consisting of fake snow and baubles, reflected them in a myriad of colours. Only the fairy, precariously perched on the top, looked the worst for wear.

"We've had her since you were a lad," said Delphina, reaching up to put her straight.

"She looks how I feel." Trevor had just emerged from his bedroom after another disturbed night's sleep.

"Merry Christmas, darling."

"What's merry about it?"

"Now, now. Don't start sounding like Scrooge. Today we are going to forget all about the trials and tribulations of the King's Theatre and enjoy ourselves. I'm doing the cooking, so all you have to do is relax and open your presents." Delphina was very proficient at taking charge of any problems hanging over her family. After all, she had had a good many years' practice. "Here you are," she added, thrusting a large red box at him.

He took his present from her and sat on the couch. "Thank you. Yours is under the tree."

"This is what I love about Christmas. Opening the gifts," she said, tearing the paper off her present. "Oh darling, it's lovely." She held up a simply designed gold bracelet with the tragedy and comedy masks hanging by a small, single loop at one end.

"I know the clasp is dodgy on that one you've had for years, so I thought this would act as a replacement."

"It's wonderful. Thank you darling." And she threw her arms around his neck and kissed him on both cheeks. "Well go on, open yours."

Trevor tore away the red paper to reveal a distinctive crest from a Knightsbridge store. On opening the box, he found a crisp white dress shirt with a perfectly starched ruffle front, topped off with a velvet maroon bow tie.

"Mother. It must have cost a fortune."

"I got it in the sales. That one of yours is looking a little worse for wear around the collar, so I thought for the opening of the next season you should have a new one."

The watery smile that had appeared on Trevor's lips when he opened his present now started to fade. "If there is a next season?" he uttered, despondently.

"Of course. We must think positive. I've decided to stick around for a little longer and organise a campaign to save the theatre."

The watery smile fleetingly returned to Trevor's face as he acknowledged Delphina's defiant stance. Watching her heading for the kitchen, a horrifying notion immediately came into his head. Which was worse? The thought of losing the theatre or his mother chaining herself to the doors like a modern-day Emmeline Pankhurst.

***

The Christmas cake decorations lay in an ordered row on the kitchen table. A team of reindeer, the sleigh and of course, Santa himself. Also, in the collection was an assortment of plastic holly berries and a deep red paper band that would eventually encircle the cake. This was Amelia's contribution, together with a very rich Christmas pudding, to her friend's Christmas table.

Preparations always started on the pudding at least six weeks prior to the big day, with the cake following about two weeks later. This gave both items a good time for the flavour to fully mature, and bring forth words of praise from her friend.

"I don't know how you do it," Elaine remarked.

"It's a tried-and-true recipe," Amelia answered, with a certain amount of muted pride. "It's been in our family for generations."

As she put the finishing touches to the cake, her thoughts again returned to her grandfather and how he introduced her to the excitement of the theatre. If only she had had the confidence at school to take part in the annual productions. If only she had pursued her secret ambition to write a play. If only she had joined the local dramatic company.

If only...

She was stirred out of her reverie by the hall clock chiming ten o'clock. Time to be going. She loaded the food into the boot of the car and set off for Elaine's house. The route took her past the King's and as she slowed down to look at the building, she muttered a few words to herself, "That's my New Year's resolution. I'll not let Craddick pull the theatre down.

I'm determined to help save the King's."

***

Sycamore Grove was a hive of activity. Beverly was up and already busy in the kitchen when Greg emerged still suffering from the effects of the office party. Their festive "open house" starting at midday, was a tradition that began the year they were married, but the front door was firmly shut at three o'clock and just the two of them sat down for the remainder of Christmas Day.

Beverly was an accomplished cook and had the kitchen organised with parade ground like efficiency. Greg was very much a private to her Sergeant-Major and obeyed her every command. The automatic timer on the oven had switched on at seven thirty that morning and a large ham was nearing completion with a twelve-pound turkey hot on its heels. A profusion of cold vegetable nibbles and dips were already arranged on various servers ready to be placed on the large dining table. Pickled onions, eggs, beetroot and walnuts, (a Bev speciality) were also awaiting their final resting place ready to be devoured by the family, relations and friends who would be dropping in.

As Greg sipped his morning coffee and attempted to look vaguely interested in what was going on around him, Beverly started to marshal him into action.

"All these need to go out onto the table — and don't forget the spiced tomato chutney." She noticed Greg's face drain of colour as he looked at the savouries and smiled to herself. For all his talk and bravado, he had a limited alcohol retention and never seemed to learn from past mistakes. She knew just what had to be done in order to get him ready for their guests. Taking him by the shoulders, she marched him to the stairs.

"Up there and have your shower," she commanded, pointing towards their bedroom door.

"I can think of better things to do in there," he said, turning to face her and pulling her close. The wry grin on his face quickly disappeared when he saw her cold stare reflecting back at him. "Won't be long," he mumbled, and trudged off.

The smile came back to Beverly's face as she returned to her kitchen. "So predictable, my husband," she thought. "But I wouldn't have him any other way."

One hour, one raw egg, one slice of dry toast and two cups of strong, black coffee later, Greg was back to his old self and helping his wife with the final preparations before the first caller rang the doorbell.

"Darling! Happy Christmas. Say happy Christmas Reggie and wipe your feet."

"Aurelia. How nice. You're always the first." Beverly forced a smile as her guest grabbed her and gave her two theatrical kisses on her cheeks with her lips at least three inches away. "Reggie," continued Beverly as Aurelia pushed past her and headed for Greg.

"Festive felicitations." chortled Reggie, swaying slightly. He handed her a bottle wrapped in cheap paper with "Merry Xmas" written on it, and followed his wife.

"Small bottle of sherry," Beverly whispered to Greg as they followed their guests into the lounge.

"It always is," he replied.

"I wanted to get here early to catch up on the gossip." Aurelia had settled herself in an armchair and already grabbed a handful of peanuts.

"Not much to tell, really."

"Oh darling, I don't believe you. There must be some little titbit. You've got that old lecher Max Pendleton in the cast for one thing. Whose skirt has he had his hand up?"

"He's got too many skirts of his own to worry about. He is playing the dame you know."

"Well, if that doesn't kill him off, nothing will. He's older than God. Why doesn't he give up and retire gracefully, like we did?"

"Still headlining we were," chimed in Reggie. "Right to the end."

Beverly sensed that they were about to launch into numerous anecdotes that littered their career and quickly changed the subject.

"Drinks?"

"Or is it too early?" Greg slipped an arm around Beverly and gave her a quick wink.

"G & T for me if that's all right," said Aurelia and, looking at her husband, added "And Reggie'll have a ginger ale."

"What?"

"You are driving, darling, and we have to call in at Ken and Erica's next." Greg moved to the small home bar in the corner of the room and prepared the drinks. Reggie sidled up and whispered to him that he might "liven up" the ginger ale. Aurelia started her probing again.

"How's Trevor been behaving?"

"Oh, you know Trevor," said Beverly. "Everything's chaotic and then somehow it all comes together. Delphina's down for the holiday to lend moral support."

"Oh wonderful. I must get to see her."

"They'll be here soon. They're calling in for a drink."

"Oh, this is just fabulous," gushed Aurelia. "We go back years you know. Did I ever tell you about the time we did *'Arsenic and old Lace'* together? Of course, we were both far too young."

At that point the doorbell rang again and Beverly raised her eyes heavenward in thanks. "I'll get it," she announced quickly and made a hasty exit.

For the next three hours or so, the Westcott home was awash with a stream of visitors coming and going. The air was alive with the festive spirit and the joy of people greeting one another and swapping stories.

"It's like Crewe station used to be on a Sunday in the old days." Aurelia had just enveloped Delphina in another theatrical embrace. "Everyone coming from one engagement and off to another. I was just telling Beverly about *'Arsenic and old Lace'*." Her voice could be heard above most of the other conversations happening in the room and every now and then a shriek of laughter made everyone's head turn.

"I suppose I ought to go and rescue mother," said Trevor, as Greg handed him a glass of wine.

"Are you feeling all right?" enquired his friend. "You look a bit washed out. Has the production taken it out of you?"

"You could say that," sighed Trevor. "Been a bit of a bugger, this one. That and everything else." He immediately bit his tongue as Greg turned to him with a quizzical look.

"Everything else?"

"Oh, you know, the usual problems we get in this business." Trevor desperately wanted to talk to someone about the threat of closure, but knew this was neither the time nor place. "Still, nothing to worry about today," he continued quickly and forced a smile.

As three o'clock approached just a few stragglers were standing chatting in the lounge. Aurelia was, of course, one of them and Reggie, who had had quite a few ginger ales "livened up" with a fair amount of whisky, was asleep in the chair.

"I'll call a cab," suggested Greg, and picked up the phone.

"Poor darling is quite worn out," laughed Aurelia, desperately trying to cover up for her inebriated husband.

After waving goodbye to the remainder of their guests and piling Reggie into a taxi, Beverly and Greg closed the front door and stood with their arms around each other in the hall.

"Well, Mrs. Westcott, another performance over."

"You have been the perfect host. Thank you." Greg knew how much Beverly liked to entertain, and the Christmas day ritual was at least a good way of catching up with friends they'd not seen for a while.

"I'd better make a start on our dinner," she added.

"But you've not had your Christmas present yet."

"That's right. Where is it?"

"You'll have to follow me," he said mysteriously and started up the stairs towards the bedroom.

***

Christmas day for other inhabitants of Seahaven passed off with varying degrees of success. Amelie's pudding and cake were a triumph as attested to by there being very little of either commodity at the end of the day.

In London, Gavin spent an energetic day with his sister and her family playing games, although he lost heavily at Monopoly as his thoughts were often straying to what Robert might be doing.

Robert's thoughts were also straying as he spent the day with his ex-lover and new partner. During the Queen's speech, his mobile rang.

"Excuse me," he said, and quickly left the room while his hosts wondered who could be calling him.

"How are things?" enquired Gavin, who had managed to slip away and make the call.

"Nothing but eating, drinking and watching TV. What about you?"

"I'm losing at Monopoly."

"I should be there advising you on what to buy and sell." They laughed and simultaneously said how much they wished they were spending the day together.

"Don't be late in picking me up tomorrow. Remember I have a matinee at four o'clock."

"I'll be outside at ten."

***

In the wilds of Somerset, the exchanging and unwrapping of presents started early in the morning. Lunch was at one o'clock and the afternoon took on a quieter air as the grandchildren played with various new toys and the adults dozed in front of the large, open wood burning fire.

Russell had only been in the country for barely twenty-four hours, but already he was getting itchy feet. He was a town person through and through. Quite the opposite to his wife who loved the wide, open spaces. On many occasions she had suggested moving into a rural area outside Seahaven, but he had vigorously opposed the idea, saying the travelling would be an added burden to his already hectic business life.

His life was certainly hectic at the moment, and not necessarily from a business point of view. For over a year, he had been indulging in a dangerous liaison with a rather nice lady called Anne, who just happened to be the wife of his partner in crime, Barrie Stone. Often knowing what Barrie's movements were, he could arrange to call around during an afternoon for more than a cup of tea.

"Just going for a breath of fresh air," Russell announced to the others.

"Would you like some company?" asked his wife.

"No, it's all right. I won't be out long. You stop and help Lisa with the tea." Pulling on his coat and making sure his mobile phone was in his pocket, Russell flashed a quick smile at his wife and left the house. Moving to the other side of his parked car and hidden from view, he took out the phone and punched in a number he knew by heart.

"Hello?"

"Happy Christmas, sexy," Russell replied, with a leer in his voice.

"Russell. You're taking a chance, aren't you? What if Barrie had answered?"

"I'd have been wishing my old mate the compliments of the season. Besides, isn't he taking your mother back to the Home after lunch? That's what he told me."

"Clever old you," said his lady friend. "Oh, by the way, Barrie's in Brighton for all of January second."

"Then I shall find a window in my busy schedule and pay a call. Anyway, don't forget you're both coming to us for New Year's Eve."

"Yes. When Barrie told me we'd been invited, I acted very put out and protested that you two would be talking business all night. But Barrie insisted, so I just had to agree."

"Now who's being a clever old thing."

They were both giggling like schoolchildren behind the bicycle sheds, when a voice called, "Granddad."

"Oh, duty calls," sighed Russell. "My grandson's tailing me."

"See you in a few days."

"Can't wait," he said, and flicked off the phone as Jamie rushed towards him holding his brand-new model aeroplane.

SCENE SEVEN
SUNDAY, DECEMBER 26TH

International Television and Films Incorporated is located in a thirty-five-story tower block on the corner of Forty Second Street and the Avenue of the Americas in New York City. It's now famous logo, seen at the beginning of a number of television blockbusters, adorns the huge smoke glass doors that lead into a plush foyer with deep red couches arranged at decorative angles. On the right wall is a bank of TV screens that constantly show clips from a multitude of programmes currently available from the company's many satellite channels.

Straight ahead is a slightly curved, mahogany reception desk behind which sit two smiling receptionists, ready with the customary welcome of, "How may I help you?" Embedded in the other wall are four shining black doors covering the entrance to state-of-the-art elevators, equipped to take employees and visitors, at high speed, to any floor. The main administration offices are located between floors three and twenty-five. The remaining floors house boardrooms, screening rooms, and hospitality suites, with the top two given over to a newly refurbished employees dining room with a panoramic view of Bryant Park opposite, and the famous Forty Second Street below, stretching from East to West.

Just prior to the Christmas break, the Corporation had

completed a multi-million-dollar deal to buy a large catalogue of films from a rival company ranging from third rate "B" movies to top grossing box office hits. After the acquisition, the race was on to produce a schedule for the following spring that would hopefully guarantee the Corporation a healthy slice of the market and keep the advertisers happy.

I.T.F. Inc. prided itself in attaining numerous awards annually for its quality programming and world market penetration. In recent years the market in Great Britain and Europe had increased, so much so that the company had opened a London office to oversee distribution and franchising.

On the team dealing with the London office was Bradley Harman, a good looking twenty-seven-year-old, who had been with the company since graduating from Cornell University in Ithaca New York, with a Masters' in Business Administration.

His clean-cut appearance was that of the All-American young businessman with a burning ambition to succeed in his chosen field. In the three years he had been with the company, his boss, Wilbur Dexter-Hawkes, had kept a sharp eye on his progress.

"Good chap, young Harman," he enthused to one of the directors at a monthly departmental meeting. "I'd like him to go to the London office for a few weeks and make sure everything's working smoothly."

Brad was told of the idea a week before the Christmas break. He readily agreed to take on the assignment and then put in a request of his own.

"I have some holiday owing, so do you think I could tag on an extra week and do some sightseeing? My folks came from England; in fact, I was born there."

"You mean you're a Limey?" joked his boss.

"Hardly. We left when I was only six months old."

"And you've never been back?"

"No sir," Brad replied, wistfully. "I've always wanted to, but with school and university and joining the company, there never seemed to be any time. My folks wanted me to go to Oxford or Cambridge, but I didn't like to be too far away from them. They're quite elderly."

"Oh, you were a late addition to the family?"

Brad looked down and answered quietly. "Yeah, their only child."

"That'll be fine," said Wilbur. "You visit your homeland. But make sure that London office is up to scratch."

The Harmans had upped sticks and moved to New Jersey when the electronics company Brad's father worked for had made him an offer that he couldn't refuse. The American market was growing at an alarming rate and expansion was the only way forward. Jeremy Harman was one of a few specially chosen executives who would oversee the U.S. operations. Originally, they were only supposed to stay for one or two years, but the American way of life, and the sight of the Manhattan skyline across the Hudson River, was too much for the Harman family to resist. The opportunity to stay presented itself and they took it.

From a very early age, Brad had taken an interest in the performing arts. On many a weekend the Harman family would take a trip into Manhattan to see a Saturday or Sunday matinee on Broadway. In high school, Brad showed a strong aptitude for literature and participated in a number of school productions. For a time during his teenage years, he contemplated an acting profession, but after a disastrous attempt at the romantic lead in *"Guys and Dolls"*, his ambition in that direction quickly evaporated. Instead, the idea of a more administrative role became his goal, much to the relief of his parents. His father had pointed out that television and the advent of home video was the way forward and Brad soon realised that was where his future lay.

His days at Cornell were some of the happiest. Always the life and soul of any party, he was never short of a girlfriend; and during his last year he started a rather passionate affair that was to pave the way towards a career with I.T.F. Inc.

Marie-Ann Porter, a stunning beauty from New York, of whom he had lusted after for a good six months, finally broke off her relationship with the hunky quarterback from the football team and turned her attentions to Brad. Lying in his arms after one particular night of passion, she mentioned that her father was on the board of I.T.F. Inc. and that she would like to introduce him to the new man in her life. The rest, as they say, is history and within a month of receiving his Masters, Brad started working for the company.

Unfortunately, his relationship with Marie-Ann came to an abrupt end when she was lured away to Europe to start a modelling career and was soon seen on the cover of a number of magazines and on the arm of a famous fashion photographer. But no matter, Brad was doing a job that he had quickly grown to love. And what the hell — there were plenty more fish in the city.

The day after Christmas would not normally find Brad in his office. The holiday was always spent with his parents who still lived in New Jersey, but this year certain events had forced him to return to the city a day early. Firstly, he had to pick up his travel documents and make final arrangements for his trip that would start on the evening of the twenty-seventh and secondly, he had received a text message on his mobile from a Mr Culvert wanting to see him as soon as possible.

"Does that mean what I think it means?" his mother asked, when she heard of the message.

"I think so."

"Brad, are you sure you want to do this?"

"I'm pretty sure." He hesitated then added, "It's just that I've thought about it for such a long time. If the information I'm after is positive and with this trip suddenly coming up — well it feels as though fate has taken a hand."

Brad walked through the doors of the building and across to the elevators.

"Didn't expect to see you today." called the receptionist, who had drawn the short straw to work the day after Christmas.

"Need to pick up a few things for the trip," he explained, as the soft two-tone bell announced the elevator's arrival.

On his office desk his secretary had left a folder containing all his travel arrangements. He quickly flicked through them whilst dialling a number on his cell phone.

"Hello? Mr Culvert? Yes, I received your message. Thank you very much. I'm back in the city and can see you whenever you like."

The voice at the other end asked if that afternoon would be convenient and after receiving an affirmative answer, arranged to call at Brad's apartment at two o'clock.

Brad spent the next twenty minutes checking over the details of his trip and finishing off a couple of things left from before the holiday. He then picked up the folder with his travel documents and left his office taking the same elevator back down to reception.

"See you in a few weeks," he called to the receptionist.

"Give my love to good old London," she called back in a mock British accent, as he headed for the doors on the other side of the lobby.

Turning to his left he walked a few yards to the Forty-Second Street subway entrance and there took the "B" train downtown to Twenty-Third Street. He had recently moved into a small apartment two blocks down. The rent was just within his budget since his last promotion, and it was much better than the two room "cupboard" he had first occupied on arriving in the city. It had a reasonable sized lounge with two bedrooms, bathroom, kitchen and, with a little help from his mother, been tastefully decorated.

The subway was fairly crowded with people returning from the holidays and shoppers on the lookout for post-Christmas bargains, but Brad loved riding it. He rarely took a cab. The noise of the other traffic and the erratic driving irritated him so much. On emerging from the subway station at Twenty-Third and Sixth, he had a short walk before arriving home. Up four steps to the front door and then up one flight brought him to his own door.

The cold, blustery New York air had already made his cheeks tingle during the journey from the subway, but on entering his apartment a warm blast from the central heating soon had him peeling off his topcoat. He made himself a cup of tea, which he much preferred to coffee (a throwback to his British roots), and sat down on his couch. The clock on the kitchen wall showed twelve thirty, so he had an hour and a half before the arrival of his visitor. There were a number of calls he had to make, mostly to friends whom he hadn't spoken to since before Christmas, informing them of his trip.

Whilst starting some provisional packing, Brad noticed a light snow had begun to fall. He crossed to the window and looked out at the crystal flakes settling on the cars across the road. The buzzer sounded and he glanced at his watch. Two o'clock. Right on time.

"It's Culvert, Mr Harman." The voice sounded tinny over the intercom.

"Come right up. First floor," answered Brad, as he pushed the door release button.

The flakes of snow that had gathered on Elliott Culvert's coat shoulders quickly melted as the warm interior air hit them. Brad shook his damp hand and invited him into the apartment. He was shorter than Brad had remembered. Their one and only previous meeting had been at Culvert's office where a large desk had separated them, so as to not give a true sense of his build. His shoulders were slightly rounded and his head, with a receding hairline, looked a little too large in proportion with the rest of his body. Mid-fifties Brad thought to himself as he closed the door.

"Thank you so much for agreeing to come out, today of all days. Shall I take your coat?"

"Thank you," replied his guest, removing the damp overcoat and handing it to him. "I got caught in this sudden snowfall coming from the subway. It looks as though we might be in for quite a covering."

Brad hung the coat on a stand by the door and then they both moved into the lounge. "I do hope not. I'm off to London tomorrow. I don't want any hold-ups at the airport."

"That's right. You mentioned your impending trip on the phone." Culvert had sat on one of the couches and began wiping the condensation off his round, rimless glasses. "Is it business or pleasure?"

"A bit of both," said Brad, sitting opposite him. "May I offer you some tea, or perhaps something stronger?"

"Very kind, but I really can't stay. I'm on my way to see my son and his family in Brooklyn. That's why I suggested I call in on you here rather than at the office. Just a short break in my journey."

"I must say I'm pleased you've managed to get back to me so quickly. I thought the process would take a lot longer."

"Actually, it was one of our more straightforward investigations. Everything you need to know is in here." Culvert handed over a large sealed envelope.

"Thank you very much," said Brad, taking the package and placing it carefully on the glass coffee table.

"Look all the information over and if there's anything more you need to know just give me a call."

"I'm sure everything will be fine. You came highly recommended. I'll write you a cheque now. Are there any other expenses?"

"No sir. Just the agreed fee."

"Splendid," said Brad, moving to a small writing desk in the corner of the room. He took his chequebook out of a drawer and wrote a cheque for five hundred dollars to Culvert and Hewitt, Private Investigators.

"There you are," he said, handing over the cheque.

"Thank you, Mr Harman." Culvert stood up pocketing his fee and looked around for his coat.

"Out into the bleak mid-winter," said Brad with a smile, as he helped the P.I. on with his coat.

"I've done jobs in worst conditions than this. I could write a book."

"I'm sure it would be a best seller," said Brad, opening the front door.

"Goodbye, Mr Harman. Have a good trip."

"Thank you. I hope it will be an eventful one."

Elliott Culvert started to trudge down the flight of steps and make his way out into the afternoon air where the wind was now whipping the snow into the faces of the pedestrians hurrying along the sidewalk.

Brad closed the door and turned back to look at the envelope lying on the table. He picked it up and for a good thirty seconds just stared nervously at it. Then, with a quick movement of his hand, he tore open the top flap and took out a bundle of papers.

Slowly he sat down on the couch and began to turn each page over. On the third page he saw something that made him stop. He picked up the piece of paper and, after staring at it for a few seconds, sank back on the couch, his head resting on a large cushion. He was looking at the façade of a large building with a group of people posing for a picture in front of it. Beads of perspiration started to break out on his forehead and his hand shook slightly.

"This is going to be one hell of a trip," he murmured quietly to himself.

***

The noise was deafening. Mrs. Nesbit had left Trevor in charge of the box office while she gave her niece, Megan, a hand on the confectionery counter. Hordes of children — mostly with parents or grandparents in tow, for which Trevor was eternally grateful — were stocking up on sweets, chocolates and crisps ready to enjoy the Boxing Day matinee. The theatre was full and Trevor noticed the plans for the evening performance looked very healthy.

"We're short on most of the chocolate bars," Mrs. Nesbit called to her very harassed looking niece. "See if there are some more in the stock room."

Megan disappeared into the little room as Mrs. Nesbit turned back to admonish a tall, spotty youth for pushing in front of a little girl.

"Wait your turn," she snapped. Then, with a smile, enquired what the little girl would like.

Backstage there was almost as much activity but thankfully not as much noise. Stage manager Stan had just called the half-hour and was making some last-minute checks of the set.

"Anything going to collapse on us this afternoon?" joked Willie Waters, who had been practising a few dance steps in the wings.

"Solid as a rock!" retorted Stan.

"I don't think Gavin would agree with you," said Willie, while executing a Vaudeville style *"Da da"*.

Stan ignored him and walked down to the Stage Door to check that everyone had signed in. He looked at the clipboard where the names of the company were printed with their signatures alongside. His face drained. Gavin hadn't signed in. Moving quicker than he had done in a long time, Stan rushed to the Green Room where he found most of the cast talking over the events of their Christmas.

"Anyone seen Gavin?" he asked, hoping someone had, and that he had forgotten to sign in.

The negative response caused his face to drain even more.

"I'm sure he'll be here," Beverly reassured him optimistically. "He'd never miss a performance without ringing in."

"I've got to find Trevor," said Stan. "Someone will have to go on."

"Isn't that the A S M's job?" called Max, as Stan started for the pass door.

"We haven't got one."

"Then it looks like it'll be you, old love!" Stan turned at the door and sneered at the half made up Max, before disappearing down the corridor to front of house in search of the Director.

***

"We're going to be late. The half-hour will have already been called. Why the hell do we have to do Boxing Day matinees? And on a Sunday, too." Gavin was now in a panic. Robert had never seen him like this. He was wringing his hands and craning his neck to try and see what the holdup was. They had been stationary in Robert's car on the outskirts of Seahaven for the last twenty minutes. Gavin had tried to call the theatre using Robert's mobile, but the battery was low and he couldn't get a signal.

"It must be an accident," said Robert, trying to sound as calm as possible.

"This is awful. I knew we should have started back earlier."

"Who wanted to take advantage of an empty house when I called round for you?"

A momentary flicker of pleasure flashed across Gavin's face before his brow once again showed deep furrows of tension. "I know, I know," he admitted. "But you should have insisted we got back. You were the one doing the driving."

"Oh, so now it's my fault?"

"No! Oh, I'm sorry. I don't know what I'm saying. I've never been late for a performance. Never."

"I'm sure we'll get there on time," said Robert, trying to sound more confident than he was.

"Yes, yes. I must keep calm." He apologised again, and laid a hand on his companion's knee.

"Here. Stop that. You'll be giving that young policeman ideas."

"Eh?"

Robert nodded his head toward a figure approaching the car and wound down the window.

"Sorry about this, sir," said a young and very handsome police constable. "A car pulling a caravan has jack-knifed on a patch of ice up ahead. The car's stuck in a ditch and blocked the road both ways."

"Do you think we'll be here long, officer?" asked Robert, calmly.

"They've radioed a garage for a breakdown truck, but being Boxing Day there's only a skeleton service operating."

"But we've got to get to the centre of town, we've just got to." The pitch of Gavin's now panicking voice was getting higher.

"What my friend means is that he's appearing at the King's Theatre and the curtain goes up in half an hour," said Robert, trying to stop Gavin reaching a pitch where only dogs would hear him.

"Oh, you're an actor are you sir?" said the policeman with a smile. "In the Pantomime? I'm taking my nephew to see it in a couple of days."

"That's if we're not still stuck in this bloody queue."

"Nerves are taking over I'm afraid, officer," said Robert, in a calm voice. "We've had a long drive from London."

"Oh, I know how it is. I did a bit of acting myself at school. Fare gives you the collywobbles, doesn't it?"

Feeling that Gavin was about to lose his control completely, Robert quickly spoke again.

"Is there any way we could turn around and find another route into town?"

"Turning round isn't a problem, but the only other way is to go back to the village of Anscombe Lacey and then take the Brighton road. It'll add a good twenty or so miles to your journey."

Gavin groaned and slumped back into his seat. "I should just about make the interval."

The constable thought for a moment and then said, "Just hold on here a second." He crossed the road and disappeared along the drive of a farm opposite. A few minutes later he reappeared and moved back to Robert's window.

"That farmer is a friend of my dad's. He's got a private road that cuts between his two fields and comes out about three miles further on. He'll open the gates so you can use it. I told him it was an emergency." He added, grinning, "Well, it is in a way. Can't keep those kiddies waiting."

"That's very kind of you, officer," said Robert, starting the car and beginning to manoeuvre out of the queue of traffic.

"Thank you. Thank you so much," echoed Gavin, as the look of panic started to fade from his forehead.

"Would you like me to radio a message through to the theatre for you?" offered the police officer.

"If you could, I'd be eternally grateful," replied Gavin. His anxious face now showing the first signs of a smile.

Robert turned the steering wheel and guided the car along the muddy driveway as the other astounded drivers in the queue looked on. True to his word the farmer stood by the open gate at the other end and waved them through. Both men acknowledged his wave as they drove down the private road.

"I'll never make a disparaging remark about our splendid police force again," vowed Gavin.

"He was rather handsome, wasn't he?" said Robert, flirtatiously, and received a slap on the knee from his now grinning passenger.

***

At the theatre the mood was anything but calm. After receiving a call from the police, Trevor had given control of the Box Office back to Mrs. Nesbit and followed Stan back stage.

"You'll have to go on," Max said, after Trevor had relayed the news to the waiting company.

"I can't. I don't know any of the lines," shouted Trevor.

"You ought to, old love. You wrote the bloody things."

"You can take the script on with you," said Stan. "We'll make an announcement that Gavin is indisposed."

"I'll 'indispose' him when he gets here. I suppose he's been out on the razzle in London and missed his train."

"I'm sure that's not the case," said Beverly, with a knowing edge to her voice.

"Can't Alex or Carl do it?" suggested Trevor.

"That would only leave one of us in the chorus," chimed in Alex. "How odd is that?"

"No more than when there's two of you," derided Max, pleased to be getting a jibe in at them for a change.

"Oh, go and blow up your sagging tits," retorted Carl.

"Stop it all of you," shouted Trevor. "We have got to do something, there's a full house out there."

"I'm sure he'll get here," said Beverly, trying to be reassuring. "What did the police say?"

"That they should be OK — as long as the roads were clear."

"You ought to prepare yourself," Max said. And then added with an air of superiority, "Of course, if you bothered to organise understudies…"

"Max", screamed Trevor, "I don't need you pontificating right now about how I run *my* company."

With the look of a scolded schoolboy, Max turned and sloped off to his dressing room.

"We could hold the curtain for about ten minutes while you get ready," said Stan.

"I suppose there's nothing for it." Trevor looked resigned. "What time is it?"

"A quarter past," said Stan checking the clock by the stage manager's desk. "I should have called fifteen minutes."

"Let everyone in the company know what's happening and hold off calling beginners until I tell you."

Trevor turned and walked into Gavin's dressing room. He sat down at the dressing table and switched on the lights surrounding the mirror. Staring at his reflection he started to shake, more with rage than nerves. What else could go wrong? When would this nightmare end?

He took off his coat and new dress shirt and bow tie that Delphina had given him for Christmas and picked up a tin of make-up. His hands trembled as he removed the lid. How he wished his mother were there to help him, she was always so good at character make-up. But Delphina had elected to go back to London that morning on the first available train to see what help she could get to assist her son's plight in saving his theatre.

Outside in the corridor the other members of the company looked at each other wondering what the impending performance held in store.

***

On returning to the main road, Robert broke every speed limit in the book and clocked up a few other potential violations as he drove his anxious partner towards Seahaven and The King's Theatre. At twenty-nine minutes past two he screeched to a halt outside the stage door as Gavin threw the car door open and leaped out.

"See you after the show," Robert called after the disappearing actor, who waved back in the affirmative.

"He's here," screamed Carl. "Abanazar's appeared in a puff of smoke from a chariot with a very dolly driver."

Gavin pushed past him and came face to face with what looked like his character double. Trevor stood in the doorway to his dressing room wearing the Abanazar costume that looked very tight on him and with so much hastily applied make-up that he took on the appearance of something between Othello and Quasimodo!

The vision was so hysterical, the nervous tension that had

been building up inside Gavin finally gave way and he burst out in a fit of laughter.

"Where the fuck have you been?" demanded Trevor.

"Don't ask, just don't ask. Am I going on, or are you?"

With the speed of light and tremendous relief, Trevor started to remove the costume. "Stan. Hold the curtain for ten minutes," he called, and threw the first garment at Gavin. He then lifted a leg and started pulling at one of the boots. Hopping around like a demented rabbit, he continued hurling abuse at Gavin and threatening all kinds of retribution for putting him and the company through the torture of the last half-hour. Gavin tried to explain what had happened, but gave up and continued getting ready.

"I could go out and entertain the troops for a few minutes?" suggested Willie Waters.

"Good idea," said Trevor, and threw the second boot at Gavin. "Stop them ripping up the seats!"

Needing no more encouragement, Willie bounded off towards the stage to once again save the day.

***

Brad had read and reread the information in the envelope left by Elliott Culvert at least five times before putting the papers away in his briefcase. He moved into his kitchen and automatically started to make himself a cup of tea. Half way through the operation he realised that he could do with something a little stronger. Switching off the kettle, he opened the refrigerator door and took out a cold bottle of beer. Removing the top and drinking straight from the bottle he looked out of the window. The snow had covered everything and was still coming down.

His thoughts returned to the information in his briefcase. Was he doing the right thing? Would the facts that the Private Detective had furnished him with change his life forever, or should he just leave everything as it was? Lost in a sea of questions to himself, he almost dropped his bottle when the sharp ring of the phone on the kitchen wall brought him back to the present.

"Hello son."

"Oh, hi Mom, I was going to call you."

"Has he been?"

"Yes."

"Did he provide you with what you wanted?"

"Yes."

For a moment neither of them spoke. Brad broke the silence.

"Look, if you and Dad don't want me to do this, then I won't."

"No, it's not that. You must do it if you want to. It's just that we don't want you to be disappointed. It's a long way to go to end up with nothing."

"I know, but I'm a big boy now."

There was a catch in his mother's voice. "Yes, you are. My big son."

"I'll call you every day from England and tell you what's happening."

"Be sure that you do," she said, knowing that he had always kept them informed of everything he did, from the time he was a young boy staying over at a friend's, to his weekly calls from Cornell.

"I love you two very much."

"We love you. Have a safe trip, son."

***

At the start of the performance, still shaken by the events of the drive to the theatre, Gavin tried to compose himself in the wings as he waited for his first entrance. He stepped onto the stage and immediately a barrage of booing rang out before he could utter his first line. Looking down at the audience, he noticed it was being led by a group of men in the centre of the fifth row.

"Ricky and his friends from 'The Crown'," thought Gavin. Of course, they had tickets for that performance. There was a lot of nudging and whispering and Gavin hoped they wouldn't start sending him up. But as he launched into his first speech, they soon settled down and, together with the rest of the enthusiastic audience, responded in all the right places.

Gavin relaxed into his part and enjoyed the banter with the audience. As he turned to make his exit, he noticed a lone figure sitting on the other side of the aisle.

The bugger, he thought to himself as he left the stage. Got himself a ticket without telling me. Then a smile broke out across his face. His *chauffeur* had come in to make sure everything was all right after the harrowing experience of getting him to the theatre on time.

The first act was well under way by the time Trevor, washed and changed back into his dress suit, returned to the front of house. Mrs Nesbit, with her niece's help, had just finished replenishing the confectionery counter ready for the interval rush.

"It seems to be going very well," she said, encouragingly. "Lots of laughter and applause. And have you seen this?" She held up a special Boxing Day edition of the Seahaven Courier. "The review is in."

135

Trevor looked at her anxiously. "Please let it be a good one," he wished to himself, and took the paper from her.

"It's not bad at all. They think the scenery is a bit tired looking, but in the main it's all right. Gavin gets a very good notice."

"He would," sneered Trevor, as he scanned down the article. "He needn't think this will let him off the hook for being totally unprofessional."

On stage Willie Waters was causing a riot in the laundry scene. As the audience warmed to him so he started adding bits of business into the slapstick. The chases got longer and the amount of soapsuds hitting Max in the face was increasing with every performance — much to the old actor's chagrin.

Trevor opened the back door of the stalls and looked in just in time to see Max slip on a slippery part of the stage and be propelled precariously close to the orchestra pit. He held his breath fearing the worst, but Willie was straight there and in his cheeky *Wishee Washee* character yanked Max back onto his rather unsteady feet.

"Steady on there, Mum. Better take more water with it!"

Max glared at Willie as the audience shrieked with laughter.

The scene eventually returned to what was scripted and Trevor made a mental note to tell Willie to cut down on the amount of soapsuds he used. He didn't want Max breaking anything. That would only necessitate him taking over *that* part. He'd had one close call in that department and didn't want another.

SCENE EIGHT
MONDAY, DECEMBER 27TH – TUESDAY 28TH

The holiday was well and truly over judging by the amount of traffic on the Long Island Expressway. The limousine carrying Brad to John F. Kennedy International Airport had taken twenty minutes to go about three miles along Franklin Delano Roosevelt Drive and across the East River. Luckily Brad had given himself plenty of time for the evening journey from Manhattan, so he sat back in his seat, unperturbed by the ranting of the driver. Turning onto the Grand Central Parkway, the traffic was lighter and his journey continued at a reasonable pace. Three quarters of an hour later he was in the British Airways terminal preparing to check in his luggage.

"Boarding will be at eight thirty through gate thirty-eight, Mr Harman. Enjoy your flight." The check-in clerk smiled at him as she handed him his boarding card.

"Thank you," he replied. Picking up his hand luggage, Brad decided it was time for a pre-flight drink.

The departure lounge was bustling with passengers preparing to board the numerous overnight flights to Europe and beyond. Having purchased a scotch on the rocks, Brad settled himself into a vacant seat in one of the many bars surrounding the lounge and looked up at the screen detailing the flight times. "Good," he thought. "The London flight is still on schedule."

He quickly finished his drink and decided to pay a visit to the Duty Free. There he bought a bottle of perfume provocatively named *"Impudence"* and took advantage of the gift-wrapping service offered by the sales assistant. Putting the package into his hand luggage, he again glanced up at the flight departure screen. *Go to gate thirty-eight* was flashing against his flight number, so he started to head for the walkway in the direction of the gate.

Some thirty minutes later he was settled in his window seat in Business Class aboard the British Airways 747 and being offered a complimentary glass of wine by the steward. At nine thirty precisely he felt a jolt as the giant plane was pushed back from the gate. Thirteen minutes later the four engines roared as it started its journey down the runway and then on to Heathrow.

Once airborne the first officer welcomed everyone on board and, after giving details about the flight, informed the passengers that the time in London was now 2.50 a.m. Brad adjusted his watch before easing his seat back to a more comfortable position. He looked out of the window into the cold, clear night sky and at the lights of Long Island below. One thought occupied his mind. What would the next few days reveal?

***

Following the success of her culinary delights at her friends, Amelia had returned home after Boxing Day lunch, fending off Elaine's entreaties to stay another night.

"There's still a lot of your scrumptious cake left. You must help us eat it."

"I'm sure there's a couple of eager little mouths that can fulfil that job," Amelia replied, beaming down at Elaine's niece and nephew.

The rest of the day was spent rereading the library book Elaine had lent her. Wilfred Latchman, the architect of the King's Theatre, had been one of the major exponents of late Victorian and early Edwardian building design. All the main cities in the British Isles boasted a Latchman creation at one time, whether it be a theatre, museum, art gallery or hotel.

An appendix to the book told the sad story of how few examples of his work were left, due to redevelopment or war damage. Apart from the King's one other theatre, with only the façade intact, was still standing somewhere in Yorkshire. It no longer housed live shows, but had given way in the nineteen eighties to the ever-popular Bingo craze.

Amelia closed the book and sat staring into space. Surely that must be reason enough to save the King's? The only remaining example fully intact of Wilfred Lachman's work. How frustrating to have to wait another day before contacting the man at English Heritage.

***

"Ladies and Gentlemen, welcome to London Heathrow. The time is 8.55 and the temperature outside is one degree centigrade. We hope you have had a pleasant flight and would like to thank you for flying British Airways."

Brad noted that they had arrived slightly early due to good following winds. He pulled his hand luggage out of the compartment above his seat and joined the queue of passengers making their way to immigration. Once through, he collected the rest of his luggage and crossed to the green sign saying "Nothing to Declare". Emerging without being stopped, he was met with a sea of faces all looking anxiously for their respective friends or relations arriving from all points of the compass.

To one side of the hordes of people he saw a group of men all holding up placards with various names and companies. Almost immediately he recognised the familiar International Television and Films Incorporated logo and his name written underneath it.

"Good morning, Mr Harman, my name is Anthony and I'm your driver during your stay in London."

"Hi Anthony. I'm pleased to meet you."

"The car is right outside the door, sir. Please let me take care of your bags." He skilfully guided the trolley containing Brad's luggage through the crowds to the terminal exit and stopped beside a sleek, black Jaguar car. With the utmost professionalism he quickly loaded everything into the boot and with a flourish opened the back door for Brad to get in.

The warm air inside the pre-heated car cocooned Brad immediately. He loosened his topcoat and settled back to enjoy the drive to the Capital.

"How far is it to the hotel?" he asked, as Anthony manoeuvred the car into the heavy morning traffic on the M4.

"About three quarters of an hour, sir," replied Anthony, and then added, "If the traffic is kind to us."

"It can be pretty hectic, eh?"

"Especially if there are road works on Chiswick High Road."

"I don't know the area, I'm afraid," said Brad, staring out

at the rather bleak scene either side of the motorway.

"Is this your first time in London, Mr Harman?"

"It's my first time in Britain since I was about six months old."

"You were born here?"

"I was, but I remember nothing about it."

Driver and passenger laughed.

"It's a pity you've come back at such a dreary time of year. I hope this weather isn't too depressing for you."

"It was snowing when I left New York, so I can't complain."

"According to the latest weather forecast it should remain dry with the chance of some winter sunshine over the next few days."

Anthony's weather report pleased Brad. His intention was to do some travelling before starting work at the London office in the New Year, so fine weather would be very welcome.

"Where exactly is my hotel situated?" asked Brad.

"It's in South Kensington, sir. The I.T.F office is a short distance away in Knightsbridge."

"I've heard all these names. I just don't know where they are."

"It's not too difficult to find your way around," Anthony reassured him. "And if you need me, I'll always be on hand."

"That's very comforting to know, Anthony. Thank you."

"My pleasure, sir."

The traffic had now built up as they approached the end of the motorway. As soon as it was possible, Anthony turned the car off the main road and took a series of side roads that he was familiar with and delivered Brad to his hotel a short time later.

As Anthony opened the boot for the porter to take the bags, Brad turned and thanked him for looking after him so well.

"I'm not expected at I.T.F until sometime after January 2nd," he added. "So I'm going to do a little sightseeing."

"May I take you anywhere, sir?" offered Anthony.

"No thanks, I'll be going out of town. Why don't you take the next few days off? Can I get in touch with you when I need you?"

"My home number and mobile are on this card, sir," said the chauffeur handing Brad his card. "Call whenever you need me. I shall be ready at all times."

"Thank you again — and have a good New Year."

"Thank you, sir." And with a curt bow he returned to the warmth of the car and drove away.

Brad's spacious fourth floor room overlooked Kensington Gardens with Hyde Park in the distance. He stood for some time gazing out over the London Parks he had heard and read so much about. After all these years he was finally here. The winter sun was now out and the partially bare trees glistened from the overnight frost that was slowly melting away. He longed to go out walking and exploring, but jet lag was starting to kick in and he knew he should rest for a few hours. Although his flight was smooth and fairly quiet, he had only managed a couple of hours sleep. Picking up his hand luggage, he moved to the large double bed that dominated the room, sat down on one side and took out the envelope given to him by the Private Investigator. After looking through the contents for the umpteenth time, he picked up the phone and within seconds a polite, perfect English accent asked how she might be of service to him.

"I'm feeling the effects of my flight, so I'm going to take a nap. Could you take any messages that might come in and wake me say..." He glanced at his watch that was now reading eleven thirty. "Three o'clock?"

"Of course, sir. Is there anything else I can do for you?"

Brad thought for a second and then continued. "Yes, as a matter of fact there is. I need details of how to get to a town on your South Coast. Seahaven." Ever since he had received the folder from Elliott Culvert, the name "Seahaven" had been engraved on his brain.

"Seahaven, yes sir. It's about sixty miles from here, not too far from Brighton. There should be a fairly regular train service from Victoria, unless you would prefer to drive."

"The train will be fine," said Brad, not wishing to negotiate London traffic. "But I would like to have a hire car when I get down there. And I need to book into a hotel."

The receptionist assured him that she would make all the arrangements for him.

"Is there anything else I can help you with?" she asked.

"Yes, there is one other thing," said Brad, taking another quick look at the contents of the envelope. "I also need the phone number of "The King's Theatre."

***

Between Christmas and New Year, the Council Offices operated a skeleton staff, as most people preferred to make a long break of it. Amelia Fothergill was not one of them. Arriving at her usual time she nodded to the receptionist before going to her office.

Only a few letters had been delivered to her desk and she

143

dealt with them fairly quickly. As she filed the last one, she noticed the time was approaching ten o'clock and wondered if now would be an opportune moment to contact English Heritage. Breathing deeply and slowly, she took the number out of her handbag and lifted the receiver.

"English Heritage, how may I be of assistance?" The voice was clear, concise and very business-like to a point where Amelia almost thought she was talking to herself.

"Oh, good morning," she said with a slight stammer, then, quickly regaining her composure, continued. "May I speak to Mister Hapgood?"

"Whom shall I say is calling?"

Amelia was again thrown slightly. She didn't want to give too much information until she knew she was doing the right thing.

"He won't know me. I'm ringing to enquire about the possibility of acquiring a preservation order on a building of some note."

The voice at the other end became hesitant. "I'll see if Mister Hapgood is available."

Amelia quickly added before she was put on hold, "Please inform him it's a building by the architect Wilfred Latchman."

"One moment please." The line went silent. Thank goodness they're not playing some awful music while I wait, Amelia thought to herself. A full thirty seconds went by before a warm, soft spoken man's voice came onto the line.

"Joseph Hapgood here. How can I help you?"

"Oh, Mister Hapgood, thank you for talking to me."

"It's about Wilfred Latchman, I understand."

"Yes, that's right. Do you know the King's Theatre in Seahaven?"

"I do indeed. I visited it some years ago. A fine example

of Lachman's work."

"Well, I have some very reliable information that it could be scheduled for demolition."

"Really? I'm not aware of any such plans. Could you tell me the source of your information, Mrs…?"

"Miss." said Amelia automatically, then added, "I'm afraid it's rather difficult as it's not yet public knowledge and…" She was now perspiring again and her mouth was beginning to go dry.

"I really need some concrete facts. If there is anything more you can tell me." The voice of the man from English Heritage now sounded a little more urgent.

"It's not something I can discuss over the phone. Is it possible for me to meet you?"

"I'm afraid my diary is full for the next few weeks."

Amelia let out a cry of despair. "Oh dear, by then it may be too late."

Joseph Hapgood sensed that this was no ordinary enquiry. The lady sounded genuinely worried about the building.

"Look," he said, trying to sound as helpful as possible. "I'm spending the New Year weekend with friends in Eastbourne. If it's any use I could stop over in Seahaven for half an hour if it would be of help."

"Oh yes, yes." The relief in Amelia's voice was overwhelming.

"It would have to be late afternoon on the 30th."

"I can be available anytime."

Arrangements were made between them to meet in the lounge bar of the King's Hotel, situated across the road from the theatre, at four o'clock.

Finally throwing caution to the wind she added, "My name is Fothergill. Amelia Fothergill."

For a full two minutes Amelia sat with her hand still on the telephone receiver, breathing deeply and wondering if she had done the right thing. Suddenly it rang making her shout out in shock.

"Hello?" she said, showing none of her usual efficient telephone manner.

"It's Elaine."

Amelia sighed with relief as she heard her friends voice on the other end of the line.

"Have you contacted English Heritage yet?"

"A few minutes ago," Amelia confided.

"What did they say? Are they going to take action?"

"It's not as simple as that," said Amelia. "But I have made an appointment to meet Mr Hapgood on Thursday."

"The day before New Year's Eve? That's a bit odd."

Amelia related her conversation with Hapgood and then asked if Elaine would come with her to meet him.

"Wouldn't miss it for the world. I'm on holiday for the whole week." said her friend enthusiastically. "Quite a covert operation it's going to be."

"Not a word to anyone, Elaine. I'll meet you at the hotel at three forty-five."

"Can't wait!"

Amelia said goodbye to her friend and feeling more confident about what she had started, decided it was time to relax and maybe treat herself. She again picked up the phone and dialled.

***

"That's one single adult for tomorrow night's performance in the name of Fothergill. Thank you very much and please pick

146

the ticket up by seven fifteen." Mrs Nesbit had received a steady stream of bookings all morning. "At least some people have read the review," she said to Trevor, who was standing beside her.

"Thank you for coming in to man the box office," he said.

"I was glad to get out of the house. My old man's done nothing but fall asleep in front of the telly since Christmas Day. I got fed up of looking at him."

"Still, your loyalty is very much appreciated."

She flashed a smile at him as the phone rang again. "Hello, King's Theatre. Yes sir, we do have a performance tomorrow night. Just one seat? No, I'm sorry, you can't sit there but will the stalls be all right about seven rows back? The stalls — that's downstairs. Fine — yes you may pay by credit card." She began to take the details of an American Express number which she punched into the computer.

"And the name on the card is?" she enquired, then repeated it. "Bradley Harman. Thank you, Mr Harman, your ticket will be at the box office." She replaced the receiver and looked up at Trevor. "He wanted to sit in the orchestra. I think he's a foreigner"

"Must be an American. They call the stalls the orchestra over there."

"Trust them to be different," said Mrs Nesbit. "Anyway, I've put him next to that Miss Fothergill who just called. I hope they get along."

Trevor smiled at her. "I'll be in the office if anyone wants me."

SCENE NINE
WEDNESDAY, DECEMBER 29TH

"That's the lot," said Tim, as he put the last of the Christmas presents in the boot of Russell's car.

"Thank you," sighed Russell, knowing full well that it would be just him who unloaded everything when they got back home.

"It's been a wonderful, few days," Hazel said, kissing her daughter and giving her a hug. "Hasn't it, Russell?"

"Delightful," replied her husband, secretly giving thanks that they were finally heading home. Russell loved his daughter and grandchildren, but five days of playing happy families were more than enough. He relished the thought of being back in his own home, back in the town and most of all back to pursue all his various activities — secret or otherwise.

"Have a good New Year," called Lisa, as Russell backed the car out of the drive.

"I'll give you a ring next week," her mother shouted and waved to her grandchildren through the open window.

"Put that window up, or we'll catch our death of cold."

"Oh Russell, don't be such a grouch. It's a lovely day. When we get back, we ought to go for a walk along the prom."

She was right, it was a lovely day. The bright yellow sun was shining in a cloudless winter sky and it remained there for the entire journey back to Seahaven.

Russell said very little apart from cursing the occasional driver and complaining about the fact that the country roads had not been completely cleared of snow.

"At least our town council keeps things moving," he boasted. His wife just smiled and nodded. She knew he would never develop a liking for the countryside and had resigned herself to being a "townie" for as long as they were together.

***

The hotel receptionist, true to her word, had made all the arrangements for Brad's trip to the South Coast. First class rail travel, a Hertz rental car waiting for him at Seahaven station and a selection of suitable hotels.

"There are two that we would recommend," she informed him. "The Imperial, which is situated on the Promenade near to the marina and the King's, which is further along towards the town. Both have plenty of availability this time of the year."

The King's, Brad thought to himself. Same name as the theatre. It must be an omen. "The King's, I think. Can I make a reservation from here?"

"I can take care of that for you, sir. How many nights will you be requiring?"

Brad thought again for a moment and then said, "Make it for two, but tell them I may stay on further."

"No problem, Mr Harman. I'll deal with it straight away."

Brad thanked her again and received a broad, perfectly formed smile.

The hotel lobby was throbbing with winter visitors as Brad turned in search of a porter. Within a few seconds one appeared at his side and was requested to take his suitcase outside and call a cab. With lightning efficiency, the receptionist completed her task and handed Brad an envelope containing his train ticket, car hire and hotel reservation details.

"Thank you for taking so much trouble," he said, putting the envelope into his briefcase.

"No trouble at all, sir. Enjoy your trip."

Outside the porter had carried out his duties for which he received a handsome tip as Brad climbed into the waiting taxi.

"Victoria station," he called out.

"'Ave yer there in no time, Guv'nor," replied the driver, as he pulled away from the kerb. Brad smiled to himself at hearing first hand a Cockney voice that, until then, he'd only witnessed on film.

***

Gavin lay in the big double bed in Robert's bedroom, looking out of the large window at the marina across the road. It was full of boats moored there for the winter, gently bobbing up and down on what little swell there was. He had moved out of his not very salubrious lodgings on the other side of town after returning from the Christmas break.

"You'll not find anything cheaper," growled his landlady, when he informed her of his immediate departure. "And I won't be refunding your week's rent in advance."

"That's perfectly all right, Mrs McGrath," said Gavin as he quickly packed his belongings.

"You're all the same, you theatricals. Here today, gone tomorrow. I don't know why I bother to take you in. My late husband would give you what for if he weren't lying cold in his grave."

"Your late husband knows where he's better off," thought Gavin to himself. She was still moaning at him for all to hear as he closed the car door.

"I'm sure you'll soon find someone to take the room — preferably someone who can endure the freezing conditions," he shouted to her as he depressed the accelerator and drowned out the stream of abuse that followed his parting comments.

Lying there in the warmth of the luxurious bed, he struggled to come to terms with the events of the past week. Robert had been very insistent about him moving in, yet they still knew very little about each other. Had he really done the right thing? Was it all going to end in misery? These and numerous other questions continued to pound away in his head.

He looked around the tastefully decorated room. Everything was so perfect. Too perfect. This sort of thing didn't happen to him. A series of short-lived flings and countless one-night stands was the sum total of his love life. The longest relationship he had experienced was with the assistant stage manager of a nine-month tour of "Witness for the Prosecution". When the tour ended, so did the affair.

"Oh well, I may as well enjoy it while it lasts," he said out loud to himself, and lowered his head back onto the soft, downy pillow.

His head shot up again as the dulcet tone of the bedside phone began to purr. He stared at it, wondering whether or not to answer. No one else knew he was there. After the fifth ring he thought, what the hell, and picked it up.

"So, Sleeping Beauty is awake at last."

"Oh, it's you." said Gavin, flopping back down onto the bed.

"Who else were you expecting?"

"No one." Gavin sounded slightly guilty. "I mean I thought it might be someone for you who didn't know I was here."

"So what? Don't you want people to know you're there?" Robert's voice sounded hurt.

"Of course I do," was Gavin's quick response. "I didn't mean... I... Oh shit."

There was a second of silence, followed by gentle laughter from the other end of the phone.

"You bastard," said Gavin, joining in the laughter. "Don't do that to me."

"Sorry. Couldn't resist it."

"Anyway, what do you mean by leaving this morning without saying goodbye?" This time it was Gavin's turn to act hurt.

"You looked so peaceful lying there, I didn't want to disturb your beauty sleep."

"How considerate! Where are you now?"

"I'm in Brighton. I have to meet a client for lunch, so I expect you'll be gone before I get back."

"Yes." Gavin silently cursed the fact they were doing a matinee every day until well after the New Year. "I'm afraid we're not going to see a great deal of each other now the holiday is over," he added.

"I could come down to the theatre and meet you for a drink after tonight's performance," suggested Robert, tentatively.

"Would you? I would love that. It's about time you met

everyone. It will save umpteen introductions at Beverly's New Year's Eve party."

"It's a date. I'll be at the stage door. Hope the performances go well."

After the phone call, Gavin threw off the bedclothes, made his way to the bathroom and indulged in a long, hot shower.

***

Settling back in a first-class apartment aboard the ten thirty-five south coast train taking him to Seahaven, Brad sipped a rather good cup of tea. He had been warned about indulging in any beverage or edible commodity provided by the rail companies, but this tasted a lot better than some of the New York restaurants had served.

He gazed out of the window at the English countryside flashing by. Large areas of land were still white from the recent snowfalls, but as the train neared the coast these gave way to brown barren fields and hedgerows patiently waiting for the first signs of spring. The outskirts of the town looked particularly depressing in the cold morning light, with row upon row of terraced houses packed tightly together.

"We are now approaching Seahaven. Seahaven next stop," announced the conductor over the PA system.

Brad stood, put on his overcoat and collected his case from the luggage rack. Alighting from the train, he made his way into the small station concourse and immediately saw the Hertz rental office in the far corner.

"Mr Harman — yes sir, we have your reservation," said the short, bespectacled office manager. "If I could just have your signature on this form."

"Of course." Brad completed all the necessary paperwork and produced his American Express card in payment.

"The car is waiting for you outside, if you would follow me." He moved around the counter and led Brad outside.

"Here are the keys, sir," he said, passing them over together with a complimentary road map covering Seahaven and the East Sussex area around the town. He then proceeded to give a brief rundown of the controls and showed Brad the handbook and emergency phone numbers.

"Now all I have to do is remember to drive on the right side of the road — or should I say left?"

The man smiled at Brad's joke. How many times had he heard an American say that? For about ten minutes Brad studied the town map and located his hotel. The recently invented satellite navigation device was available in the car, so he punched in the reference and with a little trepidation, started the car and attempted to find reverse. He was so used to an automatic, but had been told there were none available for rent. There was only one way out of the station and the road led straight down to the Promenade.

"I hope it's main road all the way," he mumbled to himself, and slowly eased the car out of the parking area.

***

Russell allowed a thin smile to creep across his lips as he drove past the *"Welcome to Seahaven"* sign situated on the outskirts of the town.

"Soon be back in our own home," he said, with considerable relish.

"Yes," replied his wife, with nowhere near as much

enthusiasm.

He turned the car onto the main road bypassing the centre of town and running down to the Promenade. This route took them towards the rear of King's Theatre. As they approached the old building, the smile on Russell's face broadened. Not long now, he thought to himself as he stared up at the one thing standing between him and a financially rewarding enterprise.

"Russell, look out." screamed his wife with such a force that his hands momentarily left the steering wheel. Having taken his eyes off the road to look at the theatre, he hadn't noticed another car turn off the Promenade and heading towards them. Regaining control of his reflexes, he quickly returned his hands to the wheel and pulled hard down to the left. The whole car shook as the front wheels mounted the pavement, narrowly missing a bus shelter and post box. A shrill screech pierced the afternoon air as Russell slammed his foot down on the brake pedal. After what seemed a lifetime, the car finally came to a stop two inches away from the plate glass window of the post office.

The other driver, having assessed what was about to happen, swung his car to the other side of the road and pulled up just short of a British Gas repair van. The two cars had narrowly missed a head on collision and for a few seconds both drivers just sat staring ahead of them.

Eyes bulging and hands shaking, Russell suddenly let fly with a tirade of abusive language directed at the other driver. His wife, who was also shaking, tried to calm him down as he fumbled with the door handle. Pulling it with so much force that it almost came off in his hand, he threw open the door and climbed out onto the road. Still shouting at the top of his voice, he started to cross, only to be stopped abruptly by the blast of a horn from an oncoming corporation bus.

"Have you got a death wish, mate?" shouted the irate bus driver, as the blue and white double-decker thundered by and on up the road.

"Don't talk to me like that. Fucking moron," yelled Russell, but his words were drowned out by the diesel engine.

By now the other driver had alighted from his vehicle and was standing beside it. Russell marched across to confront him continuing his verbal assault, much to the amusement of a small group of pedestrians who had gathered to watch the showdown.

"What the bloody hell do you think you are playing at?"

"I'm terribly sorry." The man's calm, soft American accent briefly halted Russell's rantings. "I had indicated I was turning into the hotel parking lot." He nodded towards the King's hotel situated on the corner of the road and the Promenade and then added, "I guess I hadn't estimated how fast you were going."

"Are you trying to say I was speeding?"

"No, not at all. I'm sure it was entirely my fault. I was just making sure I had the right turning. This is my first time in Seahaven."

"Oh, a tourist," grunted Russell, as Hazel, who was still rather shaken, joined him.

"I do hope you are not injured, ma'am?"

"You could have killed us all." Russell started to flare up again as his wife laid a hand on his arm.

"Now Russell," began his wife. "Remember your angina. You don't want to bring on an attack."

For a number of years Russell had suffered with the condition and this sort of situation could easily cause it to flare up at a moment's notice.

"I can't apologise enough. My name is Harman, Bradley Harman. If there is any damage, I'd be glad to pay for it."

Russell, who immediately saw the possibility of an insurance claim, opened his mouth to speak but was stopped by Hazel.

"There's not a mark on the car. Thank goodness we're all all right — if rather shaken."

As the words of abuse had now stopped, the small audience began to disperse, slightly disappointed that the entertainment was suddenly over.

"If there is anything I can do to make amends — I'm staying at the King's for a few days. Please don't hesitate to contact me."

"That won't be necessary," said Hazel, smiling at the handsome American. "As I said, there's no harm done."

"That's very understanding of you, ma'am," said Brad, returning her smile.

"Yes, well — remember — we drive on the correct side of the road over here," Russell stated with a great amount of authority. And with that he turned around and headed back to his car.

"Goodbye ma'am." Brad gave her a courteous bow of the head. "I hope we run into each other again."

"Not in our cars I hope, Mr Harman." With the tension now subsided, they both allowed themselves a brief laugh. "And don't worry about my husband. His bark is worse than his bite!"

"Hazel!" Russell was already back in the car and had started the engine. Hazel returned to the car and joined her husband.

"He was a very nice young man. He could have knocked you for six, giving him all that abuse."

"Then I'd have sued him for assault."

"But you weren't looking where you were going, Russell."

"What do you mean? Of course I was looking where I was going, woman. Whose side are you on anyway?"

Brad watched them as they disappeared towards the Promenade still arguing. He climbed back into his car and started the engine. Checking very carefully that no traffic was approaching from either direction, he slowly turned the wheel and continued his drive into the car park of the King's Hotel.

***

The curtain fell and immediately rose again as the company took their final bow of the matinee performance. The house was almost full, mainly due to a large party of scouts and guides taking up most of the Grand Circle.

The cast left the stage and headed for their respective dressing rooms. With barely a two-hour break before they were due to start the evening show there wasn't much time to leave the theatre to eat, so an impromptu tea in the green room usually took place.

As they had been running for the best part of a week, a familiar routine now began to emerge. Carl and Alex were usually first to arrive. They poured themselves each a cup of tea and opened a plastic food box containing a veritable banquet of goodies, which they devoured rapidly. Various other cast members drifted in together with a couple of the stagehands. Max would arrive with a flask of soup and the

Guardian crossword. He would always make some ribald comment to Claire Stevens, who treated it with as much contempt as she could muster before taking a seat on the other side of the room and burying her head in another chapter of an overly sentimental novel.

Last to join the company were Gavin and Beverly. They would stop outside their respective dressing rooms to swap any tit bits of gossip that had come their way and shouldn't be shared with anyone else. Then, with a quick comment to the others about how the performance went, they too would lounge on one of the well-worn couches and read or, in Gavin's case, listen to a show album on his portable disk player.

That afternoon, apart from the sound of tea being stirred and sandwiches munched, an air of quiet descended quickly on the green room.

Beverly suddenly gave a start as she heard a familiar voice hailing her from the other end of the corridor.

"Beverly? Beverly darling, where are you?"

Swathed in an old fake fur coat that she had inadvertently *"kept"* after a tour of *"Breath of Spring"* had folded prematurely in Oldham twenty years ago, Aurelia Dumont stood framed in the doorway.

"There you are," she gushed, as Beverly stood to greet her. "Darling you were wonderful as always. The way you slap those old thighs of yours — you're the best in the business."

Beverly assumed that was a compliment as she was enveloped in Aurelia's arms. Gavin looked across at Carl and Alex who had started to giggle before the latter almost choked on a vol-au-vent.

"And Max — you old letch. Still treading the boards, I see."

"Hello Aurelia, old girl. Is Reggie with you?"

His question was answered as the ageing entertainer tottered in rather unsteadily behind his wife.

"Max. Good to see you again," he said, with a slight slur in his speech.

"Fancy a cup of tea, old love?"

"If that's all you've got," said Reggie, rather dispiritedly, until Max indicated he should follow him to his dressing room.

"I've just seen Trevor in the foyer," continued Aurelia. "The poor dear, he looks as though he's got the weight of the world on his shoulders."

Beverly nodded. "Yes, he has seemed rather distracted for a few days now." A fact she had discussed with Gavin earlier. "I think the final rehearsals took it out of him."

"Well, we're none of us getting any younger, are we darling?"

Beverly wondered how many more references to age Aurelia would manage to get in during her backstage visit.

"Anyway," she persisted. "You did say to call round after we'd seen the show, so why don't we go to your dressing room and have a good long chat?"

By *"a good long chat"* Beverly knew she was going to be pumped for any juicy bits of gossip that would readily be passed on to all and sundry by Aurelia.

"Lovely show, darlings. You were all super." Aurelia announced her verdict to the ensemble then, firmly clutching Beverly by the arm, ushered her out of the green room. Beverly turned her head and mouthed "Help" as she disappeared from view.

"Who on earth was that?" asked Claire Stevens.

"It's Aurelia Dumont." Willie Waters provided the

answer. "I used to see her and her husband in creaky old tours that used to come to our local theatre when I was a kid. I didn't know they were still going."

"They're not," said Gavin. "Gave up the business some years ago due to Reggie's medical problems."

"What were they?" enquired Carl. Gavin cupped his hand as though holding a glass and made a drinking motion. Enough said.

The quiet air descended on the green room once more. Only once or twice did a shriek of laughter from the direction of Beverly's dressing room penetrate the silence.

After about a quarter of an hour Gavin decided to act as a saviour to Beverly and rescue her from the tenacious verbal grip Aurelia had on her.

"Sorry to interrupt," he said, popping his head around the dressing room door and cutting Aurelia off in mid-flight. "But you did say you wanted to try out that new bit of business."

Beverly looked at him vaguely.

"You know, the scene in the cave." He punctuated his words with an emphatic nod of the head.

"Oh of course," she said, with a look of relief. "Thank goodness you remembered."

Aurelia stood, rather displeased at being interrupted. "Well don't let me stand in the way of artistic excellence," she quipped, with more than a pinch of irony in her voice.

"Thanks for stopping by," said Beverly. "It was nice to see you and Reggie again so soon."

"Oh yes — Reggie. I'd quite forgotten about him. Where has he got to?"

"I think he's in with Max," said Gavin.

Aurelia's face lit up at the prospect of another chatty

session and she headed off in the direction of Max's room shouting "goodbyes" over her shoulder.

Beverly flopped back down into her chair and thanked Gavin profusely for coming to her aid. She rewarded him handsomely with a large G&T.

It wasn't until Stan, the stage manager, called the half-hour for the evening performance, that the Dumonts finally left the theatre. An ashen-faced Max appeared in his doorway.

"That bitch!" he announced to the rest of the cast. "That no talent, ravaged old harpy. Do you know what she did? Started by saying how wonderful my performance was, and then spent what seemed like an eternity pulling it apart."

A few sympathetic "tuts" greeted his comments as the company dispersed and prepared for the next performance. Out of earshot, Willie Waters was heard to say, "I didn't think she had such good artistic judgement."

In the theatre foyer a few people had started to arrive, eagerly anticipating the two and a half hours of fun and spectacle, they hoped would banish any post-Christmas blues. Amelia picked up her reserved ticket and then stood looking about her. Memories of her childhood came flooding back as she noticed the familiar theatrical surroundings. The architectural features that her grandfather had pointed out during her childhood visits, although slightly faded with time, were still intact. The ornately carved handrail of the staircase that led up to the Grand Circle, and the thickly padded double doors that opened into the stalls.

Another audience member was also taking in every detail of the foyer. Amelia noticed the handsome young man standing on his own next to the box office and was then slightly surprised to hear an American accent when he asked

Mrs Nesbit where the bathroom was.

After the language barrier had been broken down and the gentleman's toilet was pointed out to him, Brad crossed the foyer, giving Amelia a dazzling smile as he passed which brought a quick flush of colour to her cheeks.

More and more people were now pouring into the theatre, so Amelia decided to take her seat in preparation for the performance. Looking around at the faded, but still beautiful designs of the auditorium, she became lost in admiration for the Latchman architecture. The thick embossed proscenium arch and the delicately embroidered fronts of the four theatre boxes. All truly delightful and certainly worth saving.

"Excuse me." Brad's voice suddenly brought her out of her dreaming with a slight start. "I believe I have the seat next to you."

Amelia once again felt her cheeks tingle as she stood to let him pass her. They barely had time to exchange a few pleasantries before the house lights dimmed and the small band began the overture.

Gavin was the first to notice him. As he made his exit, swirling his cloak to a chorus of "boos", he caught sight of Brad, who seemed slightly bewildered by the audience participation. Carl and Alex spotted him at the start of the opening number and began over-emphasising every dance step and gesture in an attempt to catch his eye.

"I'm sure he was smiling at me," purred Carl, as the chorus left the stage.

"In your dreams," replied one of the girls. "It was our skimpy Chinese costumes that put the smile on his face."

The costumes were indeed skimpy, but bore more of a resemblance to the Folies Bergères rather than ancient China.

"He doesn't seem to know what's going on," added Gavin, who was looking at Brad through a spy hole at the side of the stage.

The initial surprise Brad had at the audience's reaction to this typically British entertainment, was now beginning to wear off as he sat back in his seat and started to join in the fun. Even the sight of Max in one of his outrageous frocks with enormous boobs didn't seem to bother him. It was when Beverly strode onto the stage, slapped her thigh and announced that she was Aladdin, that Brad sat forward in his seat and stared, wide-eyed, at this leggy female pretending to be a male!

"Sorry to disappoint you boys, but I think he prefers the more mature woman," she said to them all in the interval. "These good old legs of mine can still work the magic."

"Really?" queried Claire Stevens. "I thought it was me he was looking at."

"I think you've all got him totally bemused." Trevor had come backstage to check on something and heard them all talking."

"What do you mean?" asked Gavin.

"Mrs Nesbit says he's an American."

"Oh, that explains it," chimed in Max. "They don't understand pantomime over there."

The hubbub in the foyer excited Amelia.

"Nothing like live theatre, is there?" she said to Brad, who had followed her out.

"Certainly isn't; although this kind of entertainment is very new to me."

"Is it your first pantomime?"

He nodded.

"So, don't you have this kind of entertainment in America?"

"Not to my knowledge; although it does seem great fun."

"Oh, it is. Often, it's the first thing a child sees in the theatre. My grandfather used to take me every year when I was very young."

"This certainly is a lovely building," said Brad, looking around in admiration.

"Yes, and it's absolutely criminal that they're thinking of pulling it down."

Amelia suddenly froze as she realised what she had said. Her enjoyment of the show and being back at the King's, had allowed her to drop her guard and let slip the confidential information.

"Pull it down?" exclaimed Brad incredulously. "That would be criminal. Who on earth would want to do a thing like that?"

Amelia tried to make light of what she had said. He's only a tourist, she thought to herself. It won't mean a lot to him.

"I'm afraid it's what they call progress," she said casually.

Before Brad could question her further, the bell sounded for the start of the second act.

A great cheer rang out around the auditorium as the company took an extra curtain call. Amelia was blurry-eyed with emotion. As she finished clapping enthusiastically, she fumbled with a small lace handkerchief, quickly wiping away a tear in the hope that the gentleman next to her wouldn't notice. Regardless of the fact that the production was less than perfect and, in some scenes, embarrassingly bad, the whole evening had swept her back to her childhood.

Remembering years of watching productions with her

grandfather and wishing she had the nerve to be up on the stage had produced a torrent of emotional memories. The lights, the music, the colourful costumes and the pleasure the production had given to the audience over the past two and a half hours had affected her deeply. She turned her head away from Brad and continued to mop up an errant tear that was careering down her cheek.

Brad was not aware of her emotional state. He sat staring at the curtain as though he was willing it to rise one more time so as to take another look at the array of performers accepting the audience's applause.

"Did you enjoy it?" she said finally, smiling bravely and tucking the handkerchief into her coat pocket.

For a moment he didn't reply, then he slowly turned and looked at her. "The evening has been a revelation for me," he said. "I must see the show again. Do you think I will get a seat for tomorrow?"

His question took Amelia by surprise. She had noticed throughout the performance that he had responded wholeheartedly with all the audience participation and been very generous with his applause. He had been especially enthusiastic about the quality of the principal boy and girl's musical numbers, and Gavin's suitably evil, but well-defined performance as the panto baddie. He had even made some complimentary remarks about Max's performance. But to want to see the production again — and so quickly.

"I'm sure you will be able to get a ticket. You can ring the box-office in the morning."

As they walked up the aisle towards the back of the theatre, Amelia turned and said, "I'm Amelia Fothergill."

"Brad — Brad Harman." They shook hands and then

laughed at the thought of only now exchanging introductions after enjoying each other's company for the past three hours.

"And may I say what a pleasure it has been to share my inaugural visit to a pantomime, and to this beautiful theatre, with one so enthusiastic about the building," he added.

For a few moments, Brad turned and looked around the now almost deserted auditorium, drinking in the details of the walls, the ceiling and the whole feel of it.

"It would be a great pity if this theatre were to disappear," he said, then added "Something should be done about it."

His companion slowly nodded. "I'm so glad you think so. And I shall do my very best to make sure that it will."

As they moved into the foyer, Amelia thought what a good idea it would be if his voice was added to her proposed save the theatre campaign. Seahaven needed visitors. Especially foreign ones. She was just about to suggest they talk further when she heard the tail end of another conversation.

"Goodnight, Mrs Nesbit."

"Goodnight, Mr Curtis-Smyth," said the box-office manageress, pulling on her winter coat.

Curtis-Smyth thought Amelia to herself. That was the name of the person who called her office the previous week. The owner of this theatre.

For the first time since the beginning of December there was no frost that night. The day had been fine with a partial sunlight that had finally given way to a thick cloud cover ensuring the temperature stayed above freezing. A small group had gathered around the stage door hoping to get a few moments with their favourite characters. Most of the younger ones were eager for a look at Willie Waters and clung expectantly to their autograph books and programmes.

Robert had driven down to the theatre and parked in the "Dog and Trumpet" car park opposite. He crossed the road and stood a few yards from the group listening to the comments. For a moment he was acutely aware that he was the only single male there. Most of the others were schoolchildren, unattached females and wives who had dragged their rather unwilling husbands to the stage door instead of home or to the pub for a much-needed drink. As he looked around, he noticed another man walking towards him from the direction of the theatre's main door.

Brad had said farewell to Amelia in the foyer. She, in her haste to introduce herself to Trevor, had wished him a pleasant stay in the town and hoped they would meet again. He left the building and walked the few yards towards the waiting group. Stopping in the shadow of the building, he fixed his eyes on the stage door.

Robert was wondering who he knew in the company when the excited murmurings of the crowd grew with the emergence of Willie Waters. Books and programmes were thrust forward in anticipation of a signature. Full of smiles, Willie happily signed everything he was given and posed for a number of pictures with his fans.

Having got their rewards for waiting patiently, most of the crowd began to disperse just as Max appeared in the doorway.

"Hello. Sorry to have kept you waiting," he said, in a grand theatrical manner. "Now who's first?" His voice started to tail off as he saw people leaving. Two elderly ladies holding on to each other for comfort and warmth, glanced at the old actor as they moved towards the bus stop.

"Isn't that Max what's his name — the old actor?" one of them said.

"Yes," the other replied. "I thought he was dead."

Max's smile withered away as he caught sight of a smirk on Willie's face.

"Fancy a quick one across the road? My treat." Willie made the offer to deter any misunderstanding between them.

"Don't mind if I do," said Max. "Anything to get away from these autograph hunters."

Willie glanced at the remaining two men who had their hands firmly thrust in their coat pockets and led the way to the pub. Most of the company had left the theatre by the time Gavin emerged with Alex, Carl and Beverly. He moved straight to Robert's side and squeezed his arm. Brad stayed in the shadows watching all of them. After a few quick introductions they all started to move in the direction of the "Dog and Trumpet" when Alex caught sight of the lone figure observing them.

"I told you he fancied me," he preened to the others.

"Nonsense. I caught his eye in the finale and he smiled back," protested Carl.

"He's been there a while," said Robert quietly to Gavin. "Are you sure he's not one of your admirers?"

"Who cares if he is. I've got my date for tonight."

Beverly looked back over her shoulder at Brad who had moved a few paces and was now illuminated in the orange street light. "Well, it certainly ain't me he's waiting for," she joked. "It must be Claire he's after, but she's gone clubbing with the girls."

As they disappeared into the pub, Brad stood in a quandary as to whether he should follow or go back to the hotel. After a full minute he decided on the latter.

"I hope you don't mind my intruding on you like this, but

I feel I must speak to you." After saying her farewells to Brad, Amelia had quickly crossed the foyer and placed herself in front of Trevor as he headed for his office. "My name is Fothergill. Amelia Fothergill. We spoke last week on the telephone."

Startled at being stopped in his tracks, Trevor stared at the person obstructing his path and tried to recall her name.

"I'm sorry," he started. "But I don't remember—"

"It's about this building. You've had a letter from my boss. Russell Craddick."

Any trace of a smile disappeared immediately from Trevor's face as the name of his dreaded nemesis thundered in his head.

"Oh, I see. Well, you can tell Mr Craddick that I fully intend to—" His sentence was again cut short as Amelia held up her hand and stopped him in full flow.

"Mr Curtis-Smyth, I think it is shameful that anyone, let alone a member of the Town Council, should want to do anything to this beautiful theatre."

Trevor's bottom jaw hung like an open drawer as the full impact of Amelia's words echoed around his brain.

"I'm fully aware I shouldn't be saying this, but knowing what I know I can't stand by and let this appalling act be perpetrated. Something has to be done." She was staring straight at him and shaking like a leaf, fearful of the consequences of her actions. Slowly the look of anger started to fade from the director's face and a glimmer of a smile returned.

"My dear lady. If you have a few minutes, perhaps we should talk about this in the comfort of my office."

Amelia also allowed herself a smile as she nodded in

assent and said, "I should be only too pleased."

"This way, Mrs Fothergill," Trevor said, opening his office door.

"Miss," she corrected with a modicum of embarrassment. He stood back to let her pass and as she did, she looked up into his eyes that were now shining with renewed hope and anticipation. Amelia felt that, at last, she was beginning to make progress.

***

As Brad walked slowly back towards the Hotel, he stopped once more to look at the theatre. All the sights and sounds of the previous three hours swirled around in his head. Continuing on to the hotel, his whole body slowly began to shake. A gnarled, twisted pain began to take hold of his stomach and as he approached the steps leading up to the hotel's revolving doors, he clutched at the stone pillar supporting the portico. He felt as though he was going to vomit, but nothing came. Again, his stomach churned as he tried to rationalise his actions. The Night Porter, who had emerged for an illicit cigarette, saw him and, thinking he was about to collapse, hurried down the steps to his side.

"Are you all right, sir?" he said, placing an arm on Brad's shoulder.

"Yes, I'm fine. Just a dizzy turn. Probably walking too fast," Brad offered as a weak excuse and then began to climb the steps. "Thank you for your concern. Goodnight."

"Goodnight, sir." The Night Porter reached inside his coat pocket for his packet of cigarettes and said silently to himself, "Try a little water with it next time."

The motion of the lift carrying Brad to the fourth floor did nothing to help the state of his stomach and as he closed his bedroom door and lent against it, he began to piece together all he had seen and heard that evening. Slowly an uneasy calm came over him and he did what he always did when he had a lot of thinking to do — he made himself a cup of tea.

Stirring the hot, steaming liquid, he lowered himself onto his bed and sipped. After a few moments he reached for the envelope in his briefcase and again turned over the pages of information Eliot Culvert had furnished him with. Now the names, dates, places and facts contained in the file made a lot more sense to him. He finished his tea, moved to the telephone beside the bed and dialled nine for an outside line followed by a thirteen-digit number.

"Mom?"

"Brad. How are things going?"

"I'm in Seahaven and I've tracked down the theatre. It's a beautiful building. Just how you described. They have a production on, which I saw tonight."

"And?" said his mother, with a nervous edge to her voice.

"I haven't said anything to anyone yet, but I heard something interesting and have made a decision. I'm going back tomorrow night."

***

Amelia looked around the office gazing nostalgically at the many framed posters of productions she fondly remembered from her childhood. One after the other brought memories flooding back including the one advertising *"Seahaven Remembered"*. How she wished she had been able to take part in the production Trevor had reopened the theatre with.

"I hope this is to your taste. I'm afraid I only have a bottle of dry sherry in the office." Trevor handed her a glass and then sat in his chair behind his desk.

"This is perfect, thank you," she said, sipping the cheap liquid that Delphina had provided in case of emergency.

After a few introductory pleasantries, they discussed the impending closure of the King's and agreed that a campaign must be mounted to save the theatre. Amelia also told Trevor of her arranged meeting with Mr Hapgood.

"Of course, if any of this were to be traced back to me, my career would be in jeopardy." Amelia, for the first time that night, realised the enormity of her actions.

"That must never happen," said Trevor, earnestly. "Besides, we don't want our most valuable source of information to dry up. Having you on our side is more than I could have hoped for. For the first time since receiving that letter I have a feeling that the fates are with us. After what you have told me I am hopeful that success could be on our side."

"I do hope so," echoed Amelia, finishing her sherry a little too quickly.

"Would you like me to come with you to meet the English Heritage chap tomorrow?"

"I think that might be a little unwise. If we were seen together in public there's always the possibility Craddick would find out."

"Of course, you are quite right. Stupid of me to suggest it."

"I will contact you the minute I know something, Mr Curtis-Smyth."

"Trevor, please." He crossed around his desk and,

standing in front of her, took her hand. "And may I call you Amelia?"

Immediately, a tingling sensation rushed to her cheeks.

***

A roar of laughter went up from members of the cast gathered in the "Dog and Trumpet" as Willie Waters finished one of his many comical tales of working in Children's Television. He was just about to start another one when the landlord called last orders. The group broke up as most headed for the bar to purchase a last drink.

Gavin had taken great pride in showing Robert off and introducing him to the rest of the gathering. Envious looks from Carl and Alex, as well as some of the female members of the company had kept a glowing smile on Gavin's face. Beverly managed to monopolise Robert while Gavin ordered a final drink, and insisted he attended her New Year's Eve soiree.

"Well, what do you think of this motley band of reprobates I spend my working life with?" Gavin asked, as they climbed into the car.

"I have to say I was a little wary about meeting them. I didn't think we would have a lot in common. But they all seem very nice."

"Very nice?" Gavin raised his eyebrows in a quizzical way.

"You know what I mean. It's not as though I've lived with them day in, day out for the last three weeks."

"Believe me, you wouldn't have wanted to." He cut short the rest of his sentence as his eye caught two figures leaving the stage door of the theatre. "That's Trevor — and with a lady."

"What's so strange about that?"

"Nothing, I suppose. It's just that I don't recognise her as anyone on the staff."

As Robert turned his vehicle out of the car park, Gavin peered through the rear window at the two figures deep in conversation, oblivious to anything going on around them.

SCENE TEN
THURSDAY, DECEMBER 30TH

"I'm just going to pop into the office for an hour," Russell announced to his wife, after breakfast back in the comfort of his own house.

"You're supposed to be on holiday until Monday," grumbled his wife. "And there are a lot of things to do if we're having people around tomorrow night."

"It'll only be for an hour. Just to make sure everything is still ticking over." Russell gave a rather forlorn looking Hazel a quick peck on the cheek and quickly collected his coat from the hall closet before she could start on at him again.

There was no real need for him to go to the office, but the thought of being in the house while his wife rushed around getting things organised for the following evening was too much for him to bare. Demands would invariably be made upon his time, and that was something he wasn't prepared to be drawn into. So, a quick trip to the office and an hour or so in the lounge of the golf club would suit him fine.

Amelia was already at her desk looking once again at the book on Wilfred Latchman, which was open at the page showing a picture of the King's Theatre. For a short while she pondered on the events of the past week or so, and especially on the previous evening.

Suddenly an idea popped into her head and she

impulsively reached for the local telephone directory. Quickly finding the required number she lifted the receiver and started to push the buttons. A familiar voice in the corridor outside promptly stopped her actions and she replaced the receiver as the office door swung open.

"Miss Fothergill, good morning."

"Mr Craddick, I didn't expect you in until after the New Year." Her delivery was shaky and she looked as white as a ghost. Luckily, he only gave her a scant glance and didn't even notice the open book on her desk.

"I'm not stopping. Just need to get a few things I left in my desk," he stated, crossing to the door to his office and taking out his desk keys.

Quickly regaining her composure, Amelia noticed the keys and wondered if the "few things" meant the details she had discovered pertaining to the new development. She hoped there would be no further movement until after the holidays, or at least until she had met with Mr Hapgood that afternoon.

"Anything I can help you with?" she asked, shuffling some papers towards the library book and covering the picture.

"No, thank you. Any messages?"

"I've put them on your desk together with a small amount of mail," she said, finally regaining her efficient secretarial manner. "Nothing that can't wait until after the weekend."

He disappeared into his office, closing the door firmly behind him. Amelia quickly retrieved the book and put it into her bag, pushing it under her desk and out of sight.

Standing in front of the large window with its panoramic view of where the apartment block would soon start to rise, Russell turned to his desk and gave a cursory glance at the messages and letters Amelia had left for him. He permitted himself a brief smile when he saw there was nothing from the King's Theatre or Curtis-Smyth.

"Must be too busy with his tacky travesty of a show to have read my letter," he muttered to himself under his breath. Twirling the desk keys in his fingers, he turned his attention to the drawer that he kept locked. Opening it and extracting the file, he slowly leafed through the various papers and once again began to relish the thought of how much there was to be made from the back handers he would receive from the project. Especially from Barrie Stone.

"All I've got to do now is make sure Stone gets the contract," he said to himself, whilst replacing the file and locking the desk drawer. Suddenly his intercom rang out with the call tone. "Yes, Miss Fothergill?"

"It's your wife, Mr Craddick." Amelia heard an audible sigh before Russell reluctantly told her to put Hazel through.

"What is it? I am rather busy at the moment," he snapped, leaning back in his chair and surveying the empty desk in front of him.

"I need you to pick up a few things on your way home, Russell. Have you got a pen handy?"

Realising his sojourn to the golf club was now in danger of being cut short, he started to protest. But it was to no avail and as he left his office, gruffly bidding a "Happy New Year" to his secretary, she noticed he was clutching a comprehensive shopping list.

The door closed firmly and for a few moments Amelia sat wondering if there was a chance that he may return. Eventually she lifted the receiver and once again dialled.

***

After two hours of tossing and turning, and thinking about what the night had revealed to him, Brad finally fell into a deep sleep. The bedside phone rang three times before he stirred himself from his slumbers and picked up the receiver.

"Hello?" he croaked.

"There is a call for you, Mr Harman," the voice of the receptionist purred in his ear.

"Thank you," he said, slightly surprised and wondering who could be calling him.

"I'm terribly sorry to intrude on your time like this, Mr Harman. It's Amelia Fothergill."

"Amelia Fother…" His brain finally clicked into wake-up mode as he recalled his theatre companion of the previous evening. "Oh of course, good morning."

"I hope I'm not disturbing you? I thought I would wait until you had finished breakfast before calling."

Breakfast? Brad had not yet had his customary early morning cup of tea. He squinted at the clock radio that was showing ten thirty. "No, you're not disturbing me at all," he fibbed. "What can I do for you?"

"I hope you won't think this an imposition, but after our delightful conversation last evening, I was wondering if I might interest you in adding some weight to my proposed campaign for saving the King's?"

Amelia's request had wiped away any trace of tiredness that Brad still had as he swung his legs to the side of the bed and sat bolt upright. "What sort of thing had you in mind?" he asked.

"Well as a visiting American who obviously took a great interest in the history of the theatre, perhaps you could write a letter…" Her voice trailed off as she realised how feeble her idea seemed when put into words.

"I would be only too happy to," he said, enthusiastically. "But how am I supposed to know about the planned closure?"

Amelia, for the second time that morning, lost her composure. "You're quite right; it was foolish of me to suggest it. I'm so sorry for wasting your time."

"No wait. I really would like to help. You see I have an interest in the theatre. I'm sort of in the entertainment business myself."

Brad told Amelia what his line of work was and how, many years ago, he had aspired to be an actor. Finding a kindred spirit, Amelia poured out the details of her conversation with Trevor and how she planned to meet with Mr Hapgood that afternoon at his hotel.

"What say we have dinner together after your meeting and before I leave for the theatre?"

"You are still intending to see the show again tonight?" Amelia thought his enthusiasm might have worn off in the cold light of day.

"You bet."

They arranged a time to meet and said their farewells. Brad immediately picked the phone up again and dialled the theatre.

***

"That's odd," said Mrs Nesbit, as she finished taking another booking. "I'm sure that was the American gentleman who saw the show last night. He's reserved a seat for this evening. Very insistent he had one as far forward as possible."

"Perhaps he's a fan of someone in the company. Claire Stevens, no doubt. She's had a few admirers in and I noticed she was playing directly to him on more than one occasion last night." Trevor was standing in the doorway to his office looking at the morning mail that consisted mostly of invoices. "Still, I don't care how many times people come back to see her or anyone else in the company. We need all the ticket sales we can get." To emphasise his point, he held out a handful of bills.

"Bookings are not too bad. Beginning of next week is a bit thin, but there's been a steady stream of reservations and enquires." Mrs Nesbit turned to look at him with a sudden glint in her eye. "You know what we need?"

"What?"

"A bit of publicity. Oh, I don't mean an advert in the local rag. Something with a bit of interest. Even a bit of scandal. That always gets people in."

"I hardly think a scandal would help us, Mrs Nesbit," retorted Trevor.

"You'd be surprised. Look what happened last year at the Theatre Royal, Brighton when that chap in the company was arrested for soliciting in the bus station. The place was packed for the rest of the run."

"I suppose you've got a point. I'll give the matter some thought," he said, turning back into his office and closing the door. If the news broke now about the proposed closure and redevelopment of the site, what sort of public interest would it generate? He felt like ringing the newspaper and getting them to blast it on the front page of the next edition, but then he remembered about the meeting between his newfound ally and the man from English Heritage.

***

A light drizzle had started as Amelia rendezvoused with Elaine at the entrance to the King's Hotel for their meeting with Mr Hapgood. As they moved through the reception to the lounge bar, the large, gold faced clock above the door showed the time as three-fifty.

"I do hope he's on time," said Amelia, anxiously. "Driving conditions are not very good, and I heard on the radio that the weather was much worse in London."

As they passed through the open doorway into the lounge, they noticed a few people having afternoon tea. No one was sitting on their own and no one looked like they were waiting for anyone.

"Shall we sit over there?" Elaine was pointing to a vacant table in one of the two bay windows overlooking the sea front. They crossed the room and made themselves comfortable before ordering a pot of tea for two from a young waiter who was hovering in attendance.

Both ladies silently peered out of the window at the theatre across the road. The lights of the foyer lit up the pavement area in front of the theatre, and brought a welcome bit of colour to what otherwise was a gloomy, rain-soaked Promenade.

Lost in thoughts of what might happen to the old building, neither of them noticed a gentleman appear in the lounge doorway, quickly look around the room, and then cross over to their table.

"Miss Fothergill?"

Amelia gave a start at the sound of her name and then

realised the soft tones in his voice were that of her expected guest.

"Mr Hapgood," she said, with a relieved smile on her face. "I'm so pleased you could come." She stood, extended a hand in greeting and introduced her friend. All three sat down and another pot of tea was ordered.

"Could I have lemon with my tea?" requested the man from English Heritage. The waiter smiled and nodded in assent before leaving with the order.

Amelia looked at Joseph Hapgood. He was everything she has imagined after speaking to him on the phone. Immaculately dressed in a three-piece suit and bow tie, his round face and slightly large nose supported a rimless pair of spectacles. His thin, mousy coloured hair was neatly combed with a straight parting on one side. To Amelia's well-trained eye everything was in place. A perfect example of someone meticulous about themselves and their profession.

"I arrived slightly early," Hapgood said. "So I availed myself of the time by taking another look at the theatre." With a slight nod of his head, he indicated the King's on the opposite corner. "It really is a fine example of Lachman's work, especially the foyer and grand staircase."

"Then you think it is worth saving?" Amelia wasted no time in getting to the point of their meeting.

"Oh, indeed I do," replied Hapgood, enthusiastically. "There is a slight problem though inasmuch as the rear of the building is not part of the original. I understand it was rebuilt after the Second World War."

Amelia sat back in her chair and her expression of high expectation momentarily started to fade.

"It was an authentic rebuilding programme," chimed in

183

Elaine. "I did extensive research on the theatre for a project some years ago," she added, proud of the work she had done on the production of *"Seahaven Remembered"*.

"Oh yes, I'm quite sure that doesn't diminish the case for getting a preservation order on the building. It's just that we must be ready for any objections that may come along."

Amelia seemed encouraged by his words. "Then you'll go ahead and stop any redevelopment?"

"My dear lady, I'm afraid it's not as simple as that." Amelia's immediate response was stopped by the arrival of the waiter with their tea. Elaine took it upon herself to be "mother" and for a moment nothing was said while all three stirred their hot beverage and took a sip.

Anticipating Amelia's question, Hapgood continued. "The next phase would be to contact the Department for Culture, Media and Sport."

"Where are they?" asked Amelia.

"In London. Don't worry, I have plenty of contacts there. They will need a detailed report on the building and reasons why the area is up for redevelopment." Hapgood took another sip of his lemon tea and then looked Amelia straight in the eye. "Which brings me to my next question," he said slowly. "Where did you obtain your information from and, who wants to pull the theatre down?"

Again, there was a moment of silence. Amelia looked across at Elaine with an impassioned plea of what to do on her face.

"I think you've got to tell Mr Hapgood all you know," said her friend, earnestly.

Taking a deep breath, Amelia launched into the entire synopsis of how she had come by the information.

When she had finished, Hapgood slowly removed his glasses, took out a pristine, white handkerchief and meticulously polished them. Finally, he said, "So Mr Curtis-Smyth has received a letter stating the Council's intentions, but nothing has been made public yet?"

"That is correct," confirmed Amelia.

"Then we have a slight advantage." His words encouraged Amelia, who again looked at her friend but this time with a much-relieved expression. "No doubt your boss, Mr Craddick, intends to make a splash with the Council's proposals, so I will start proceedings as soon as I get back to London on January second."

"You will?" Amelia's voice rose in volume so as to attract the attention of a few other tea drinkers.

"If I may also suggest," continued Hapgood, in much quieter tones. "That you let Mr Curtis-Smyth handle all the publicity from now on. As you say, if the fact that you knew about this proposal gets out, your position would no longer be tenable in Craddick's employ."

"He's right, Amelia," said Elaine.

"Now I really must be going if I'm to reach Eastbourne by dinnertime." Hapgood rose from his chair and all three said their goodbyes. The two friends waved as he drove his car out of the hotel car park. Their spirits were high.

The rain had stopped and a watery evening sun on the horizon made a golden pathway of light up to the door of the theatre. "I wonder if that's an omen," thought Amelia to herself.

***

"It's like déjà vu," said Alex.

"Pretty weird," added Carl.

"I hope he's not a stalker," said Claire Stevens. "Why don't you go and ask him what he wants, Gavin?" she continued giving Gavin a nudge.

"Why me?" he retorted. "He's probably just a frustrated amateur who's desperate to break into showbusiness. Silly bugger."

The group at the stage door started to laugh and Brad, the object of their conversation, eased back into the shadows of the building. He had seen that evening's performance after having dinner at his hotel with Amelia. She had related the events of her meetings with both Trevor and Mr Hapgood, and he had reiterated that he would be willing to do anything he could to help with the cause.

During the performance his mind careered through a jumble of facts revealed in the Private Investigators report and what he had learned since arriving in the English seaside town. By the time the curtain fell he had made a decision.

Next to emerge from the stage door were Max and Beverly. The others pointed out the mysterious "Stage-door Johnny" as they all crossed to the "Dog and Trumpet". Once inside, Max was pleased to have a group of ladies from the local Townswomen's Guild come up to him for autographs. Beverly and the rest of them moved to the bar where her husband was waiting for her.

"For my hard-working wife," said Greg, handing her a large gin and tonic while giving her a kiss on the cheek. "How's the show going?"

"It'll be better when we get back to doing two matinees a week instead of every day," Beverly said and then took a long drink from her glass. "God, I needed that."

After ordering drinks, they all sat at a vacant table in the middle of the room and chatted in general about the show. Their collected attention was suddenly focused on the door when it opened and Brad walked into the pub. No one made a comment as he moved to the bar and ordered a scotch on the rocks. Interpreting his request as whisky with ice, the barman produced his drink, which he downed in one gulp. The group at the table watched him as he turned to look at them.

"I do believe he's coming over," whispered Carl, as Brad started to move away from the bar.

"Good evening," said Brad, as he approached the table.

"American," uttered Alex weakly, as he stared into Brad's eyes.

"May I say how much I enjoyed the performance," continued Brad.

"As much as last night?" enquired Gavin.

"Oh, you noticed I was in both nights."

"We certainly did, dear," gushed Alex, and received a dig in the ribs from Carl. The whole table was gazing at Brad who, after slowly looking at them all, had let eyes linger on one or two of the performers.

"I'm sorry to intrude on your time, but I wonder if I may buy you all a drink?"

Everyone now relaxed under the charm of their new admirer and a round of drinks was ordered. Max noticed something was going on and managed to extricate himself from the group of ladies, one of whom had started to sing his famous "Dreaming" song.

"Another autograph hunter?" he asked expectantly.

"An American," hissed Greg under his breath. "He's

buying a round of drinks."

"Very civil of you, old love," said Max loudly, as Brad looked over towards him. "Mines a Famous Grouse if that's all right." He held out his hand to Brad. "The names Max. Max Pendleton."

"Brad Harman."

"Here from the Colonies?" joked Max.

"Just for a few days. I have some business in London."

"What sort of business are you in?" asked Greg, as they all resumed their seats after introducing themselves.

"I'm in films and television," replied Brad, to a stunned audience. "Here's my card."

He took out of his wallet, one of I.T.F's personalised cards and it was passed around the table.

"You're not here talent scouting, are you?" said Gavin, tentatively. For one brief moment they all had a fleeting picture in their minds of being cast in the next Hollywood blockbuster.

"I'm afraid not," said Brad, bursting their imaginary bubbles filled with fame and fortune. "I'm in franchising for the European market."

"And what brings you to this part of the country and to our little pantomime two nights in a row?" Beverly asked the question."

"Nothing important. Just doing a little bit of personal research."

"How intriguing," said Beverly, flirtatiously.

"Don't embarrass the man," said Greg, as he noticed a flush of colour cover Brad's face.

The conversation became concentrated on life in New York and the Broadway theatre until someone reminded the group that there was an early New Year's Eve matinee the next day, and the evening began to break up.

"It was very nice to meet you all," said Brad, as everyone started to leave the pub.

"If ever we're in New York we'll look you up," teased Alex and Carl.

"Please do, any of you," said Brad, wondering if he had done the right thing in issuing an open invitation.

"Had a wonderful time in the Big Apple back in the seventies with Richard and Liz," began Max, on another of his flights of fancy before Gavin interjected.

"We're here after the show most nights if you want to join us."

"That's very kind of you."

"We're a very hospitable group," said Beverly. "Don't be a stranger."

Brad walked back to the hotel with a slight spring in his step. His stomach was perfectly calm, his head was clear and there was a smile on his face.

He had crossed the first hurdle and knew exactly what to do next.

SCENE ELEVEN
FRIDAY, DECEMBER 31ST

"Darling!"

Swathed in a chic, if rather old fake fur that she often wore, Delphina stood posed in the doorway to Trevor's apartment like Norma Desmond in Sunset Boulevard.

"Mother, how lovely to see you." If her son sounded less than enthusiastic to see her, she ignored it and breezed into the apartment. "I didn't think you'd be back until next week," he said, closing the door.

"What? And miss celebrating the start of a new century with my talented son. I had to come back. Besides, I have some news."

"Oh?" Trevor began to show a little more interest.

"But first I need a drink. The train journey from London was an absolute nightmare. Hardly a seat to be had and I was forced to sit next to this overweight Scot who I'm sure, by the smell of him, had started celebrating Hogmanay at the beginning of December. He fell asleep, snoring loudly, and used my shoulder as a pillow."

"If you will travel on a holiday, what do you expect?" Trevor handed her a gin and tonic and poured himself one. "Anyway, what's this news you bring?"

Delphina took a sip of her drink and leaned back into a comfortable position on the sofa.

"Wilfred Latchman!" she declared, grandly.

"What about him?"

"Do you know who he is?"

"Of course I do. Part of the show 'Seahaven Remembered' was about him."

"Ah, but do you know how significant his name is?"

"You mean as a designer whose architecture should be preserved?"

"Exactly. And especially the architecture of the King's Theatre."

"Yes, well as a matter of fact you're the second person to come up with information on Mr Latchman."

"Oh?" said Delphina, with a deflated look as the wind was quickly taken out of her sails.

Sitting opposite his mother, Trevor proceeded to relate the conversation he had had with Amelia two days ago and the contents of a phone call she had made to him earlier that day.

"So, the wheels are already in motion to put a stop to Crabbage or Caddy, or whatever his name is, going ahead with his evil little scheme?"

"Yes, but very slow motion at the moment. Amelia—"

"Amelia?" said his mother, with a slightly quizzical look.

"Miss Fothergill," continued Trevor. "Says the English Heritage chap suggests that, as I've been sent a letter of intention from the Council, we go public before they do. Get one over them, so to speak."

"Splendid idea," said Delphina. Then, grinning like the proverbial cat with the cream she added, "And I have a further piece of information that will top this whole story off rather nicely."

"All right mother," said Trevor, wearily. "You may have

the final bow."

Delphina rose from her position on the sofa and crossed over to replenish her glass looking every bit the Grand Dame of the theatre preparing for her curtain speech.

"Not only was the King's Theatre designed and built by Latchman to commemorate the beginning of the reign of George V, but when the Royal Family paid a visit to the town, they were so taken with the theatre they commissioned a model replica."

Trevor was now giving Delphina his full attention.

"Apparently, it's all to scale, with the intricate design of the façade completely replicated down to the last detail. And would you believe it is still in existence in Buckingham Palace to this very day." She stood as though waiting for a tumultuous round of applause to break out. Instead, Trevor crossed to her, beaming with delight and gave her an affectionate embrace.

"This is wonderful news," he said, and kissed her on both cheeks. "It's bound to add a lot of weight to the campaign. But how did you find all that out?"

"Reggie and Aurelia's old agent, Bernie Belchard, is also a theatre historian. I rang him and asked him to find out what he could for me, and he came back with all that information."

Trevor could not contain the joy he felt at that moment. He walked around the room with a slightly inane grin on his face and with the feeling that a great weight had been lifted from his shoulders. Finally, he stood still, took a deep breath and said quite cogently, "I'm going down to the theatre to see how the matinee is going. You know I feel I can start to the New Year, the new Millennium, with a lot more optimism than I had a few days ago."

"Talking of New Year," said Delphina. "Be a darling and

drop me off in the town, would you? I've a million things to do before we leave for Beverly's party."

**

Pushing back the duvet, Brad sat up in his large double bed and rubbed the sleep from his eyes. He had slept soundly for the first time since arriving in Seahaven and, after being gently lulled back into consciousness by Brahms Violin Concerto coming from Classic FM on the radio alarm, he found his head clear and his mind fixed on what he must do before the day was through.

After an invigorating shower, he ate a hearty breakfast in the hotel dining room and then stopped by the reception desk to look at a rack of brochures advertising various places of interest to visit. Most of them were closed for the winter, but one of the recreation areas, just outside the town with "spectacular views of the surrounding countryside", caught his eye. Picking up the brochure, he made his way back to his room and consulted the complimentary Seahaven map.

The recreation area was about five miles outside the town on the road that passed the Marina. "Not too daunting a drive," Brad thought to himself. And it would hopefully be somewhere quiet where he could finalise his plans.

The weather looked bright and the overnight cloud cover had meant there was no frost. Having worked out his route, Brad drove out of the hotel and turned onto the Promenade. There was very little traffic about and he assumed most people were preparing for the evening festivities.

He was soon passing the Marina and heading out of town on the coast road which climbed quite steeply. Apart from a couple of traffic lights and a round-a-bout, which confused him at first, there were no major road problems and soon he saw a sign for the recreation area car park.

"It's a pound all day this time of the year," he was informed by an aged attendant wearing a large black overcoat and fingerless mittens.

"I'll only be here for an hour or so," said Brad, glancing at the clock on the dashboard that showed two forty-five p.m.

"Still a pound," sniffed the attendant, as he produced a ticket in return for the coin Brad had given him. "Park where you like. We're not exactly packed out."

Indeed, they weren't. Brad saw only five other vehicles as he drove across the tarmac and pulled up in a space with a perfect view of the ocean. Looking through his driving mirror he noticed three of the cars were empty. Another one to his left contained an elderly couple who seemed to be bird watching, and the fifth one parked way down at the far corner was a mobile home with all the curtains closed.

After the drive from the hotel the car was warm and Brad wondered whether to stay there or venture out to stretch his legs. Finally, he decided on the latter and, making sure his thick winter coat was buttoned up, he opened the car door. His eyes stung slightly in the cold air and the chill breeze immediately made him think twice about going any further. But as he was now out of the car he may as well continue. He pulled the collar of his coat up and started to walk towards a sign that said "Cliff Path".

This took him right to the edge of the cliff and gave a rather splendid view of the beach and rocks below and out over the bay. A lone oil tanker could be seen on the horizon and, turning to look East, Brad saw a breath-taking vista of the surrounding countryside and in the distance the bay of another seaside town. Slowly he turned a full circle until he was facing back to where he had come from. The whole of Seahaven could be made out in great detail. He could see the Marina, the Promenade and the King's Theatre lit up for the matinee performance.

He turned another three hundred and sixty degrees taking in the view. The brochure had been perfectly right in its description; it was a spectacular sight. He decided to explore further and moved along the path that started a cliffside descent. In the shade of the cliff the wind subsided and, as the sun was now out, the temperature felt a little warmer than would have been expected for the last day of the year.

Holding on to the safety rail that ran all along the path he looked down at the jagged rocks below. The tide was in and the waves were pounding the rocks, their white foam sending up a spray that caught the morning sunlight and created a brief rainbow. It reminded Brad of the permanent rainbow Niagara Falls made, and that in turn reminded him of home. His parents had taken him to Niagara and Toronto for his eleventh birthday and he had been back many times since.

How far away everything seemed at that moment. His home, his job and his parents. Thoughts flooded back into his mind as to what he was doing in this little English seaside town. What did he hope to achieve here? Was he doing the right thing? Questions, questions. He thought he had answered them once already, but now they were gnawing away at him again. Staring at the waves pummelling the rocks below made him feel dizzy and his grip tightened on the rail.

"Good afternoon."

The voice made him step back quickly from the rail and

turn to his right. The elderly bird watchers were coming down the path towards him.

"We saw you brave the weather and decided to do the same," said the man. They were a couple well in their seventies Brad thought, but looked fairly sprightly for their age. He wore a raincoat and flat hat and she, thick women's trousers, a long coat and headscarf. Both of them carried binoculars around their necks.

"It doesn't seem as windy here," said Brad, smiling at them.

"Oh, you're an American," said the woman, pushing back a wayward piece of hair that had escaped from under her headscarf.

"I am that," replied Brad. "Although I was born in England."

"We've never been to the USA," the old man informed him. "My wife's not one for flying."

The smile vanished from the woman's face and Brad detected a look of sorrow come over her countenance.

"That's a shame. I think you'd like the country, especially the New England States. The scenery is beautiful, and looks stunning in the Fall. Not unlike parts of Britain, so I'm told."

The woman looked at him again and attempted a smile, but it vanished again when Brad mentioned how quick the flying time was compared with some years ago.

"I'll just go and sit over on that bench for a minute," she said to her husband, and wandered away to a seat set in the rock face.

"You'll have to excuse my wife," said the man in hushed tones. "Any mention of flying or aircrafts tends to upset her."

"I'm terribly sorry," apologised Brad. "I didn't realise..."

"That's all right. You weren't to know." It was now the man's turn to show an expression of sorrow. "You see our only son was killed in a plane. He was in the Royal Air Force and there was an accident during a training exercise."

Brad went cold. Not from the effects of the weather, but from the feeling of the tremendous loss this couple must have suffered.

"I — I don't know what to say."

"Oh please, you weren't to know. It was some time ago now; back in the seventies." The old man went on to explain how keen they had always been on bird watching and how they had travelled all over Europe and to Africa. But now, since the accident, they just visited places around the British Isles.

"We were too old to have any more children," said the man, with heavy regret in his voice. "You don't realise what you've had until you've lost it, do you?" He looked straight at Brad and noticed the American staring straight out in front, lost in thought.

For a few seconds neither of them said anything, until the old man broke the silence. "Well, I'd better be getting Edith back to the warmth of the car. Don't want her catching pneumonia."

"Of course," said Brad, coming out of his reverie. "It was very nice to meet you."

"You too. Have a pleasant stay." The old man shuffled off towards his wife and Brad watched as the two of them, holding very tightly to each other, made their way back along the path.

Brad remained looking out to sea for a few more minutes before quickly returning to his car. A look of determination was fixed on his face as he reversed out of his parking space and headed for the car park exit. The attendant was dozing inside his hut as Brad turned with a little too much speed onto the main road.

"It's got to be now or never," he said out loud, and pressed his foot down harder on the accelerator.

Crossing the town boundary line, he noticed a sign stating that the speed limit was forty and that cameras were in operation. He took the pressure off the accelerator and, keeping within the law, drove back to the hotel. In his room he took two or three papers from the envelope Culvert had given him. Putting them safely in the inside pocket of his jacket, he made his way out of the hotel, across the road towards the King's Theatre.

He started up the steps of the theatre leading to the foyer, but then stopped and looked at his watch which showed 4.50. The afternoon performance would be finishing very soon, so changing his mind, he walked the short distance to the stage door. As he opened it, he heard the sound of laughter coming from the afternoon audience. Momentarily stopped in his tracks, he looked around at the unfamiliar surroundings. Immediately to the left was the stage doorman's office. As Trevor hadn't the funds to employ a Stage Doorman, it was unmanned. Slowly, Brad started to walk towards where the laughter was coming from when a voice said, "Can I help you?"

He turned round to see a man in a bright, glittery Chinese costume coming out of one of the rooms. "Oh, it's you." said Carl. "And what can we do for you, dear?"

"I-I..." Brad started to stammer, when Alex joined them.

"You've not been in to see the show again, have you?" he asked of Brad, who was now thinking he ought to abandon his visit.

"No, I have some business to discuss…"

"With Trevor?" Carl chimed in inquisitively, before Brad could finish his sentence. "He'll probably be Front of House."

Brad was about to answer when the PA system crackled and Stan's voice announced, "Full cast on stage for the finale."

"Oh, got to go," continued Carl. "If you just wait here, he's bound to come back stage after the finale." And he and Alex both scurried off in the direction of the stage.

Brad looked at the doors leading off the corridor. He moved along until he saw the name on the door he recognised. Slowly, he reached out a hand and knocked.

No reply.

Of course not. Everyone was on stage.

The familiar music of the finale started and the sound of clapping and cheers filled the backstage corridor. Another couple of minutes passed and then Brad heard the sound of chatter as members of the cast headed off stage. Not wanting to be seen standing in the corridor, he quickly opened the dressing room door and went inside. The smell of stale air and greasepaint filled his nostrils. His heart was beating faster as he looked round at the array of costumes hanging up on makeshift rails and heating pipes. With a last-minute change of mind, he turned to leave the room.

Too late. A familiar voice was heard outside the room and the handle of the door turned.

Brad backed away until his retreat was stopped by the dressing table. Staring at the door, he held his breath as the occupier of the room entered.

"Well," the person exclaimed. "The boys said you were waiting to see someone, but I never thought it would be me."

"I must apologise for having come into your room

uninvited, but there is something very important I have to say to you."

"How intriguing. Do sit down."

Brad sat on an old Bentwood chair next to the dressing table.

"Now what is it you've got to tell me?"

"I'm afraid there's no easy way to say this." said Brad, and took a deep breath, "I think you... Are my mother."

Reaching for the ever-present bottle of gin, Beverly froze.

END OF ACT ONE

ACT TWO

SCENE ONE
FRIDAY, DECEMBER 31ST (CONTINUED)

Jeremy and Martha Harman had never kept any secrets from their son. From an early age when he was able to understand, they had informed him that he was adopted. When he was older, they told him that if ever he wanted to find out who his real parents were, they would not stand in his way. It had never bothered him during his school years, but a documentary on adoption made by I.T.F had started him thinking that maybe he should find out where his roots lay.

Living in America could have made the job of tracing his beginnings a little more difficult. But with the help of his parents providing places, dates and his original birth certificate, the information passed on to Eliot Culvert enabled the detective to track down who Beverly Potts, Seahaven's Beauty Queen of 1971, had become.

The words of Brad's revelation bounced around in her head. Eventually the power of speech returned, and in shock rather than anger, Beverly spat out, "What are you talking about?"

"I know this must come as a total surprise to you, but I felt we needed to be alone and with everyone always around..." He didn't complete his sentence.

"My baby died at birth. I never even knew if it was a boy or a girl." Beverly's voice was shaky and faltering as the vivid picture of the moment she was told of the events filled her mind. "How can you be my son? How can you?"

"I have some documents to show you," he said, almost inaudibly.

But Beverly wasn't listening. Her mind flashed back to those harrowing days in the Brighton hospital where she had suffered excruciating pain giving birth to what she was told had been a still-born child. Had she been lied to by her aunt, or was this some sick hoax that had been concocted to ruin her perfect life with her devoted husband?

Brad never took his eyes off her. He waited until the glazed look that had taken hold of her slowly changed, as if she was coming out of a trance. He saw the face that had been smiling and welcoming now contorted with anguish.

Silence.

And then in a quiet, almost disbelieving tone, she spoke. "Documents?"

Reaching into his inside coat pocket, Brad pulled out a crumpled birth certificate and laid it down on the table in front of her. "I was born on July 15th 1972 in Brighton, England. The name of the father is listed as 'unknown', the mother, Beverly Potts." Brad then took out a photocopy of a newspaper article and picture showing the crowning of "Miss Seahaven 1971" as seventeen-year-old Beverly Potts. "Is that you?" he asked, quietly.

Even through the layers of greasepaint the colour seemed to have disappeared from Beverly's face. She sat totally immobile for what felt like an age, just staring at the pieces of paper in front of her. She was unable to speak, unable to feel any sensation in her body. She was numb — totally numb. Only her mind was active, rushing backwards in time, rewinding her life to a period she had desperately tried to wipe from her memory.

London. That awful club with its clientele of leering men and their false promises. And then the feeling of despair and humiliation at returning home with nothing to show for her excursion into the big wide world except an addition to her life that she didn't really want.

Or did she?

Exiled to Brighton, wondering what was going to happen to her. Feeling very scared, but being told no need to worry. Aunt Flo will take care of everything. All she had to bear was the pain. The excruciating pain. Then finally the relief, the blessed relief that it was all over. On July 15th 1972. A date Beverly would never forget.

From that day on nothing was ever mentioned about "the incident". It was as though that chapter in the life of Beverly Potts had been totally erased.

A new life for her. A new beginning.

As the days and months and years passed, the recollection of those anguished times grew dimmer. On occasions when friends gave birth or she saw parents with happy children playing on the beach, the memories would suddenly come flooding back of that awful time — and of the child she never saw.

And now there, a few feet away from her, someone she never knew existed. A child, no — a man. A son.

Her first instinctive reaction was to dispute his statement. She didn't want to know. She didn't want anything rekindling those harrowing days of her youth. It was all in the past. Her life with Greg was a good one. She didn't want anything to disrupt it.

But then slowly her eyes moved to look at the reflection in the mirror of the person beside her. A son who had grown into a fine, handsome young man. The son who had now come looking for his mother.

Tears welled up in her eyes and started to cascade down her cheeks as she turned to face him.

"Please don't cry," he stammered. "I needed to know and I didn't want to just phone from the other side of the Atlantic. I thought if I came here and saw you — met you first; then decide whether or not to tell you who I was. Well... I thought it was the best way." The words had started to flow quicker and then, suddenly there seemed nothing more to say.

They stared at each other for a few seconds, then Brad continued. "I don't want to be the cause of any upset to you or your husband. If you want me to go, I'll understand. I just needed to see you once and talk to you."

Beverly said nothing. Then, with the emotion of a mother touching her child for the first time, she tentatively reached out a hand and softly stroked his cheek.

Finally, the words came. "My son." Simultaneously, their arms went out as they clung to each other in an emotional embrace.

"I'm sorry, I'm sorry," was all that Brad could find to whisper in her ear. "I'm not here to make trouble. I just wanted to know." They broke from their embrace and Beverly, with her finger pressed to his lips to stop him apologising, was nodding her head.

"Shh," she said, through a torrent of tears. "It's all right. Truly, it's all right." She could see the emotion of the moment had overtaken him. Half laughing, half crying they clung to each other again.

Their reunion was suddenly interrupted by a knock on the door.

"Come on, you old slapper. Aren't you ready yet?" The jocular insult came from Gavin. He and some of the cast, were going to the pub after the New Year's Eve matinee.

Wiping away tears, make up and mascara with a tissue, Beverly called back, "I'll give it a miss. I need to take a shower and then there's so much to be done before tonight's party."

"OK. We'll see you later." Then he added, "You haven't seen that handsome American hunk, have you. Apparently, he was hanging around the stage door."

"No such luck," called out Beverly, staring across at the face Gavin had so accurately described.

"I should go," said Brad, after he heard Gavin and the others leave.

"But we must talk. There's so much to say. So much I need to know about you."

"But not now. We will talk if you would like to."

"Like to?" Beverly's voice rang out with a joyous resonance.

"I can stay around for a few more days. Maybe we can meet up tomorrow."

"Tomorrow nothing. You're coming to my party tonight."

"Oh no. I don't think that would be a good idea."

"Nonsense. You can't be on your own; not tonight of all nights."

What about your husband?"

"Greg and I have never had any secrets. I told him everything about my life before we got married."

"But the others. What will they say?"

"They don't need to know anything just yet. I'll say we

bumped into each other outside the theatre and as you were all alone on New Year's Eve, I invited you along."

Brad looked doubtful.

"I'm an actress darling. I'm used to improvising. Especially in a Curtis-Smyth production."

A smile broke out on both faces. Any tension that was initially there had now gone.

She gave Brad her address and arranged that he would come early so as to meet Greg "officially". "Obviously I'll need to tell him what's happened, but there won't be any problem, I promise"

As Brad turned to leave, she caught hold of his sleeve and turned him around to face her. "Gavin was right", she said tenderly. "You are a handsome hunk."

***

"Barrie, Ann, how lovely to see you both." Russell extended a welcoming hand to Barrie Stone and gave his wife an affectionate kiss on the cheek. "So pleased you could both come."

"Very kind of you to invite us again this year," said Barrie, crossing the Craddick threshold and removing his coat.

"New Year's Eve wouldn't be the same without your nearest and dearest around to celebrate it with," chortled Russell, managing to place an unseen hand on Ann Stone's posterior as she followed her husband into the house.

"Where's Hazel?" Ann asked her secret admirer.

"Being the industrious housewife in the kitchen. Hazel," he called. "We have guests."

Apart from the Stones, Russell had invited a number of

other contacts from his rather shady list of business associates. Hazel had managed to include some old personal friends, so the evening wasn't all one sided.

A four-course meal had been prepared for the special evening, and as each of his guests arrived, Russell, playing the jovial host, organised the pre-prandial drinks.

Barrie was already engrossed in conversation with the managing director of a building supply company as Russell crossed to Ann Stone with a sweet sherry.

"You're looking particularly ravishing this evening," he whispered.

"A little too loudly," she thought. "Behave yourself," she said, through clenched teeth.

"Ravishing and ready to be ravished," he continued. Ann decided he was playing too dangerous a game and moved to speak to a group of wives on the other side of the room.

The party progressed into the dining room where they all enjoyed the exquisite meal Hazel, with very little help from her husband, had spent the entire day preparing. Before they all retired to the lounge for coffee and liqueurs, Russell rose from his place at the head of the table to propose a toast. For a fleeting moment Hazel thought it might be to her in grateful thanks for her culinary efforts, but it was not to be. Instead, he wished them all a prosperous New Year and a large return on all their projects, which brought a round of applause accompanied by hearty sounds of "hear, hear".

Back in the lounge, the group again split into male and female camps. Russell made a number of arrangements to meet with some of them to discuss "something on the horizon". He didn't give a lot away, but whetted a lot of appetites.

After the obligatory singing of "Auld Lang Syne" as the new millennium dawned, the party formally broke up. Russell managed another furtive word with Ann as he helped her on with her coat. "See you in a couple of days," for which he received a subtle smile.

Closing the door after the last guest had gone, Russell returned to the lounge and poured himself a large brandy. As Hazel busied herself clearing away the remnants of the meal, he sat in his favourite armchair and thought comforting thoughts of what the next few months had in store.

Little did he know that events unfolding at a party on the other side of town were to have grave repercussions on his underhanded schemes.

***

Beverly decided to forego the dubious delights of the theatre's antiquated shower system in favour of a long soak in the bath when she got home. She was so relieved she had declined the offer to join the other members of the cast in the Dog and Trumpet. The last thing she wanted to do was indulge in idle chatter with the events of the last hour whirling around in her head.

After Brad had left her dressing room, she had sat quietly by herself slowly coming to terms with the enormous change that had taken place in her life. She knew Brad was not there to make any trouble; that he genuinely wanted to meet her and in so doing complete the jigsaw puzzle that was his life. What a brave decision it was of his, she thought, to come all this way to seek out his roots.

The more she thought the more she realised how much she

wanted to know about him. Where and how he lived, what his life was like, what his adoptive parents were like? So many questions, but for now, they would have to remain unanswered. She had a house full of guests arriving in a few hours for the party. How she wished she didn't have to act the perfect hostess when all she wanted to do was be with her husband — and her son.

Arriving home, she drew a bath and laid out the outfit she had already chosen for the party. The water was warm and comforting as she closed her eyes and relived the moment of revelation. The moment when a dashing young man from another world suddenly entered hers and changed it forever.

"Dreaming of your lover?"

So removed from the present was Beverly, that she hadn't heard her husband arrive home with a car full of beer, wine and spirits. She hadn't heard him coming up the stairs or seen him put his head around the bathroom door.

"Oh!" she gasped, opening her eyes with a start.

"Sorry to give you a jolt. Were you asleep?" He leaned over and kissed her forehead.

"No," she said, catching her breath.

"The Cash and Carry was heaving. I managed to get everything — I think. Plenty of gin and whisky, so we're all right. The others can fend for themselves." He moved back to the open door. "I'll unload, put the car away and have a G and T waiting for you when you come down."

"Thanks," she shouted, as he left. Then added quietly to herself, "I'll need it."

True to his word Greg had a drink waiting for her when she eventually came down stairs. He had settled himself in front of the television and was watching the final minutes of

"Gone with the Wind".

"That's right Rhett, treat 'em rough." he said, playfully grabbing Beverly's hand and pulling her down next to him on the sofa.

As the credits rolled, she reached for the remote and switched off the television. Greg turned to his wife with a look of surprise, but before he could say anything she had started to speak.

"Greg. I've got something very important to tell you."

Their relationship had always been built on the solid understanding that they never kept anything from each other. Any problems, any minor irritations that affected them individually, or as a couple, were always talked about and resolved as quickly as possible. They had got through twenty-five years of marriage that way with hardly a ripple to rock the boat. But Beverly's revelation produced, if not a tidal wave, certainly a large swell.

Greg stared at her while trying to comprehend the immensity of what he had just heard. Eventually, and quite quietly, he found the words to respond. "I can't believe it. I can't believe that someone could be so cruel as to tell you your child had died."

"Not someone. My fucking Aunt Flo," Beverly said. "I hated her. I always hated her." The loathing in her voice immediately started another flow of tears.

Greg moved quickly and cradled his wife in his arms. "Hey, shh," he said, stroking her hair.

"All those years. All those lost years." Beverly was still crying her eyes out, so much so that Greg's sleeve was turning quite damp. He moved his arms from around her shoulders and held her facing him. "Now listen to me. This should be a great occasion. You've said what a nice man he seems. He just wants to get to know you. He's not asking to move in or anything."

"I know, I know," she wailed.

"Then what's all the crying for? Aren't you pleased he's come looking for you?"

"Yes, of course I am. It's just so sudden, so unexpected. And today of all days."

"What better way to start the New Year? The New Century." He handed her a tissue to wipe her tear-stained face and then kissed her. "Now you'd better go and repair your make-up, ready for your guests. And your son."

Grabbing another handful of tissues, she stood up and gazed adoringly at her husband.

"Oh Greg, thank you."

"What for?"

"For being the best. The very best husband anyone could ask for."

As she left the room, Greg crossed to the fold down bar and poured himself a very large whisky. As he brought the glass to his lips, a thought flashed into his mind. Suddenly, he wasn't just a husband, he was a stepfather! The stepfather of someone who had bought him a drink in the pub the night before.

***

Amelia sat in her armchair staring at the television. A particularly gruesome war film was half way through and the other channels carried the obligatory holiday fayre of game shows and situation comedy repeats. "Such a lot of rubbish they put on at holiday time," she thought to herself as she

213

flicked over the pages of the TV guide.

New Year's Eve had come to mean very little to Amelia. She had always felt rather guilty at the idea of leaving her mother alone. Feeble attempts at trying to make the evening an entertaining one had always fallen flat; and long before the firework displays on the television had started, her mother was complaining of tiredness and wanting to go to bed.

Elaine had invited her to a supper and dance being held at the Seahaven Conservative Club, but as she was going with a gentleman co-worker from the library, Amelia politely declined the offer.

"Amelia, I'm not going to let you spend tonight on your own", insisted Elaine.

"But you will be with all your friends", began Amelia.

"And you're one of them. I'll pick you up at eight thirty."

So, there she was, sitting with a cup of tea, waiting for the time to pass.

"Amelia Fothergill, this won't do at all," she told herself and stood up defiantly. "I know what you need!" She moved to the large, rather antiquated sideboard that once belonged to her parents and opened one of the cupboards. There she found a bottle of very expensive sherry — a Christmas present from her cousin in Ipswich. Pouring herself a generous measure she moved back to her chair.

"That's more like it," she said taking a sip. Then pushing a button on the TV remote, she changed channels and started to watch a documentary about the life and habits of the rhinoceros in East Africa. After a few more sips of sherry, she found herself giggling at a sequence where a male rhino was squaring up for a fight with a rival. Facing head on to the camera, the rhino momentarily reminded her of Russell

214

Craddick in a particularly bad mood.

She giggled again as the rhino charged and missed. Lifting the glass to her lips for another sip, she was suddenly startled by the ringing of the phone.

"Who on earth could that be," she said out loud, putting down her glass and turning down the commentary on the TV.

"Seahaven 68435."

"Miss Fothergill. Amelia?"

"Yes" There was a slight tremor in her voice as she recognised the familiar voice of the caller.

"It's Trevor Curtis-Smyth here. I hope you don't mind my calling you?"

"Not at all," she stammered. "How nice to hear from you."

"I've told my mother all about our meeting and what you are doing for our cause."

"Oh, it's nothing."

"Believe me, it means a great deal to us both. Mother is here and would like to have a few words."

Amelia knew all about Delphina Curtis and had seen her in a number of productions over the years.

"Amelia, darling," bellowed the actress down the phone. Amelia felt like dropping into a curtsey at the sound of theatrical royalty. "I just had to tell you in person how grateful we both are for your help."

"Oh please—" began Amelia.

"It's people like you who are so important in keeping our great theatres in Britain alive and operating."

"Well, I've always loved the theatre."

"We humble actors would be nothing without the support and dedication shown by the public."

"That's very kind—"

"You don't know what an inspiration your actions have been to Trevor in this hour of desperation," ploughed on Delphina.

"Thank you, Miss Curtis."

"Delphina, please. I know we're going to be the best of friends. Until we meet, au revoir."

There was a slight pause and then Trevor came back on the line.

"Sorry about that," he apologised. "Mother is apt to get a little emotional at times."

Amelia heard Delphina remonstrating in the background.

"She was very kind in what she said."

"Anyway, all I wanted to do was to thank you again and to wish you a Happy New Year."

"And a Happy New Year to you, Trevor," she said coyly, before adding, "And I hope it *is* a happy one."

As she replaced the receiver, Amelia felt herself glowing all over — and it wasn't from the sherry. Now she was ready to go out and have a good time.

***

By ten thirty that night, the party at Sycamore Grove was in full swing. All the guests had arrived except Trevor and Delphina, whom everyone assumed were going to be fashionably late. As well as the King's company of Thespians there were business associates of Greg's and close friends and neighbours. Sounds of lively chatter and laughter pervaded the air as the guests greeted each other and immediately launched into all the gossip since they last met.

Earlier that evening, by prior arrangement, Brad had

arrived and officially met Greg. Mother, Stepfather and Son stood nervously in the hallway until Greg broke the ice by warmly shaking Brad's hand and offering him a drink. All three chatted for over an hour, with Brad telling a very truncated version of his life story.

There was so much more for them to say, but the conversation was interrupted by the arrival of their first guests; none other than Aurelia and Reggie Dumont.

It had been decided that the reason for Brad's presence at the party was that, as a fan of the show, he had already met some of the cast and, as he was on his own at New Year, Beverly, in her usual big-hearted way, had invited him along. Everyone accepted this as a perfectly natural thing to do, and soon Brad was enveloped in numerous conversations and began to feel more relaxed than he had done in days.

Another relative stranger at the party was Robert. He stayed close by Gavin's side, desperately trying to remember everyone's name as he was introduced to them. When he was finally introduced to Brad, the two realised that they were the "newcomers" to the circle of mainly theatrical folk, and fell into conversation on topics of a more general nature.

"New Jersey?" exclaimed Robert, after hearing where Brad had been raised. "I have a cousin who lives just outside Atlantic City. We were at school together, but before going to university, he decided to take a year out and travel around the USA. Instead of coming back he met a girl, got married and now has three kids and sells insurance."

"Have you ever been out there?" asked Brad.

"A couple of times. Once to see him after his first child was born and then on a holiday to San Francisco three years ago."

"What a great city."

"So is New York."

"Ah, you've sampled the Big Apple?"

"Only for a couple of days at the end of my first trip. I'd love to go back. It's so alive."

"The city that never sleeps." smiled Brad. "You're welcome to come and stay anytime. Both of you," he added, as Gavin arrived with a replenishment of drinks.

"What are you two cooking up?" he said, with mock suspicion.

"We've just been invited to New York."

"Really?"

"Where abouts are you?" enquired Robert.

"Twenty-First Street in Chelsea. And it's just a short walk to Greenwich Village," he added, with a knowing wink.

"Sounds perfect," beamed Gavin, slipping his arm around Robert's shoulders.

"As long as you don't expect me to do the conducted tour of the bars," warned Brad. "My watering hole is further uptown." All three burst into laughter and continued chatting and drinking.

"Everything seems to be going smoothly," observed Greg, as he topped up his wife's glass.

Beverly was looking across at her son. "Yes, thank goodness. I've been on tenterhooks all night in case people started asking too many questions."

"All anyone is interested in is eating, drinking and having a good time. And talking of time, where have Trevor and Delphina got to?"

"Just arriving by the sound of it," said Max, as he tottered by on the way to the drinks table.

A chorus of "Darlings" went up near to the living room door. As the crowd parted, there stood Delphina with Trevor hovering behind her.

"Look at her," said Max, filling his glass. "You'd think she'd just opened in the West End."

"Now Max, said Beverly. "You know Delphina loves to make an entrance." And with outstretched arms, she crossed the room to greet her final guests.

"I hope we're not too late," said Trevor apologetically. "Mother had a few phone calls to make."

"One has to remember, at this time of the year, those poor dears who haven't seen me for ages," announced Delphina, as though half the theatrical profession wouldn't be able to function without a call from her. "Now who's here?" she continued, surveying the sea of faces in front of her.

"Whisky?" Greg said quietly to Trevor. "I have a rather good malt hidden away."

"You read my mind," said Trevor, and they both headed off towards Greg's study.

Delphina commandeered Beverly into introducing her to anyone she didn't know. This consisted mainly of the neighbours and colleagues of Greg's, who were fascinated at meeting a "celebrity" from the London stage, even if her name was only vaguely familiar to most of them.

Brad had wandered over to where the buffet was laid out and helped himself to a few sandwiches, when Claire Stevens (who had been eyeing him up all night) jostled his arm.

"I'm so sorry," she exclaimed, "I didn't make you drop anything, did I?"

"Well, that's a new line." said Alex, and got an icy stare from the young actress. He and Carl had been watching her attempts to get an introduction to the American ever since she arrived.

"No, I'm fine," smiled Brad, as he turned to face her.

"I'm Claire Stevens. I'm in the pantomime at the King's."

"Yes, I've seen you on stage. Brad Harman." He juggled his plate of food as he attempted to shake hands.

"So, you've seen our little show?"

"Yes. Twice, as a matter of fact."

"Twice?" Claire thought that anyone sitting through it once deserved a medal for endurance. But twice.

"I thought you were very good. The duet with Beverly was very — er — good."

"Thank you. She's great to work with and knows all the tricks of the trade. Mind you she has been doing it for long time." Not realising that her seemingly innocent comment had been overheard by the two chorus boys, she wondered why they were convulsed with laughter. Then, looking around to see her hostess standing behind her, she realised what she had said and turned beetroot red.

"Oh — er, I didn't mean... Excuse me," she stammered, and beat a hasty retreat to replenish her glass. Beverly started to laugh when she saw Brad's slightly bewildered look.

"Sweet girl," she said. "The trouble is the lights are on but there's no one at home." She knocked on her head to demonstrate the point, which caused Brad to join in the laughter. "Brad, I would like you to meet an old friend of mine."

"Not so much of the 'old'." Brad saw an imposing figure looming up behind Beverly.

"Delphina Curtis, this is Brad Harman."

"It's a pleasure to meet you," said Brad.

"Brad is a fan of the pantomime," explained Beverly.

"An American with taste. How original."

"Delphina!" said Beverly, in a slightly admonishing tone, but Delphina ignored her and took Brad by the arm.

"So, what brings you to this part of the world? Surely not just to see a British Pantomime?"

"Actually, I'm discovering my roots."

Beverly's face suddenly registered alarm as she feared Brad might inadvertently reveal the real reason for his visit.

"Really?" said Delphina inquisitively.

"Yes. You see my parents were born near here." He glanced with a wink at Beverly, who visibly relaxed again. "They often spoke of the town and of visits they made to the King's theatre just after they were married."

"How interesting."

There was quite a crowd around them by now. The inclusion at the party of this young American had puzzled a number of the guests, and now his explanation of how he came to be there was drawing a lot of interest.

"And what do you think of our beautiful theatre?" enquired Delphina.

"It is beautiful, quite beautiful. And to my mind it is shameful that anyone could even consider tearing it down."

Bombshell!

The chattering stopped as the effects of Brad's remark hit the rest of the guests like a tornado. Delphina's smiling features started to crack like a cartoon character who had just been hit in the face with a sledgehammer. People looked at each other, wondering if they had heard correctly. The silence was shattering.

Brad slowly opened his mouth to continue. "That is right,

isn't it? The Seahaven Town Council proposes to redevelop the site?"

No one moved for a few seconds and then a low murmur started up.

"What's he saying?"

"Can't be, we've heard nothing."

"Must have the wrong end of the stick."

"Ladies and Gentleman!" The loud authoritative voice caused the chatter to subside once more as everyone turned to see Trevor Curtis-Smyth standing on the other side of the room.

"If I may have your attention for a moment." His face showed a solemn countenance as he looked across at his mother. Delphina made a move to speak, but was stopped by a motion from Trevor as he began to explain the situation.

"I was hoping to get through tonight without dampening anyone's spirits with talk of closure."

The hubbub started again, "Closure? Who's talking of closure? What does he mean?"

Trevor held up his hand and silence once more descended on the room. "But it seems our young friend here has inadvertently let the proverbial cat out of the bag."

It was now Brad's turn to feel his features drain of colour as the gaze of everyone in the room fell on him. "I'm sorry," he started. "I thought everyone knew about it." His voice tailed off as he realised the enormity of his innocent comment.

"They would have by tomorrow. I was hoping to at least finish the year on a happy note."

Brad felt as if he wanted the floor to open up and swallow him. He was sure that everything Amelia had told him over their dinner together was common knowledge amongst the company. All the talk of campaigning and seeking his help he assumed was a build up to challenge the Town Council. Never for one minute had he thought that only a few people knew of the proposals. His comments had put an instant damper on the evening, and he stood there exposed as the harbinger of bad tidings.

After what seemed like an eternity, he felt a comforting arm around his shoulders. He turned to look at a gentle face that had all the hallmarks of a protective parent.

Beverly looked towards Trevor. "I think you had better tell us everything," she said, quietly.

For the next few minutes Trevor explained to a shocked audience the contents of Russell Craddick's letter and the involvement of English Heritage. He made sure that Amelia's name wasn't mentioned and, with a warning glance in Brad's direction, stated that the anonymity of the person who had provided such valuable help was paramount — at least for the immediate future.

He concluded by saying, "I know it will probably be an impossible task for most of you, but the longer we can keep this between ourselves, the more chance we have of surprising this Russell Craddick and the Council with a preservation order."

A chorus of voices immediately agreed with Trevor, and he thanked them for their support and determination to overcome whatever the Council threw at them.

The mention of Russell's name stirred a note of pessimism among the assembled group. Many of the town's businessmen, Greg included, knew that all too often the Seahaven Courier had carried articles about how Russell Craddick was aiming to change the fortunes of the ailing seaside town with numerous projects. Projects that to the man in the street seemed fine, but to a trained eye and ear were littered with signs of dubious deals and suspicious transactions.

"Well, you certainly know how to make an impact on people," Greg said to Brad, giving him a large whisky, he seemed to be in great need of.

"I feel awful," groaned Brad. "I should have kept my big mouth shut."

"I think what you said might be for the best in the long run. I knew something was bothering Trevor. He shouldn't have had to bottle it up for the sake of the company."

"I agree," said Beverly. "We should all be involved. It's our livelihood as well as yours, Trevor."

The director and his mother had joined them and Brad apologised once again.

"It's not your fault. You weren't to know. And thank you for not mentioning a certain person's name."

"That's very mysterious," began Beverly, but realised that Trevor would not be forthcoming with any more information. Not tonight, anyhow.

Brad made his excuses and left the room. Beverly, sensing how upset he was, followed to find him in the hall putting on his coat.

"What are you doing?" she asked.

"I have to leave. I've caused enough trouble for one day."

"What do you mean, 'trouble'?"

"Blurting out all those things about the theatre and on top of that, giving you and Greg the biggest shock of your life. Tonight, of all nights. I've really loused things up." Unable to look her in the face, he headed for the front door.

"Brad!" Beverly let out a yell causing a few guests just

inside the room to look round with interest. Closing the door, she continued in a calmer voice, "You can't leave now. No one here is blaming you. It was a misunderstanding. Trevor wasn't to know you had any knowledge of the situation. It could have happened to anyone."

"But it happened to me. Just when I thought everything was starting to work out."

"It is. Please don't leave now. We..." She paused and corrected herself, "I want you to stay."

Brad slowly turned round. "I really think it would be best—" His words were interrupted by someone's voice shouting from the lounge.

"Thirty seconds to midnight everyone."

Mother and son looked at each other.

"Stay," pleaded Beverly. "At least for another minute. I would like to see the New Year in with my son."

His vision blurred by watery eyes, Brad moved towards the woman he had travelled over three thousand miles to find. They embraced and he slowly started to remove his coat.

As they re-entered the lounge everyone joined in the final countdown to the end of the year. Greg moved to one side of Beverly while Brad stayed on the other. They all held hands tightly as the singing of Auld Lang Syne took place followed by ten minutes of hugging, kissing and well wishing. Everyone then charged their glasses in a toast to a happy and prosperous New Year which, following the recent revelation, had a very pertinent ring to it.

Brad was persuaded to stay a little longer by Trevor, who wanted to have a few words with him about Amelia. Delphina continued to play the Grande Dame and managed to avoid any questions about the future of the theatre. Beverly hardly ever took her eyes off Brad, which caused Alex to comment to Carl, "Do you think they're having an affair?"

"The way Greg's been chatting away to him, it's probably a ménage à trois!" sniggered Carl. "Oh well, good luck to them. I only wish it were me helping to further Anglo-American relations."

About an hour later the party began to break up. Although the next day was a Saturday, it had been decided to only do an evening performance as most people would be recovering from the celebrations. This enabled the company to look forward to a lazy and relaxing day.

Beverly walked Brad to his waiting taxi. "Would you like to come to lunch? It'll be just the three of us and we can talk away without interruptions."

"I'll like that very much," replied Brad. He gave her an affectionate kiss on the cheek and climbed into the taxi.

"One o'clock?"

"I'll be there."

She watched until the taxi disappeared into the night and then slowly made her way back into the house.

Closing the door as the final guests left, Greg turned to see his wife sitting pensively on the stairs. "What a day," he said, with a deep sigh.

She nodded silently in reply as he sat down beside her. "All these revelations. It's almost too much to cope with."

Slowly she looked into his eyes as he put a comforting arm around her.

"Greg," she whispered. "Do you think I'm too old to be a mother?"

**

In his room at the King's Hotel, Brad was awoken from a light sleep at five a.m. by his bedside alarm. He had set it knowing the five hours' time difference meant it was midnight back home.

"Happy New Year, Mom," he said, when a familiar voice answered his call.

"Happy New Year, son. How are things?"

"Fine," he said, stifling a yawn. "Just fine."

SCENE TWO
SATURDAY, JANUARY 1ST 2000

"Happy New Year, Mom."

"Robert! How lovely of you to call."

"Sorry it wasn't sooner. Had a bit of a late night."

Next to him in the bed, Gavin stirred and opened one eye. "What time is it?" he grunted.

Clapping a hand over Gavin's mouth, Robert continued talking to his mother. "Big party at a friend's house. It went on a bit."

"I hope you had a good time."

"Yes, it was fine. What did you do?"

"Oh, we just had a few friends around. Nothing too grand."

"That's not like you. Couldn't you prize a few more quid out of the old miser?"

"Robert," said his mother, with an admonishing tone. "You shouldn't talk about your father like that."

"Stepfather. And calling him that is bad enough. Where is the old goat, anyway?"

"Having a shower. We're going to the golf club for lunch."

"Good grief. Has he made a New Year's resolution to treat you more like a wife?"

"Robert, please don't. Not now."

"I'm sorry," said Robert. "I'll call you tomorrow and we'll

get together for coffee. Just the two of us."

"I'd like that."

Robert replaced the receiver and lay back on the pillow staring straight up. Gavin, who was now wide awake, leaned up on one elbow and carefully brushed a black curl from Robert's forehead.

"What was that all about?" he enquired.

For a moment Robert didn't respond to his question. Then, slowly sitting up, he took a deep breath and started to speak.

"Gavin, I've something to tell you," he began, a little too seriously for Gavin's liking. "I was hoping not to bring this up for some time yet, but in the light of last night's revelations about the theatre I feel you ought to know."

"Know what?"

"The letter that Trevor received — it's from my stepfather, Russell Craddick."

***

"I'm ready to leave now, although why in God's name I agreed to this I'll never know." Delphina had just put the finishing touches to her make-up and was reaching for her hat. "Lunch with Aurelia and Reggie is the last thing I wanted to do today. He'll be pissed before dessert and she will keep pumping me for information about the theatre. She's a rotten cook if my memory serves, so I'll probably end up with food poisoning as well."

"It's your own fault for having too much to drink yourself last night. Not only did you agree to lunch, but also with her suggestion that I revive *"Arsenic and Old Lace"* for the two of you!"

"Heaven forfend!" exclaimed his mother, dramatically slamming a wide-brimmed hat firmly on her head.

"Have a *lovely* time," Trevor said sarcastically. "And don't drink. Remember you've got my car." He waved as she headed down the corridor towards the lift, then closing the door to his apartment, gave a sigh of relief at the peace and quiet. Mother's visits occasionally had their uses, but most of the time it was like living in the eye of a hurricane.

Grateful for the time to consider what next to do, he thought it only right to telephone Amelia and bring her up to date on the events of the previous night. She seemed genuinely pleased to hear his voice and on the spur of the moment he enquired whether she would like to join him for lunch.

"It's only a casserole," he said, apologetically. "I hope that will be all right?"

"It sounds perfect." Amelia would have settled for baked beans on toast in order to spend time with her new-found acquaintance.

"About two then?"

"I look forward to it." She took down the address and, replacing the receiver, stood looking at her reflection in the hall mirror.

Anyone who knew her well — and not many people did — would have thought her actions over the next hour to be entirely against character. She went upstairs and drew a hot bath adding to the water a blue liquid from an Egyptian looking glass bottle bearing the label "Nectar of the Orient". It was a birthday present from her cousin Amelia had privately considered far too provocative for the likes of herself to indulge in, and banished it to the back of the bathroom cabinet. Now, as the aromatic scent filled the air, she conceded that her original decision might have been a little hasty.

As the bath water changed colour and began to foam, she undressed and stepped in. The bubble bath felt smooth and relaxing against her skin, and she indulged herself for a full twenty minutes. Wrapping herself in a large, thick white towel with a smaller one wound like a turban around her wet hair, she went into her bedroom and slid back the wardrobe door. The array of dresses and suits that she possessed afforded her little choice for her luncheon date. Sensible, practical and not very appealing was her verdict of the selection facing her. In the end she decided on a light blue skirt with a not too fussy pink blouse.

After drying herself she sat in front of her dressing table and opened a rarely used make-up box. Carefully applying lipstick, eyeliner and just a touch of rouge, she then turned her attention to her hair. It was fairly long and she usually wore it up and pinned at the back. Catching her reflection in the mirror she saw how naturally it fell in a simple style onto her shoulders. With another impetuous moment of decision making, she brushed it vigorously until it shone and left it cascading down.

With her make-up complete, she dressed and, checking herself in the mirror, rashly left the top two buttons of her blouse undone. Impulsively, she dabbed an Yves Saint Laurent perfume (another present from an earlier birthday) behind her ears completing the transformation. Fifteen minutes before two o'clock she left her house for the short drive to Castle Hill Mews. Sitting in her car staring up at the building, she tried to quell the butterflies playing havoc with her stomach. Finally, after telling herself it was just lunch and nothing to get excited about, she approached the outer door and pushed the intercom.

"You look lovely," said Trevor, taking her coat and showing her into the lounge.

Blushing slightly, Amelia accepted his compliment. "Thank you. Your invitation was a lovely surprise"

"I'm so pleased you could come. Do sit down."

Amelia looked around the room and chose the paisley covered couch. He poured two glasses of sherry and sat beside her. "Here's to your very good health and a long and happy friendship between us." She blushed again and nervously stroked her neck wondering if it was a wise decision to leave the two buttons on her blouse undone.

Over lunch, Trevor acquainted Amelia with the happenings of the previous night. On hearing about Brad's revelation, a look of horror appeared on her face.

"I never gave it a thought," she exclaimed. "I thought he was just a tourist. I didn't know he had anything to do with the company."

"He doesn't. In fact, I never found out why he was there. He seemed to know Beverly quite well." Trevor made a mental note to ask Delphina when she got back if she knew who the mysterious American was.

"He seemed very keen to help when I spoke to him over dinner."

"Oh, you've had dinner with him?"

Amelia felt the colour building in her cheeks yet again. "He very kindly asked me," she said hesitantly. "And he did say he would write to the newspaper."

"Ah, the paper. That's the next step."

Amelia was glad that he had moved the subject away from her and Brad. Over coffee, she reiterated Elaine's offer to contact her cousin who was the deputy editor of the Seahaven

Courier.

"I'll ring her this evening," she offered.

"Why not now?"

Slightly taken aback by his sudden eagerness, she got up from the table and dialled her friend. After receiving a brief resumé of events, Elaine said she would get hold of her cousin straight away.

True to her word she phoned back twenty minutes later with the news that her cousin and a photographer would be at the theatre at ten o'clock on Monday morning. Furthermore, if anything official came in from the Council, the paper would hold it over until the next day.

Trevor was ecstatic and beaming with delight; something he had not done for a number of weeks. "Oh, this is marvellous," he exclaimed. "I can't tell you how grateful I am for everything you have done."

"I'm just so pleased I could be of help," replied Amelia, also beaming and looking quite radiant. Trevor impulsively gathered her in his arms and gave her a big hug almost smothering her.

So lost were they in a euphoric state of excitement, they failed to observe a figure looming large in the doorway.

"What a God-awful afternoon. I need a bloody great drink."

They jumped apart to see Delphina back from her lunch at Aurelia and Reggie's, which had been followed by a grilling that had left her feeling as though she had suffered at the hands of the Gestapo.

***

"Do you mind if I ask one final question?"

Beverly, Greg and Brad had just finished a tradition British lunch of roast beef and Yorkshire pudding, followed by chocolate cheesecake and cream. They were sitting in the lounge that, thanks to Greg and the dishwasher, was completely devoid of any signs of the previous evening's festivities.

All three had talked none stop for two hours in an honest and open-hearted way about their lives and what it meant to each of them that they had finally come together.

No recriminations, no ill feelings. Just the obvious disappointment that, certainly on Brad's part, this had not happened sooner.

Brad had waited until Greg was in the kitchen making coffee before quietly making his request to Beverly.

"No, of course not," she said, although she was pretty certain what it was going to be.

"My father? My real father? The birth certificate said 'unknown'."

Beverly, felt riddled with guilt. She cast her eyes down, unable to look at Brad while she answered him. "I'm afraid that's because I didn't know." She paused and nervously fingered the fringe on a cushion cover.

"It's not that important," began Brad. "What I mean is — well, I just had to ask."

"I know," she said, quickly lifting her head to look at him again. "And I wish I could tell you. The ironic thing is that I think he was an American. An air force pilot from an American base on a twenty-four-hour pass. But I could never be completely sure."

Emotion started to overtake her again as she recalled how

pathetic she had been in her teenage years.

"Please don't upset yourself. I really shouldn't have brought it up."

"Of course, you should," she said, reaching for a tissue. "I was so young and inexperienced. I went off thinking I knew how to look after myself in the big wide world. Deluding myself into thinking I was going to be the next Elizabeth Taylor or Vivien Leigh."

"Or Delphina Curtis," said Brad, with a wry smile. He had broken the sensitivity of the moment and they both started to laugh.

"Heaven forbid," Beverly said weakly, as Greg arrived with the coffee.

"What have I missed?" he asked, placing the tray on the coffee table.

"Brad was just comparing me to Delphina."

"Oh no I wasn't. From what I have seen you are an actress in your own right. And I'm sure your legs are better than hers."

The room was now bathed in a warm, family atmosphere that no one would have expected in so short a time. Brad was genuinely pleased he had pursued his goal and Beverly, still reeling slightly over the events of the last forty-eight hours, was becoming more and more entranced by this handsome young man who had come so unexpectedly into her life.

"I've decided to stay a little longer, said Brad. "If that's all right with you?"

"All right," exclaimed Beverly. "I want you to stay for as long as you can."

"I'm not expected at the office in London for a few days — and it will give us more time to get to know each other. There's no problem with the hotel room, the place is half empty."

"You're more than welcome to stay here," said Beverly, a little too eagerly.

"No, the hotel's fine. Besides it's only across the road from the theatre and that's where you will be spending most of your time."

"True. I'd forgotten we're back to twice daily from Monday."

"There is one other thing, said Brad, tentatively. "What about everyone else. Won't they start asking questions if I'm always hanging around?"

"He's right," said Greg. "Why don't you tell everyone. It's not as though you're ashamed of each other."

"On the contrary," retorted Beverly. She looked across at Brad. "I'm very proud of what a fine young man you are and what you have done with your life."

"There you are then. What do you say Brad?"

Brad looked at Beverly still with a radiant smile on his face. "I'd be proud for anyone to know that you're my mom."

SCENE THREE
SUNDAY, JANUARY 2ND – MONDAY, JANUARY 3RD

Sunday seemed interminable to Trevor. Monday morning couldn't come quickly enough for him. The previous day's news that the Seahaven Courier would be covering the story of the King's Theatre and its battle with the Council, had given him such a boost that he was wishing the day away.

At his mother's suggestion, Trevor spent the morning working on the script for his interview with the reporter. Delphina continually interrupted him with numerous suggestions of what he should say.

"I've had years of experience dealing with the press," she stated.

"Yes, but mother, this time they are on our side. We're not defending a production that has been annihilated by the critics, or refuting any connection with the latest theatrical scandal."

"I have never been part of any scandal." she said most emphatically.

Trevor was about to recall the headlines in the Evening Standard some years ago, after she was photographed leaving a dubious party in Kensington with an Egyptian Sheikh, following a drugs raid. But he hadn't the time or the patience to argue, and eventually she decided on a trip to at the January sales, leaving him to prepare for his meeting alone.

Driving to the theatre the next morning, Trevor had to lower the visor in his car as the bright winter morning sun was dazzling his eyes. The weather forecast had predicted a fine day with temperatures above the seasonal norm as a warm front was approaching from the South West.

He turned his car into the parking area alongside the theatre and noticed it was five to ten. To his surprise and delight, waiting for him on the steps were two people who looked very much like gentlemen of the press.

"Jack Shepperton," said the taller of the two. "I'm deputy editor of the Seahaven Courier, and this is Guy, our photographer.

"Trevor Curtis-Smyth." The three men shook hands. "Deputy editor? I'm very impressed! I was just expecting a reporter."

"After my cousin, Elaine, called me, I contacted my editor with the story. I thought the paper would be interested in covering the events as they unfolded. He was more than enthusiastic and suggested I take it on myself."

"I am very grateful to you — and your cousin," said Trevor. "You can't imagine how awful the last few days have been for me and the members of the company."

"If I could get a shot of you on the steps with the theatre sign behind you," suggested Guy, arranging his equipment and adjusting his lens to get the best angle.

"Of course," said Trevor, posing in the manner of an old actor-manager such as Garrick or Kean in front of the Old Vic.

"Now just relax a little, mate," said Guy. "Give me a look as though your whole world has collapsed around you."

"It very nearly has." muttered Trevor, as he changed his position and expression to one of forlorn despair.

238

"That's more like it," said Guy, clicking away.

After the photographer had got all the shots he required outside, Trevor led them into the foyer. Mrs Nesbit had just arrived and, curious as to what the press was doing there, was told by Trevor that he would be calling a meeting of the staff and company between shows. He left her to man the box office and suggested to Jack they go into his office.

For a full fifteen minutes Trevor bombarded the assistant editor with as much information about the King's as he could. How he had saved the theatre from obscurity and, using a large amount of his own money, brought it back to a flourishing house of entertainment. He then proceeded to tell Jack that the Council hadn't even contacted him personally about their plans, but just sent him a formal letter of their intension not to renew the lease.

"Ah, the letter," said Jack. "Do you have it with you?"

Trevor produced it from his inside pocket.

"Splendid. How about a shot of it Guy?"

"We need a bit more to make it an interesting picture," said the photographer.

"Some of the principals in the company should be backstage," Trevor informed them. He had rung a few of them the previous evening and they had readily offered their help.

"Yes," said Guy. "Why don't we do a group on the stage holding the letter in front of them?"

"Even better," added Jack, and they all headed off for the stage.

Beverly had arrived, as had Gavin, Willie Waters and Claire Stevens.

"If you wouldn't mind putting on one of your costumes," suggested Guy, to which they all agreed.

A number of shots were taken during which Jack got comments from the cast members. Just as the session was coming to an end, Max came hurrying onto the stage.

"Morning all," he shouted. "Who wants a photo?"

"I think we've got all we need," said Jack, as Guy started to pack away his camera.

"An interview then?"

"Are you part of the company?"

"Part of the company," exclaimed Max to the suppressed amusement of the others. "I'm Max Pendleton."

"Oh?" said Jack, the name not registering with him at all.

"Widow Twankey."

"Oh yes, I saw the photo in the foyer. You've got a bust like my mother-in-law."

This was too much for the rest of the group, and they all left the stage roaring with laughter. Max started to remonstrate with them as Trevor led the newspaper men back into the foyer.

"This should make front page news in tonight's edition," said Jack, as he shook hands with Trevor.

"I'm grateful for any help you are able to give us."

"This is a grand old building and deserves to be saved. Besides, if you keep this to yourself for the time being, I'll let you into a little secret." Trevor's eyes widened as Jack continued in confidence. "I wanted to cover this story myself when Elaine mentioned the name Russell Craddick. I've got a personal grudge against that individual. Some years ago, when I was an eager young reporter, I got wind of something going on between him and Granville Stone, the builder. There were murmurings of shady deals and back-handers, but when I started to investigate, my then editor, who was a personal friend of Craddick's, told me to drop it. I protested and was informed that if I didn't, I would be looking for another job. I've continued to keep my ear to the ground for tit bits of information, but haven't managed to uncover anything. He's a bit of a slippery customer is Mr Craddick. Now the paper has a new editor and I've been promoted to assistant editor, I'm in a much better position to do a bit of delving. I've been waiting a long time for a chance to nail that bastard."

"Let's hope the time has come," grinned Trevor, pleased to hear he had another ally.

***

Amelia finished taking dictation and snapped her pad shut with suppressed anger. Sitting opposite Russell, having to look at him was more than she could tolerate, knowing what she knew.

He had arrived in the office with a look of jubilation spread across his face. Wished her "good morning" and actually whistled as he entered his office. A quarter of an hour later he had summoned her in to deal with the mail that had accumulated over the holiday. Five pieces of correspondence needed his immediate attention; the others, he said, could wait.

"I have an appointment this morning," he said, glancing at his watch.

Amelia's reaction was one of surprise as there was nothing entered in his diary.

Russell noticed her enquiring look. "It's a personal matter, Miss Fothergill. I should be back in the office after lunch."

"Very good Mr Craddick," she said, rather tersely Russell thought. No matter, he remained in good spirits and, as she left his office, she heard him *"Pom-pomming"* an unidentifiable tune.

Something's up, she thought to herself as she sat back at her desk. To her knowledge he had very rarely whistled in the office and never sang.

Starting work on transcribing her dictation, she realised she needed a reference number from a file in Russell's office. Moving swiftly back to the dividing door, she knocked and opened it. Russell was on the phone and had the biggest Cheshire Cat grin on his face. As soon as he saw Amelia the grin disappeared and his manner became instantly formal and business like.

"Fine, fine," he said brusquely into the phone. "I'll see you at the arranged time. Goodbye." He replaced the phone and looked at Amelia.

"Sorry to disturb you Mr Craddick, but I need the reference number for the new bus depot project."

"Yes, yes. You know where it is."

Amelia noticed his manner had changed back to its usual gruff self. He didn't like being disturbed, she mused to herself as she pulled the file from the filing cabinet. I wonder who he was on the phone to?

Russell left the office half an hour later and Amelia noticed that his unusual light-hearted manner was back.

"He's definitely up to something," she said, this time out loud. Letters from the morning's dictation were almost finished, and then there were a number of routine things for her to be getting on with. "Nothing that can't wait a little longer," she continued the conversation with herself. Then, in another impetuous spur of the moment decision, she quickly put on her coat and grabbed her bag. Leaving the office, she moved swiftly to the fire escape stairs and started to descend.

The adrenaline was pumping again, as she realised she had begun yet another covert operation. She needed to know where Craddick was going, and the only way was to follow him. Arriving at the bottom of the stairs, she pulled open the fire escape door and let out a stifled yelp.

"Amelia. What the bloody hell are you doing back here?" She had come face to face with Thomas, one of the security guards, who was taking a cigarette break. Amelia tried bravely to regain her composure and mumbled out an excuse about being late for a dental appointment, realising at the same time that in the excitement of the previous week she had missed her rescheduled one.

Making a mental note to phone them, she continued her journey around the back of the building and stopped in another doorway near to where her car was parked. She was now exposed to the large glass windows of the ground floor and could see into some of the offices and the reception area. There, amid the constant stream of Council workers and visitors, was her boss chatting to one of the young secretaries.

She thrust herself back against the wall and waited for his next move. What was she doing, she asked herself? Why, after the nerve-wracking incident when she was trapped under his desk, had she once again put herself in jeopardy of being caught?

No immediate answers came to mind, and she abandoned her self-questioning as she saw Russell walking towards the main doors. His car was in one of the reserved spaces at the front of the building, while hers was right in the middle of the parking area.

After taking two or three deep breaths, Amelia finally decided to make a run for it. Pulling her coat collar up and keeping her head down she dodged around the lines of vehicles like a commando running through a minefield. Almost slamming into the side of her car, she thrust her hand into her handbag, feeling for her keys. Her fingers probed among the items in her bag, but no keys could be located. Panic set in again as she fervently searched every corner and crevasse, but nothing was found.

Suddenly, she detected a movement on the other side of the car park. Her eyes fixed on a black Audi reversing slowly out of a reserved parking space. Russell was at the wheel and she knew that once the manoeuvre was completed, he would turn and see her. She crouched down beside her car door with lightning speed and in doing so, banged her hip. Wincing with pain she put her hand on the tender spot and then felt something bulky. The car keys. They were in her pocket all the time.

With shaking hands, she pulled them out, unlocked the door and slid rather ungainly down into her seat, keeping her head as low as possible. Slowly she eased herself up to see Russell driving towards the exit. He paused while the automatic barrier lifted to let him pass and then waited for a gap in the traffic on the main road.

Amelia pushed herself upright in her seat and then heard a loud ripping noise. The lining of her coat had caught on the brake handle when she bundled herself in the driving seat.

"Bugger," she shouted loudly, and then immediately gasped as she realised what she had said. But there was no time to remonstrate with herself; Russell was already indicating to turn and she had to follow now or give up the chase. She turned the key in the ignition and depressed the clutch. Her leg was trembling so much that she crunched the gears. Finally, she eased the car out of the parking space and headed for the barrier. By now Russell had joined the line of traffic, unaware that he was being tailed three cars back by the unlikeliest of spies.

Traffic lights at a major junction brought them all to a standstill and Amelia noticed that Russell was indicating to turn left. He's heading away from town, she thought as the lights changed to green. The two cars in front of her continued straight ahead and by the time she had turned, Russell had increased his speed and left a reasonable gap between them.

The road was quieter and Amelia kept well back, all the time watching where Russell was heading. Eventually he indicated left again and took a tree-lined avenue that came to a junction with the coast road. With nothing approaching, he turned and joined the road. By the time Amelia arrived at the same point a double decker bus and two car transporters were bearing down too close for her to pull out. She waited while they thundered by before picking up the chase.

The road twisted a great deal and every so often Amelia caught a glimpse of the black Audi ahead of the convoy. Half a mile on, the bus pulled up at a stop and then the transporters slowed down and eventually turned left into a large car dealership going by the name of Greg Westcott. Now Amelia had a clear view of the road ahead, but to her horror it was empty of traffic.

Where had he gone? Having to slow down behind the transporters meant that if he had turned off somewhere, she wouldn't have known. Confident she hadn't passed any turnings, she drew to a halt and twisted her head round to look back along the road. Suddenly she noticed to her right what looked like a concealed entrance and what she thought was a flash of black. Without thinking, she quickly turned the steering wheel and heard the front tyres squeal under the sudden pressure. She also heard a deafening blast from a horn. Behind her another driver was making very suggestive hand gestures in response to her lack of signalling.

The concealed entrance turned out to be a small cul-de-sac with no pavement, serving four very large houses all in their own grounds; two to the right, two to the left. A fifth house, still in the process of being built, lay on an angle at the end of the cul-de-sac. Amelia stopped her car and wondered if she dared go any further for fear of being spotted. She turned off her engine and wound down her window. Everything was still. Then she heard a car door slam and the sound of feet. She froze. Were they coming towards her? Once again, she slid down in her seat with just the top of her head peeping above the steering wheel.

Out from behind a large hedgerow a few yards further up on the other side of the road, Russell emerged and started to walk towards the second of the houses. Luckily, he didn't look round or notice the surveillance vehicle parked a short distance away, but turned into the private drive.

Amelia heard his fading footsteps on the gravel, then voices, but too far away to be able to decipher what was said. Finally, she heard the sound of a front door closing.

After waiting for a few moments in case Russell should emerge again, Amelia decided to take a closer look. With no pavement the car was right up against a hedgerow, so that meant getting out of the passenger side. Avoiding the handbrake, she carefully slid across and slowly opened her car door. Once out, she crossed the road and, keeping close to the hedgerow, inched her way passed the first house. A large stone wall, at least seven feet high, enclosed the second house, with two wrought iron gates dominating the entrance to the drive.

Cautiously, Amelia peeped around the wall and first gate. The front of the house was very impressive with two large bay windows either side of an imposing front door surrounded by a portico representing a classical Roman design. In a room behind one of the bay windows Amelia could make out two figures. One was definitely Russell and the other appeared to be a woman.

Whose house was this and what was he up to? More to the point, who was that woman? It certainly wasn't his wife. The questions were whirling around in Amelia's head when suddenly the woman moved to look straight out of the window and in her direction. Amelia quickly pulled her head back and flattened herself against the wall. She felt very exposed standing there in full daylight, spying on her boss. After a few seconds she looked around again, but this time the room was empty. Her eyes searched the other windows for a sign of movement. Then, in an upstairs room at the far corner of the house, she noticed some movement behind the thickly patterned net curtains.

Realising she couldn't remain where she was, Amelia had to make a decision. Should she leave now and return to the office, or should she try to find out more?

Curiosity, and the adrenaline already flowing through her body, made up her mind for her. Looking around for a better vantage point and hiding place, she noticed that the half-completed house at the end of the road seemed deserted of workmen. She headed for it.

The shell of the property was complete except for doors and windows; and on closer inspection Amelia found the stairs were in place. Impulsively she climbed them and made for a large front room that overlooked the house next door. On the dusty bare concrete floor lay an empty Sainsbury's carrier bag that once contained lunch for one of the builders. Amelia put it to good use as a kneeling mat in front of a windowless hole in the wall. There she peered across at the house where her boss was being entertained by a mysterious woman.

"You're sure he's away for most of the day?"

"I told you on the phone, he's got a meeting in Brighton. He left just after eight thirty."

"And I'm not expected back in the office until after lunch, so that gives us a couple of hours at least." Russell grinned rather seductively and moved toward Ann Stone who was sitting on the end of a luxurious King-sized bed.

"So contrary to popular opinion, the planning department won't grind to a halt if you're not at your desk," teased Ann, as Russell kissed her neck and ran his hand up her body.

"The planning department can go hang itself."

She let out a little whimper as he started to nibble her ear lobe. His hand had now reached her blouse as he unfastened the buttons, one by one.

The morning sun was shining so brilliantly that Amelia had to shade her eyes as she peered at the upstairs window in the house across the road. She also noticed another window in the side of the house that opened onto a small balcony, but that too was covered by a full-length net curtain. From her semi-recumbent position, she noticed the shadows had disappeared. "No prizes for guessing what they're up to," she muttered quietly to herself.

Deciding that there was little more her surveillance operation could achieve, she stood up and began to move away. Just at that moment another vehicle turned into the cul-de-sac. A powder blue Jaguar with a familiar figure at the wheel. It moved slowly up the road and turned into the gravel drive of the house Amelia had been watching.

She quickly resumed her lookout position with eager anticipation of what might happen, as the tall, imposing figure of Barrie Stone got out of his car.

Ann's blouse was now off, as was her skirt. Russell had removed his shirt and his trousers had just dropped around his ankles when the sound of wheels on the gravel drive caused them both to freeze.

The expression on Ann Stone's face had immediately changed from one of lust to one of horror. "It can't be," she gasped and, in a flash, rolled off the bed and ran to the window. "My God, it is!"

"What?" said Russell, looking faintly ridiculous in his half-undressed state.

"It's Barrie," she cried, and attempted to retrieve her skirt from where it lay on the floor.

"What?" Russell let out a yell and took a step towards the window, completely forgetting the trousers manacling his ankles. He fell headlong to the floor catching his chin on the board at the foot of the bed.

"Be quiet, he'll hear you," hissed Ann, as she saw her husband getting out of the car.

Russell was groaning in pain as he rolled over and attempted to pull up his trousers. Ann grabbed her blouse and furiously began to fasten the buttons. They could both hear the crunching sound Barrie's shoes made on the gravel as he approached the front door.

"What are we going to do?" said Ann. "If he finds you

here, he'll kill you. He's a very jealous man."

Russell stood rather unsteadily. He felt a warm trickle of blood running down his neck from a small wound on his chin. "Tell him I called around to see him."

There was the sound of a key in the front door lock.

"Ann? Ann, are you home?"

The guilty couple upstairs looked at each other in blind panic.

"And what are we both supposed to be doing in the bedroom?" she whispered. Russell, not usually at a loss for words, could say nothing. His bottom jaw opened and closed without a sound, resembling a fish, floundering on the beach.

Ann quickly opened the bedroom door and stood on the landing leaning over the banister rail. "I'm up here," she called to her husband in the hall below. "What are you doing back so soon?" To a shrewd detective her manner would have seemed erratic and jumpy, but Barrie was not in a mood to notice.

"The bastard cancelled the appointment," he grumbled. "Came down with the flu over the holiday. You'd think he could have let me know sooner. Has he never heard of a mobile phone? I just turned around and drove straight back."

Still flustered at the thought of Barrie coming upstairs to find her lover and his business partner were one and the same person, she called out, "How about a cup of coffee? I was just going to make one."

"I'll put the kettle on." And to her immediate relief, he headed for the kitchen.

Back in the bedroom, Russell had managed to stop the flow of blood from his chin with his handkerchief.

"What am I going to do?" he pleaded.

Ann pointed to the window with the balcony. "Get out

there."

Russell looked at the window. "Are you mad? I'll be trapped."

"You'll be worse than that if he catches you," she said, opening the window and pushing him out.

Downstairs Barrie had switched the kettle on when his wife joined him.

"What a waste of a morning," she said, forcing a smile.

"Were you doing anything special upstairs?" he said idly.

"I was going to change the bed linen. But it can wait till later," she replied, attempting to keep a light-hearted note in her voice.

He looked at her with a slightly inquisitive expression. "Did you know you've buttoned your blouse up crookedly?"

Across the road Amelia couldn't believe her eyes. Thirty seconds after Barrie Stone had entered his house, her boss exited via the upstairs balcony. He was carrying his jacket and appeared to be in a state of panic.

Shivering in the cold air, he quickly put on his jacket and looked over the side. There was a drop of about four feet onto the roof of the double garage. Tentatively he put one leg over the balustrade and then swung the other one over to finish in a sitting position.

Amelia suppressed a giggle as she watched the ludicrous figure inch slowly forward until he had no option but to jump onto the garage. Once there he hurried over to the far end and again peered over the side. The drop was a good ten feet to the ground and Amelia knew that if Russell attempted to jump, he would more than likely end up by breaking his neck. She watched him frantically looking for something to climb down. The only available means of escape was a drainpipe on the front corner of the garage. He had spotted it and was now lying on the roof and manoeuvring into a position from where he could start his descent. The whole spectacle so amused Amelia that, unable to control herself, she let out a laugh, immediately stifling it with her hand.

"If only I had a camera with me," she murmured to herself.

"Never again," Russell vowed to himself as he desperately felt around for a foothold. His shoe finally came into contact with a clamp holding the drainpipe to the garage wall. He pushed himself backwards and tried to feel for another clamp with his other foot. Yes, there was one, and he lowered himself down about four feet. He started to repeat the process, searching in vain for another clamp. With one leg dangling alongside the pipe, his other was bent double and the knee was scraping his chin. This caused the bleeding to begin again.

"Bugger, bugger, bugger," he said through clenched teeth. The flaying leg at last came into contact with another clamp and for a few seconds he rested. An awful thought suddenly hit him. What if one of the neighbours was witnessing his unconventional departure from the house? They may suspect him of being a burglar and inform the police. How could he possibly explain his actions to them or to Barrie? Mental pictures of him being led away in handcuffs renewed his effort to continue his flight. He was just about to start feeling around for another foothold when the whole pipe gave a judder. Clinging on for dear life, he quickly glanced up to see the clamp above him protruding two inches away from the wall.

Oblivious to the cold wind blowing around the corner of the house, Russell felt the temperature of his body rising.

Sweat was pouring off him and the moisture on his hands made them slip on the pipe. "Bloody crap builders," he cursed, completely forgetting that Stones' Limited were the contractors for that particular housing project.

Another judder and this time the clamp shot out like a missile, landing with a thud against the boundary fence. Russell looked down and reckoned there was about five feet between him and the concrete path running alongside the garage. The drainpipe was starting to bend under his weight, leaving him no option but to jump before the whole lot broke loose. With a couple of short intakes of breath as though he was preparing for a parachute jump, he let go of the drainpipe and threw himself backwards.

An agonised yelp pierced the air as he landed badly and crumpled to the ground. Pain was now surging through his body from two sources. One was around his left foot and he realised straight away that he had twisted his ankle. The other was in his chest. Russell suffered periodically from angina, and at that moment he was having an attack.

"What was that?" Barrie heard what he thought was a cry and looked out of the kitchen window. Ann had kept him talking in the hope that Russell had somehow managed to get away.

"Next doors dog I imagine." Her voice came rapidly in short, nervous spurts. "You know he's only a puppy and they do yelp a lot."

"As long as it doesn't start yelping and barking at all hours of the day and night. You don't think it's got into our garden, do you? It sounded quite near." Barrie moved towards the kitchen door.

"There's no way it could get over the wall. More coffee?"

Ann said, hastily trying to divert his attention away from outside.

"No, I'd better get back to the office, I've wasted enough time already today." He took a last mouthful of coffee and walked into the hall with Ann quickly following. "Oh, I forgot. I've got those letters to post. Where are they?"

"On the desk in your study I think."

Barrie turned towards his study as Ann darted to the front door. Opening it an inch she saw a figure lumbering haphazardly towards the gates at the end of the drive. It was now her turn to give a little yelp.

It was like watching some far-fetched action movie. The events that were unfolding in front of Amelia hardly bore credibility. If she hadn't witnessed them with her own eyes, she would never have believed them. Her boss, the pompous Russell Craddick, behaving like an escaped convict. Climbing out of windows, shinning down drainpipes and now injuring himself as he finally reached terra firma.

She watched as he hobbled along the side of the front garden and headed for the gates. Now she caught sight of the front door opening. Who was coming out and would Russell be caught?

The door quickly closed again as Russell staggered through the gates and came to rest by the high wall. Hurriedly, he took a spray out of his pocket and held it to his mouth. Breathing deeply, he continued limping to where his car was parked. The front door opened a second time and Barrie Stone came out followed by his wife. He got into the Jaguar and, with a quick wave, drove away from the house and down to the main road. No sooner had he turned out of sight than Russell's Audi emerged from its hiding place and followed the same route.

Still in her kneeling position, Amelia paused for a few moments reliving the whole scenario. She needed to remember everything she had seen so as to be able to relate it accurately to Elaine; and most importantly to Trevor.

The sound of another vehicle approaching made her look up. It was a Stones' Builder's lorry coming down the cul-de-sac and onto the makeshift drive of the house where she was hiding. Now it was her turn to affect an escape.

She moved quickly to the landing and saw two beefy looking men with a younger, slimmer one, get out of the lorry and head towards the hallway. With no other way out, there was nothing for it but to brave the situation and call on her limited acting skills.

Slowly making her staircase entrance, she called to the surprised workmen. "There you are. I've been waiting for ages, so I decided to look around on my own."

The workmen just stared at her as she drew near to them. "I'm sure it will be very nice when it's finished," she stated in a patronising manner. "But it's not really what I'm looking for. I need something bigger, possibly with a swimming pool; and not so close to those other little houses. Goodbye." She completed her grand exit with a high regal wave of her hand.

Three bemused faces watched as she walked smartly out into the winter sunshine. Back in her car at the end of the road she could no longer contain herself. She threw back her head and, rather uncharacteristically, roared with laughter.

***

Meanwhile, backstage at the theatre, before the start of the evening performance, Trevor briefed the entire cast and crew on the situation so far. A number of stunned faces greeted the news that their jobs were in jeopardy if nothing could be done to save the theatre.

Spirits were raised slightly when someone came in with the evening paper trumpeting the headlines "Council to rob Seahaven of Historical Landmark". It gave full front-page coverage to the story and a double centre spread with photos, plus a favourable editorial comment.

"It's not a bad picture of me for once," said Beverly, as the paper was passed round.

"I'm hardly recognisable," moaned Claire Stevens.

"It's a jolly good one of me — and you, Gavin," said Willie Waters.

One person who took scant notice of the paper was Max. "I don't know why they didn't have one of me. My reputation should carry some weight." The fact that he hadn't even been mentioned in the article, put him in a bad mood for the rest of the day.

"The circle bar will be open after the performance if everyone can stay; and there is someone I would like to introduce to you all." Trevor's mysterious comment created a buzz of interest as the company dispersed to ready themselves for the show.

A few sandwiches, crisps and nuts, kindly prepared by Mrs Nesbit, were laid out on the end of the bar for the actors and crew. They all made their way to the circle lounge after the audience had left the building and were greeted in grand style by Delphina who had insisted on being there. After purchasing drinks — Trevor had drawn the line at a free bar — they stood around in groups continuing to chat and speculate about the major topic of closure.

"Ladies and Gentlemen, if I could have your attention for a few moments." Trevor stood by the double doors with Delphina hovering close by. "I'm grateful for your time and I hope you have a relaxed evening after suffering the shock of today's news." A sympathetic murmur ran through the ensemble and then subsided as Trevor continued to address them.

"Since I spoke to you earlier, certain events have come to light that I think you should be aware of. But first I would like to introduce you to a lady whom I have had the great pleasure of recently meeting. Someone who is a dedicated supporter of the King's Theatre and firmly on our side in fighting for its survival. Miss Amelia Fothergill."

Rather sheepishly, Amelia came from behind one of the lounge doors to a round of applause from the company.

"It's the woman we saw him with outside the theatre the other night," Gavin whispered to Robert, whom he had phoned during the interval and arranged to meet at the theatre.

Trevor went on to explain how Amelia had provided him with the original information and how she had got English Heritage involved. Between them they related the recent events, carefully avoiding any mention of who her boss was.

"I'd rather not give too much away just yet," Amelia had said to Trevor earlier that evening. "I know it's now public knowledge about the theatre, but I still have to work with Craddick, and the less he knows the better."

"Couldn't agree with you more. But I think your story of his extra marital affair is a classic."

Another round of applause greeted the news of Amelia's involvement with English Heritage, and Trevor confirmed that he had also been in touch with Mr Hapgood. He had been told to expect encouraging information in the post within the next couple of days.

Bolstered by what they had heard, a party atmosphere descended on the gathering of performers and staff. Greg and Brad had both turned up after Beverly called them with the news. All three sat down at a table and were joined by Gavin and Robert as Brad began telling them about how he had met Amelia during his first visit to the pantomime. He had since made it clear he would give whatever help he could.

"That's my boy," said Beverly, and received a look of curiosity from Gavin and Robert.

"You'd better tell them," sighed Greg, "as it seems to be a day for revelations."

"You don't mind?" Beverly asked Brad.

"Of course not."

It was now Beverly's turn to relate her story to the company who, if at first were very taken aback, soon swarmed around them with genuine affection and warm congratulations. Trevor was the only other person outside her immediate family who knew of what had happened all those years ago.

"You must be very proud of him," he said, taking her to one side and giving her a kiss on the cheek. "He's a fine young man."

Amelia offered her congratulations as did Delphina who, having had one scotch too many, started effusing about the delights of having a son, much to Trevor's embarrassment.

The party slowly started to break up, as everyone realised they were still doing two shows a day and needed their sleep.

Greg, Brad, Gavin and Robert waited in the foyer whilst Beverly retrieved her bag from the dressing room. Last out of the circle lounge was Trevor supporting Delphina and a slightly tipsy Amelia. The excitement of her daytime escapade, and being hailed as a saviour of the King's Theatre, had been overwhelming; and after imbibing rather too many sherries, her cheeks had begun to glow like the Seahaven lighthouse.

"Can we offer you a lift?" Beverly said to Amelia, as she returned with her bag.

"It's all right Bev, I'll make sure she gets home," said Trevor.

"That's very kind of you," gushed Amelia. "I'm afraid I've overindulged quite reprehensibly."

"I should take tomorrow off if I were you," suggested Brad. "You deserve it."

"I may treat myself to an extra half-hour in bed. Craddick phoned this afternoon and said he wouldn't be in the office at all tomorrow because he's sprained his ankle. Said he tripped over a kerbstone. Kerbstone my eye. He fell off a roof." Amelia realised what she had said and bit her bottom lip. But it was too late. The sea of inquisitive faces in front of her meant she had to relate her entire day's activities.

The description of her boss clinging perilously to the drainpipe brought a gale of laughter from all except one. Robert was so incensed at hearing about his stepfather's extra-marital activities, that he found it impossible to enjoy the story.

He managed to suppress his anger until he and Gavin were alone in the car.

"That bastard. That conniving, scheming bastard. How dare he treat my mother like that? I've a good mind to go round there and beat the living daylights out of him."

"Well, you could," said Gavin thoughtfully. "But on the other hand you could scare the shit out of him."

"What do you mean."

"Oh, just a quick anonymous phone call claiming to know all about his drainpipe experience."

The scowl on Robert's face began to fade as Gavin's suggestion started to take shape in his mind. A flicker of a smile appeared as he turned to look at his partner. "And who do you propose can do that?"

"Have you forgotten there is an actor wot is in the family!" came the convincing Cockney reply.

SCENE FOUR
TUESDAY, JANUARY 4ᵀᴴ

Some people can take a certain amount of pain. A nagging toothache, a thumb that has come in contact with a hammer, even a twisted ankle. Russell Craddick was not one of those people.

He slowly moved himself to the side of the bed and tentatively brought his injured foot in contact with the floor. The pain shot up his leg causing him to cry out.

"Bloody thing."

He paused before reaching for a walking stick that had been found in the garage. Inch by inch he pulled himself up and balanced on his good foot. He was in dire need of the bathroom and knew his wife had already left the house. She had been ordered to go to the nearest chemist for more aspirins. Also, to pick up a copy of the Seahaven Courier.

Events over the last eighteen hours in the Craddick household had been anything but normal. After his death-defying act with the drainpipe, Russell had somehow managed to drive back to his house and convince Hazel that he had tripped over a kerbstone whilst having an angina attack, thereby twisting his ankle.

"Why didn't you go to the hospital?" she asked. "It could be broken."

"I'd know if it was broken," he shouted, as he flopped into

an armchair. "All it needs is a cold compress and bandaging up. If I'd gone to the hospital, I'd have waited hours in A & E for someone to look at it."

Hazel began muttering about better to be safe than sorry, but was cut off by Russell bellowing for ice. She complied with her husband's request and finished the job by tightly binding the injured foot with a crepe bandage.

He stayed in the chair for the rest of the afternoon, moving only slightly to call Miss Fothergill and inform her of his accident. Hazel served him his dinner on a tray, after which he was then packed off to bed with a glass of hot milk and two more aspirins.

He slept soundly right through until eight the next morning unaware that there had been a phone call from Barrie Stone.

"I'd unplugged the phone in the bedroom so you wouldn't be disturbed," Hazel told him, as she placed a breakfast tray by the side of the bed.

"What did he want?" asked Russell, cautiously. Had he been spotted hobbling out of the Stone's driveway? No, surely not. If Barrie suspected anything, he would have been round to the house personally and Russell would be in bed with more than a sprained ankle.

"He didn't say, but he sounded rather upset," said Hazel, vaguely.

"Upset?"

"Yes. He asked if you had seen the headlines in last night's Seahaven Courier. I told him we never read that paper."

"What were the headlines?"

"He didn't say. Just asked if you would phone him as soon as you were up."

Hazel, under orders from her husband, left the house to take the short journey to the newsagents at the corner of the street. Russell managed to eat a couple of pieces of toast and drink a cup of tea provided by his wife. It was then that nature called and he began his expedition to the bathroom. Midway through relieving himself the phone rang. Russell cursed continuously as he quickly washed his hands and started hobbling painfully back to the bedroom. No sooner was he within reaching distance of the receiver, the phone stopped ringing. More cursing as he dialled 1471 only to hear that the caller had withheld their number.

Feeling exhausted after his short trip, he poured another cup of tea and eased himself back into bed. The clock radio showed eight forty-five. Time to ring Barrie and find out what he wanted. Then he realised his address book was down stairs and he didn't know Barrie's new number. His mobile phone had it stored for his illicit calls to Ann, but that too was downstairs. There was nothing for it but to wait for Hazel to return.

Five minutes later the phone rang again. Russell put down his cup of tea and lifted the receiver.

"Hello?"

"Russell Craddick?" The voice was slightly muffled and one that Russell didn't recognise.

"Yes, who is this?"

"Oh, you don't know me, but I know you."

Russell now detected a faint Cockney tone. "I beg your pardon?"

"How is your ankle?"

"Very painful!" he said, automatically. "Look, who is this?"

"You've been a very silly boy, haven't you? Climbing down drainpipes at your age."

Russell's mouth suddenly went dry and he drained of what little colour he had. "What d-do you mean?" he stammered.

"If you play away from home, you should take a little more care." The Cockney impersonator on the other end was enjoying himself so much that he had to cover the mouthpiece while stifling a laugh.

"Look here," said Russell, trying to regain his composure, "I don't know who you are or what your game is—"

"It's not my game that is at issue 'ere," interrupted the caller. "Your daredevil escape act yesterday was witnessed; and that's gonna cost you dearly."

Russell was now trembling with a mixture of terror and anger. "Are you blackmailing me?"

"Wot a nasty word," said the Cockney voice, with mock indignation. "I think we had better terminate this conversation — for the time being."

There was a click.

"Hello! Hello!" But the line was dead.

Still shaking Russell lay on his bed with the receiver gripped tightly in his hand. Who was that? Who had seen him clambering across the roof of Barrie Stone's garage? Had they got photographs? How much was this going to cost him?

The questions were reverberating around Russell's head and he felt the pain in his chest returning. A prescription spay was always kept by the bed and he applied some of the contents under his tongue. Lying back on the pillow, he heard the front door opening.

Hazel was back.

The phone box at the entrance to the Marina was almost shaking on its foundations. The two men inside were convulsed with hysterics.

"I wish I could have been a fly on the wall. I would have loved to have seen him squirming." Robert was relishing the moment. "Your performance was Tony award winning." And he gave his partner a congratulatory kiss on the cheek.

Gavin was attempting to wipe away his tears of laughter. "It wasn't bad, if I do say so myself. I didn't think I could keep it up for much longer." He thought for a moment and then his expression changed to one of a Machiavellian style. "You don't think we could screw him for a few thousand, do you?"

"Gavin." Robert playfully pushed him out of the phone box.

"Just a thought. A reward for my Tony award winning performance."

"If it's a reward you want, I think something can be arranged." He gave him a friendly dig in the ribs and they both started to run back towards the apartment.

***

"Bloody Hell!" Russell's second shock in five minutes came as Hazel held up the front page of the Seahaven Courier. "They were quick off the mark." He took the paper from his wife and started to read the article.

Hazel took the breakfast tray and started out of the bedroom.

"Bring my address book up, will you?" It was more of a

demand than a request, but Hazel was used to that. She returned with the book and Russell dialled Barrie Stone's number.

"You've read the article then," said the builder.

"We're going to have to move fast," said Russell. "

"What's all this about the King's Theatre being a 'landmark building'?"

"I've no idea. It can't be anything special, or I'd have known about it."

"You'll have to issue a statement from the Council, and lay it on thick how the redevelopment is going to be good for the town."

"I'll talk to the paper this morning. I'm surprised they haven't been on to me already. Usually, they want a counter argument when anything contentious comes to their notice."

"Maybe they've rung the office. Are you going in today?"

"I wasn't going to," came Russell's gruff reply. "I can barely stand on this wretched foot."

"Hazel told me that you had sprained your ankle. How did you manage that?"

Russell told his now well-rehearsed lie about tripping over a kerbstone.

"Sue the Council!" joked Barrie.

"He wouldn't be so jovial if he knew what had really happened," thought Russell, and then added, "I'll talk to you later today. Will you be in your office?"

"Yes. I wasted enough time yesterday going to Brighton and when I got back, I found some idiot had pulled the drainpipe away from the side of the garage. Kids I expect. They'll get what for if I catch them."

"I thought it was a secluded neighbourhood you had

moved in to," said Russell, with the images of him clinging to the drainpipe vividly dancing around in his head.

"You've not been to the new house, have you? I was only saying to Ann, we must have you and Hazel over for a meal. I can show you over the place."

"I've already seen more than enough of it," thought Russell, as they said their goodbyes.

***

Still in a state of euphoria and exhilaration following her exploits of the previous day, Amelia walked briskly into the Council Offices giving everyone she met a dazzling smile accompanied by the compliments of the day.

"Spring seems to have come early for Amelia," said Jane Tilbury to the receptionist after witnessing Amelia's somewhat out of character light heartedness.

"And she's late in," observed the receptionist. "I've never known that to have happened before without a reason."

Trevor had delivered Amelia home safely after leaving the theatre and dropping Delphina off first. Arriving outside her house he escorted her to the front door and tentatively suggested they meet for lunch the next day. She readily agreed and he wished her "goodnight", planting a kiss lightly on her cheek.

She had drifted off to sleep in a state of blissful contentment and, not having set her alarm, risen that morning three quarters of an hour late. Having very little care for what would normally be regarded as a total lack of self-discipline, she casually got herself ready for work, arriving at nine twenty instead of her usual eight forty-five.

The morning post was already on the desk waiting for her.

She casually flicked through the envelopes, stopping only when the crest on one of them caught her eye.

English Heritage.

Slowly she picked it out of the pile. It was addressed to Russell Craddick, but didn't contain the words "personal" or "private", just "urgent".

Should she open it? Normally Russell would go through his own mail and then hand over any general correspondence for her to deal with. When he was away for any length of time, she dealt with everything except those letters marked personal.

Curiosity was taking over. She could ring Mr Hapgood of course to find out if he had been successful with the Department of Culture, Media and Sport. Also, Trevor may have a letter waiting for him at the theatre. Or she could steam the letter open!

"No," she told herself out loud. "No more espionage work."

She dealt with the rest of the mail, made a few phone calls informing certain people that her boss wouldn't be in and then turned her attention back to the letter from English Heritage. Her fingers tentatively moved towards the corner of the gummed flap when, suddenly, the phone rang.

She gave a little start then immediately regained her efficient secretarial manner. "Good morning, Mr Craddick's office."

"It's me, Miss Fothergill. Is everything all right there?"

"Yes, Mr Craddick. I've dealt with the post and cancelled your appointments." She looked again at the remaining unopened envelope, then continued with a slight air of mystery in her voice. "There is one letter that is marked urgent. It's from English Heritage."

"English Heritage?" Russell paused and thought for a moment. "What could they be writing to him for, unless..."

"Open it please, Miss Fothergill."

Amelia beamed with delight. He had taken the bait. Quickly she ripped open the envelope and pulled out the letter. "It's about the King's Theatre."

Russell almost dropped the phone. "What about it?"

"Well," said Amelia, relishing the moment. "It seems they have instigated proceedings to acquire a preservation order on the building. They say that you'll be hearing from the Department of Culture—" Her sentence was cut short by an expletive from Russell.

"Leave it on my desk, I'm coming in."

"Are you sure, Mr Craddick? What about your foot?"

"Damn the foot. Just make sure I won't be disturbed this afternoon."

The phone went dead.

Amelia couldn't contain her elation over the contents of the letter. She immediately dialled Trevor who was already at the theatre. He verified that he had also received a letter from Mr Hapgood informing him that the wheels were in motion. They confirmed their arrangement to meet for lunch at midday, and once again Trevor poured out his thanks for all her help.

Amelia sat at her desk with not a care in her head for matters concerning the Council. All she thought about was the King's Theatre being saved — and Trevor.

***

After attending to Russell's needs and making him comfortable in bed, Hazel informed him she was going to town, having lunch with Robert and then going on to her afternoon bridge club. Russell knew she played bridge at least twice a week and sometimes of an evening.

Once or twice the bridge club had played matches against teams as far away as Boulogne and even Paris. This suited Russell down to the ground as it left him free to pursue his other personal *activities*.

But today he needed her there and protested about leaving him — an invalid — to cope on his own.

"Oh, all right, I'll cancel if you want me to," she said, with a certain amount of irritation in her voice. It was to her surprise when, half an hour later, she found him half dressed with the intention of going to work. She even offered to drive him there, but was told his foot felt a lot better and that he could manage.

"Something very important has come up and I need to be there," he said, hobbling towards the bathroom.

"As long as you're sure," she called after him, suppressing a smile of delight that her plans had not been disrupted after all.

With great difficulty Russell eased himself into his car and began the painful drive to the office. Once on the main road, he flicked open his mobile phone and pushed one of the stored numbers.

"Barrie? It's me. You'd better get yourself to my office as quick as you can. We've got problems."

***

"Only four more days of twice daily left," Gavin called to Beverly through their respective open dressing room doors.

"I can't tell you what a relief that will be." Beverly had

just arrived at the theatre from having lunch with Brad.

They had dined at the King's Hotel across the road where Brad had informed her that he was going back to London the day after tomorrow.

"So soon?" she exclaimed. "But we've hardly had any time to spend together."

"It'll only be for a few days. Besides, you're tied up with the show and I don't want to encroach on all your spare time."

"You couldn't possibly do that. I want to spend as much time as I can with you."

But Brad was insistent. "I'll be back next week when you are down to one performance a day. It'll give me a chance to sort things out in London; and I think you need a little time to come to terms with what has happened."

"Of course, you're right," she said, reluctantly. "I have to get used to you not always being here. You do have a home three thousand miles away."

"You'll have to come and visit me in New York. I would love you to meet my parents." He suddenly stopped and corrected himself. "My adoptive parents."

"Your parents," said Beverly, softly. "They will always be that. I just hope I can be a small part of your life from now on."

"You will be." He took her hand across the table and gave it a squeeze. "I'm so pleased things have worked out. This time last week I was all for abandoning my trip."

"I'm glad you didn't."

As they left, they recognised another couple sitting in an alcove on the other side of the dining room.

"You'll never guess who we saw having lunch together?" said Beverly, continuing her conversation with Gavin between dressing rooms.

"No, who?" he said, crossing into her room and shutting the door.

"Trevor and Amelia Fothergill."

"Really? Is something going on, or were they just talking about the theatre?"

"I don't know, but they seemed pretty close."

Gavin crossed the dressing room and pulled up a chair. "I've got something to tell you if you promise not to breathe a word just yet."

It was now Beverly's turn to be intrigued. "You know me dear, silent as the grave."

Gavin had promised Robert that he wouldn't reveal who his stepfather was until the situation with the King's was clearer, but he felt he could trust Beverly. He also recounted the incident of the anonymous phone call earlier that day, much to Beverly's amusement.

"Are you going to do it again? Give him another shock?"

"Oh yes. But Robert wants him to stew a little first."

Beverly was still laughing when a knock came at the door and Trevor's head appeared.

"I thought you'd like to know I've heard from the chap at English Heritage and also the Department of Culture, Media and Sports. They're coming down to look at the theatre in a couple of days. They've also instructed Craddick that nothing must be done before they get here."

"That's wonderful news, Trevor," said Beverly, standing and giving him a hug.

"I'm going to tell the others." He beamed, and turned to leave.

"How was lunch?" asked Beverly, with that all too familiar twinkle in her eye.

"Er, lovely," Trevor replied with a tinge of embarrassment, and quickly closed the door.

***

Russell sat behind his desk fuming. He had just taken a call from the Department of Media, Culture and Sports informing him of their decision. Before that he had spent a quarter of an hour answering questions from the over enthusiastic and probing assistant editor of the Seahaven Courier, whose name was nagging at the back of his mind. His foot was shooting pains up his leg from the exertion of driving to the Council House and staggering up to his office. He then found that his secretary had taken an early lunch.

While he sat there waiting for Barrie to arrive and Amelia to return, his thoughts went back to the anonymous phone call earlier that day. His hands started to shake as he thought of the implications his actions may bring down on him.

"If he calls again," he thought. "I'll call his bluff. See what he'll do then. Besides, it's his word against mine — unless there are any pictures." He was just about to reach into his drawer for the bottle of malt, when the door opened and in walked his lover's husband.

"You look terrible," said Barrie Stone, to an ashen Russell.

"You'd better have one of these," said Russell, bringing out the bottle and two glasses.

"What on earth's happened?"

Pouring two large whiskies, Russell showed him the letter from Hapgood and related the phone call from the Department. "I've also had some bastard reporter on from the paper wanting to know why the Council wants to destroy part of the town's heritage. It's a bloody nightmare."

Barrie sat back in his chair and took another sip. Eventually he looked Russell in the eye and said, "I think, my old mate, we'd better pull our horns in on this one."

"What do you mean?"

"Well, all this publicity. It won't look very good for me if it's known my company is involved."

"You mean you want out?"

"It's not a case of wanting out, but just think a moment. If it becomes public knowledge that you and I unofficially had a land deal before everything had been agreed by the Council, we could both find ourselves in deep water."

Russell stared straight ahead. Bit by bit he could see his plans disintegrating around him. After a few moments he slowly stood and limped towards the window. The pain from his ankle was the last thing on his mind as he looked across at the King's Theatre and watched groups of people going into the matinee performance.

For a full minute neither of them said anything.

"What if..." began Russell slowly, still looking out of the window. "What if it wasn't there?"

Barrie gazed at the back of Russell's head, not totally comprehending what he was saying. "What do you mean, 'what if it wasn't there'?"

Russell held onto the windowsill for support and turned to face Barrie. "What if that old flee pit wasn't there?"

"But it is."

"Yes. But what if it wasn't?" A glimmer of a smile appeared on Russell's lips as he moved back to sit at his desk.

The full meaning behind the remark was now dawning on

Barrie.

"You're not suggesting…?"

"It's an old building. I'm sure the wiring is a bit faulty in certain areas."

"Russell. Are you talking arson?"

"Be quiet!" said Russell, with authority. Barrie stopped talking. It was now his turn to lose a little colour. Russell continued in a slow, calculating manner. "I'm sure we've got some plans of the place around here. You could find a weak spot. Fix it so it looked like negligence. Put the blame on Curtis-Smyth for lack of proper maintenance and not adhering to health and safety. No one would be any the wiser."

It took a few moments for Barrie to take in the full weight of what Russell had proposed.

"No Russell. It's too dangerous," he said. "What if we're caught? We'd both go down for a long time."

"Not if we're careful."

"I don't know. There are too many risks involved."

"Risks are part of this business," said Russell. "But think about all the money we stand to make on the new development. Have you forgotten about that?"

"No, but—"

"But nothing. I'm not going to let this fall through now. I've put too much time and effort into it."

Barrie Stone sat motionless. He had been depending on this deal to finance a number of other projects he had in the pipeline. Many a time he had sailed close to the wind over enterprises with Russell in the past, but these were treacherous waters.

After a few moments of silence while he thought through everything that had happened, temptation finally overtook

Barrie, and he looked at his colleague with an artful smile. "All right, I'm in," he said. "But how do we go about it?"

"That's more like it. A right chip off the old block, you are."

Barrie began to protest. "My father would never have done anything like this."

"Oh, no? What about the fire at the old Palace Ballroom? That site gave us a much better entrance to the Springville Estate."

"That was started by vandals," said Barrie.

"Vandals my arse."

"I never knew."

"Clever bloke, your old man. Always knew where he was heading. That was until he walked under some scaffolding without wearing his hard hat."

The two partners looked at each other with wry smiles on their faces. Eventually Barrie asked the all-important question.

"So, who do we know who can do this little job for us?"

"You just leave that to me," said Russell, as he poured another two drinks.

***

News about the intervention by English Heritage had spread around the theatre like wildfire. The whole company was buoyant and upbeat during both houses and delighted that the Council's guarded response in the Seahaven Courier, denying any knowledge of the historical value of the King's Theatre, had been relegated to page four.

Trevor had also been on to the paper and told Jack Shepperton about the correspondence from English Heritage.

"Splendid," was the assistant editor's response. "We'll do a follow up piece tomorrow if that is all right."

"Anytime you say," said Trevor. "I'm sure the company will be more than willing to pose for more pictures. The publicity can only do us good."

"And it's another one in the eye for Craddick." Jack was relishing this. He had already given Russell a hard time on the phone and written a pretty damning article.

After the evening's performance, most of the cast crossed the road to the Dog and Trumpet, where they began debating various ways they could help the "Save the Theatre" campaign.

Get members of the audience to sign a petition. Put up posters and ask the general public to write to the paper, were a couple of the suggestions.

"I think we should all march to the Council House in costume and form a picket line," said Carl.

"What, and do a couple of numbers from the show?" quipped Beverly.

"You could throw yourself under the wheels of that Craddick's car and die for the cause." camped Alex.

Laughter broke out as the ideas became wilder.

"At least the atmosphere's more relaxed," said Trevor, quietly to Delphina. They had wandered across from the theatre and joined the others in the pub.

"You seem a lot more relaxed as well," observed Delphina.

"Well, this intervention by English Heritage has turned the whole situation around."

"I think there is another factor to take into consideration."

Trevor looked at her. "What do you mean?"

"Oh, just that you seem to be giving a lot of attention to a certain person who also holds the King's Theatre dear to her heart."

"Miss Fothergill has been of great help."

"*Amelia* has got the *hots* for you."

"Mother." said Trevor, in an admonishing tone.

"It's true. A mother's instincts."

"Please spare me the matchmaking act."

"You should be flattered that someone is taking an interest in you. Good God I was beginning to think I'd never get you off my hands."

"What do you mean?"

"You've not exactly had a multitude of lady friends, have you? There was a time when I thought you might be batting for the other side."

Now acutely embarrassed, Trevor glanced around to see if anyone else could hear Delphina openly discussing his private life. "Mother, will you keep your voice down?"

"I'm an actress of the old school, darling. I was taught to project."

"I will not have you talking like this in public." He was now as red as a beetroot.

"Oh, come on," said Delphina, sotto voce. "From what I've seen of her she seems a very nice woman. You could do worse — and nearly did a couple of times."

Trevor was immensely relieved to hear the landlord call "time", and quickly marched Delphina to the car before she started issuing wedding invitations.

SCENE FIVE
WEDNESDAY, JANUARY 5TH

The day hadn't started well. With so many things buzzing around in his head, Russell had completely forgotten about his foot when he got out of bed. Stubbing his toe against the bedside cabinet caused him to let out an agonising scream.

Hazel shot up from her deep sleep. "What on earth is the matter?"

"Sodding cabinet. Bloody foot," cursed Russell, sitting back down on his side of the bed.

"It's only seven fifteen," said Hazel, glancing at the clock.

"I know it's only seven fifteen," said Russell, in a patronising manner. "I can't sleep any more. I'm going to make a cup of tea."

He pulled on his dressing gown and began a painful journey to the kitchen. His ankle wasn't really as bad as he had made out, but getting sympathy under false pretences was another of Russell's manipulative ways.

Having made a pot of tea, he sat at the kitchen table staring out at the slivers of early morning light starting to appear above the garden wall. His sleep had been disturbed with thoughts melting into dreams that became nightmares, which woke him with a jolt. First and foremost was what to do about the theatre.

Common sense would be to do what Barrie had suggested

and cancel the whole project. But it had become an obsession with him. He wanted it out of the way. He wanted his dream of luxury holiday apartments to rise from the rubble. He wanted the money he knew he could make from the deal.

Another thought that kept nagging away at him was the mysterious phone call. Who was he? How did he know about his exploits at the Stone house, and what did he intend to do about it?

Every time the phone rang the previous day, Russell expected the Cockney voice to start making demands. "If he rings today," thought Russell. "I'm going to have it out with him. I'll ask for proof. Pictures."

"I'll threaten him with legal action", he muttered. "After all it's his word against mine."

"What is, dear?" Hazel overheard his grumbling as she came through the kitchen door.

"Don't creep up on me like that," he snapped.

She ignored him and poured herself a cup of tea. Eventually she ventured another question. "Are you going into the office today?"

"Of course I am. Can't let this foot stop me from working. Too much to do."

The martyred act didn't wash with Hazel, who just accepted his statement and remained silent.

"What about you?" he asked. "What are you doing today?"

"Nothing special. I have some things to get from the dry cleaners and that's about it. Don't forget it's my bridge club night tonight. There's a supper afterwards, so I may be quite late."

Russell took a little more interest than usual in the fact she would be out of the house that evening. "Oh yes, tonight. Well, enjoy yourself. No need to hurry back on my account."

"Don't worry, I won't," Hazel thought to herself as he left the kitchen.

***

"I'm going to be working from home today," Robert informed Gavin as they sat drinking coffee and eating slices of toast and marmalade. "I've got masses of paperwork to get through and the office is just constant interruptions."

"Does that mean that I can't interrupt you?" teased Gavin.

"You will have to behave yourself if you're staying in," replied Robert with a smile as he grabbed the last piece of toast.

"Don't worry, I won't be under your feet. There's another publicity call at midday. A follow up to the article the paper did on Monday."

"Oh good. What did they all think about that pathetic interview my stepfather gave?"

"It was a tremendous lift as you can imagine. Trevor thinks we've got Craddick on the run. And speaking of your beloved stepfather, do you think another phone call is in order?"

Both men allowed a crafty grin to spread across their respective faces.

"If your Cockney friend is ready for another performance, I'm sure he'll find that deceitful old seducer in his office this morning." Robert got up from the table and picked up his personal organiser.

"Here you are," he said, writing something on a piece of

paper. "That's his private mobile number. Not many people have it, so he'll be even more surprised that you're ringing him on it."

Gavin took the paper. "Blackmail is kind of sexy, don't you think?" he said, looking up at Robert with a seductive smile

***

"Bastard. Fucking bastard," shouted Russell, as he almost threw his phone across the office. He was incandescent with rage and hit the surface of his desk with such force he was in danger of spraining his wrist.

The words of the Cockney blackmailer had a more menacing tone than that of the previous day. Russell had demanded proof of what had been seen and was told in no uncertain terms that there was — and this is where Gavin felt he had been truly inspired — video evidence of the perilous descent from the rooftops.

"I'm still contemplating what would be a satisfactory figure for such a wealth of information," concluded Gavin, sounding more like Alfred Doolittle. "Rest assured, I'll be in touch again."

Russell heard a click as the line went dead. He sat there shaking with rage. The turmoil of the last two days was taking its toll and his head felt as though it was about to split apart. He pulled open the right-hand desk drawer and looked at the contents.

"No," he said to himself and firmly shut the drawer. It was too early for a drink, even though he felt he needed one. He had to keep a clear head for the rest of the day. There were plans to make.

Since his conversation with Barrie Stone the previous day, Russell had been trying to locate a certain phone number. He hadn't spoken to the person it belonged to for a good many years, and hoped he was still around. Finally, he had found it in an old address book in his desk at home. Taking out the piece of paper he had copied it down on, he dialled the number.

No reply.

"At least it's still connected," thought Russell. "I'll try later." He then tried Ann Stone at home.

Also, no reply. Frustration was creeping up on Russell.

Rising from his chair, he walked carefully across the office. He was still using a stick, but again this was more for sympathy rather than necessity.

"I'm just going to the planning store room," he told Amelia, who was busying herself in the outer office.

"Anything I can do for you, Mr Craddick?" she asked.

"No." He felt that was rather a sharp retort and immediately remedied it by flashing a smile and adding, "Mustn't expect people to run about after me all the time."

Amelia wondered what he needed from the store. Old files and specs on previous Council projects and buildings were kept down there, together with fading blue prints and plans.

She watched as he returned with a large, grey box folder that looked the worse for wear.

"Miss Fothergill, I don't want to be disturbed again before lunch, and no phone calls."

"Very good Mr Craddick."

The oak panelled door shut with a bang leaving Amelia burning with curiosity yet again.

Clearing most of the papers and objects off the top of his

desk, Russell opened the folder and removed a well-worn, rather dog-eared plan, and unfolded it. He laid it carefully on the desk and smoothed out the creases. In large letters across the top were the words, "King's Theatre — Stage Area".

The plan was divided into two parts, the stage and backstage area, and the rooms and space under the stage. Moving his fingers over the drawing, Russell traced the route from the stage door to the wings. He saw clearly marked towards the upstage part of the left wings, a trap door that covered a set of steps leading down to an old wardrobe store. He saw too where the dressing rooms were and the props store.

Next, he pulled out a plan that showed the auditorium and foyer areas. Originally the lighting was controlled from the left-hand side of the stage, but over various refurbishments, it was now operated from a room at the back of the circle. Finding nothing to interest him in the second plan, he turned his attention back to the first.

For a good twenty minutes Russell studied the plan intensely. He then made a few notes on a pad, tore off the top sheet and put it in his pocket. Reaching for his mobile phone he dialled the number on the paper a second time.

Still no reply.

Damn!

***

"That's right, now give me a big smile. Show me how happy you are with the good news." Guy, the photographer, was back on stage with his equipment, taking more pictures of the company for the Seahaven Courier. Jack Shepperton had done another interview with Trevor, this time with Delphina chipping in when she could.

"We've had quite a few letters and calls from our readers after the first article," Jack told them. "A lot of support for the old theatre."

"I should think so too," remarked Delphina. "All these theatres closing around the country; it's a national disgrace. I blame the Government."

Trevor doubted very much whether Delphina knew which party was in power, but made light of her comments as he led them into the auditorium and onto the stage. "Thank you all for coming," he said to the assembled company.

"We'll have one of you in the middle of the cast if we can," said Guy, and guided Trevor to a suitable position.

"This will really put the cat among the pigeons as far as Craddick is concerned," Jack whispered to Trevor, as the photo session came to an end.

"It's very kind of you to give us so much of your time."

"It's a pleasure; and I hope there is another story to come. A happy ending."

"So do I," said Trevor, as the two men shook hands.

The company began leaving the stage and heading back towards the dressing rooms when they heard a commotion at the stage door.

"What do you mean the press have been taking more photographs?" Max Pendleton stood in the corridor snorting like a ferocious bull. "Why the bloody hell wasn't I told about this?"

"I sent a message with Stan asking everyone if they could be in by midday today," explained Trevor.

"You were in the pub last night with us all," confirmed Stan.

"Well, I never heard you," snorted Max.

"Too busy with his fans from the old folk's home," quipped Willie Waters.

"Or pissed," added Alex.

"I heard that, you pansy," yelled Max.

"Oh, sticks and stones, Mary," sneered Alex.

Max was now purple and started towards Alex with his fist raised. Quick as lightning, Gavin and Stan moved either side of him and restrained his actions.

"That will do." Trevor's voice boomed out with authority and the company fell silent. "I'm sorry if you missed the announcement Max, but that does not give you the right to take it out on everyone else. In the present circumstances, we need to act as a concerted body. Any publicity is good for us and not meant to be used for personal gain. Now I suggest we all calm down and get ready for this afternoon's performance."

Everyone agreed with Trevor's comments and moved away leaving Max still smarting. "It's a conspiracy, that's what it is," he moaned, and shut himself away in his dressing room until Stan called beginners for the matinee.

Between performances, Beverly asked everyone if they would like to join her and Greg in the Dog and Trumpet for a farewell drink to Brad.

"He would like to say 'goodbye' to everyone, although he will be back before the end of the run."

They all said they would love to, and Gavin called Robert to invite him along.

"How did the phone call go?" enquired Robert. "Another Tony award winning performance?"

"I could almost feel him shaking in his shoes," said Gavin.

"I think we'd better lay off for a bit. Don't want to give

the old sod a heart attack."

"Oh," said Gavin with mock disappointment. "Just when I thought I was getting to grips with the finer nuances of the part."

***

Amelia returned to her office after lunch to find a note from her boss saying he would be out for the rest of the day. She had taken the opportunity of the hour break to walk to the library and bring Elaine up to date.

"Craddick seems in a complete dilemma. Apart from the obvious discomfort from his foot — (Elaine had revelled in Amelia's description of her boss and his death-defying escape from a first-floor balcony) — his mood swings are quite violent. They happen every time he gets a phone call or opens the mail."

"What's next?" asked the librarian. "How are things going with Trevor?"

Amelia no longer blushed when his name was mentioned. She had been a different woman over the past few days. Outward signs of the first buds of romance were now beginning to show.

"He phoned me just before I left for lunch and asked me to join him and the company tonight after the show."

"Amelia Fothergill, you'll be introducing him to the family next."

""I'm taking things as they come," said Amelia, with a modicum of decorum. They looked at each other, and then with total disregard for the library's silence rule, giggled away like pubescent schoolgirls.

Russell left the office and headed for the golf club. Due to the inclement weather, only a few of the members had braved the course before quickly heading for the nineteenth hole. He passed an hour or so idly chatting with some of them, had a drink and a light lunch and then phoned Ann Stone again. This time she answered.

He told her about the threatening calls and asked if she had received any. Getting a negative answer, he warned her to be on her guard and suggested that they cool their relationship for the foreseeable future.

Then he tried the other number for a third time.

Success.

A low, hesitant voice answered.

Russell immediately recognised it and, after a few vague pleasantries, arranged to meet the person in half an hour at Rosie's Roadside Café.

"Rosie's" was not the most salubrious of establishments, but it was the only place far enough away from town for Russell not to be recognised when he walked through the frosted glass door. The single fluorescent light afforded a dim picture of the eating area. Dotted around the room were tables and chairs that hardly matched, where a few men sat eating various plates of fried food and drinking tea out of chipped mugs.

Hidden behind a grubby copy of the Seahaven Courier was a lone figure seated at a corner table. He looked up as Russell walked in and nodded to the vacant chair opposite. Russell was about to decline the offer of a mug of tea from a large buxom woman, who presumably was Rosie, but thought better of it when he saw her piercing eyes and steely look. After placing his order, he made his way past the other diners and sat down.

"Hello Benny," he said. "Thank you for meeting me at such short notice."

The man opposite him folded his paper and glanced around the room, checking to make sure they weren't being overheard. "Nice to see you again, Mr Craddick. It's been a long time."

Benny Roffey was a squat, sallow looking man whose age was almost impossible to tell. The deep lines on his face and the fact that he hardly had any neck meant that he could be anything between forty and fifty-five. His ever-shifting eyes were set deep into his head, and when he spoke his mouth hardly opened.

"From the sound of your call you've got something pretty urgent that needs taking care of," he said, almost in a whisper. His thin lips slightly parting in a smile which afforded Russell a glimpse of his yellowing teeth.

"I do as a matter of fact."

Benny sat back in his chair. Russell was about to continue when a muscled and heavily tattooed arm appeared in front of him. An equally large hand placed a mug of what was commonly called "builder's tea" on the table.

"Yer tea," grunted Rosie. "That's one fifty."

Normally, Russell would have complained about the quality of the tea and the price, but he had more important things to deal with. Producing a two-pound coin, he waved her away indicating she should keep the change. Once she was out of earshot, he continued speaking quietly to Benny.

"It's something that I know you have experience of. A similar job to the one you did for old man Stone."

The deep-set eyes slowly began to grow wider as Benny started to recall an incident from a good many years ago.

"You mean the Palace Ballroom job?"

Russell nodded.

"So, what's standing in the way of progress this time?"

Leaning across the table, Russell whispered, "The King's Theatre on the promenade."

Benny didn't move for a few seconds, then his tongue appeared and circled his mouth, wetting his lips. "It won't be easy. It's a very conspicuous building; and it's on a main road."

"I know that, but can you do it?"

"Oh, I can do it all right, but it will take a bit of planning."

Russell shook his head. "I can't afford to wait. It has to be tonight."

"What?" cried Benny a little too loudly, so as to attract the attention of a couple of lorry drivers.

"Keep your voice down," hissed Russell. "Tonight, or tomorrow night. But it has to be soon."

"Then I'm afraid I'm going to have to say no to this one."

"Why?"

Benny pushed one of his feet right under the table and carefully pulled up his trouser leg. Russell looked down to see a police tag firmly attached above his ankle.

"I'm on a curfew. Have to be at home by a phone at seven o'clock each evening."

"Oh bugger," groaned Russell. "What the hell did you do?"

"Got nicked for drink driving and running into the back of another car."

"And they sent you down for that?"

"The other car was driven by an off-duty copper and I threatened to knock his lights out. I got six months, but they've let me out on one of these for the last five weeks. There's another eight days to go, so I've got to keep my nose clean, or I'll be back inside."

"Shit! Why didn't you tell me this on the phone?" said a very exasperated Russell.

"You never asked. Besides, I thought you just wanted someone warning off or roughing up a bit." This was Benny's usual line of business. Arson was bigger, more dangerous, and much more expensive.

Russell suddenly thought of his other problem and envisaged Benny and his thugs beating the living daylights out of his blackmailer, but decided that would have to wait.

"Sorry Mr Craddick. You know I've always seen you all right in the past. It's just this time…"

"Yes, yes, I understand."

"I could give you a couple of phone numbers."

"No, that won't be necessary."

"Well, you know how to get hold of me," said Benny, with a faint smile that once more revealed his yellowing teeth.

Russell nodded and made his way out of the café and back to his car. His foot was still giving him some pain, and this compounded his frustration. He sat at the wheel thinking hard about what to do next. In the end he came to only one conclusion. He took out his mobile phone and rang Barrie.

"So now what do we do?" asked Barrie, after Russell had explained the situation.

Slowly and deliberately, Russell answered him. "We do it ourselves."

Barrie nearly dropped his phone.

"When I say we do it, I mean you," continued Russell.

"Me? Are you mad?"

"Well, I can't with this blasted foot."

Barrie started to protest but Russell cut him off.

"Listen, it'll be quite simple." Russell explained his plan to an increasingly nervous Barrie.

"Well, are you up for it?"

"Tonight?"

"Yes. We can't afford to wait any longer."

After a few more minutes of discussing the situation, Barrie reluctantly agreed and arranged to meet Russell in the car park of the Dog and Trumpet at ten o'clock.

"You can tell Ann you're meeting some business associates for a late drink. Oh, and make sure you bring some dark clothes to change into."

"Is that all?"

"Yes. I'll see to everything else. Just don't be late."

Russell clicked off and continued his journey home. On opening the front door, he found his wife on the phone.

"Yes, everything's fine for tonight. I'll see you about eight."

"Who were you talking to?" he asked, when she had finished her conversation.

"A member of the bridge club, of course. That's where I told you I would be tonight."

"That's right," he said absently. "You're going to be in late, aren't you?"

Hazel smiled and nodded before returning to the kitchen to start preparations for dinner.

After another delightful meal, to which Russell gave no

thanks or even much attention, Hazel disappeared upstairs to get ready for her evening out. Russell turned on the television and sat resting his foot on a small stool while he watched the early evening news. But his mind took little notice of the world's problems. Instead, he sat thinking about the dilemma facing him at that very moment.

The phone rang twice giving him a nervous reaction each time for fear of it being the blackmailer. But he needn't have worried. The first was a wrong number and the second was from his daughter. She had heard about his injury from Hazel, and wanted to know how the patient was. As he finished the call, Hazel appeared, ready for her evening out.

"I'll be off then," she said. "Don't wait up for me, you know how these things go on."

"Right," said Russell, absently. He stood and watched through the window as she manoeuvred her car out of the drive and up to the end of the road where she turned left. As soon as he saw it disappear from view, his whole manner changed rapidly. A fixed determined look covered his face and silently, but very definitely he gave an affirmative nod to the plan that had been forming in his brain.

Still limping, but now disregarding any pain from the ankle, he climbed the stairs and, in his bedroom, changed into a completely black set of clothes. He then returned downstairs to the kitchen and proceeded to rifle through cupboards and drawers until he found where Hazel kept an emergency supply of matches. Two boxes were thrust into a carrier bag together with a torch. Crossing the kitchen to a door leading to the garage, he opened it and turned on the light.

He started moving around the garage like a man possessed, grabbing at paint tins and pots on the shelves.

Suddenly he stopped as his eyes alighted on what he was looking for. A tin of barbecue lighter fuel. He snatched it off the shelf and added it to the items in the carrier bag before depositing it and a small toolbox in the boot of the car.

For the next half an hour he sat at the kitchen table going over and over his plan and checking the drawing he had made of the backstage area.

***

"Second act beginners," called Stan over the PA system.

"Time to entertain the little darlings for another hour," said Gavin, as he joined Beverly on the side of the stage.

"Is Robert coming down for a drink later?" asked Beverly.

"You bet. He wanted to see Brad off."

"Oh? I hope you don't start getting jealous."

"No need," said Gavin, with a wink of supreme confidence. "I'm pretty sure Brad is firmly on the other side of the fence."

The music began the introduction to the second act and was greeted with whoops and cheers from the Wednesday night audience. Brad was in for a third time and considered himself a seasoned panto aficionado, responding to all the audience participation bits in a loud American accent, much to the amusement of the people sitting around him.

Amelia had arrived during the interval and she and Trevor watched the second act from the rear of the stalls. Delphina, who hadn't seen the show since opening night, was back in the royal box gazing down on the populace below.

Max had kept himself shut away in his dressing room when not performing, still smarting over missing another photo session. He heard his cue coming up and began to make his way to the stage.

"Pst! Max!"

Max turned to see Reggie Dumont coming through the stage door.

"Reggie, what are you doing here?"

"Aurelia has gone to her sisters in Worthing for a couple of days and taken the car," explained Reggie. "I was fed up of being on my own, so I decided to hop on a bus and pay you a visit."

"Great to see you, old love. I'm just about to go on, so why don't you see the rest of it from out front and we'll have a drink after the show."

"Will do," said Reggie. "See you across the road?"

Still not happy about socialising with the rest of the company, Max thought for a moment and then said, "No, I tell you what. Come back here and we'll have our own little party. I've got a couple of bottles of scotch tucked away."

"Better still." Reggie turned to go through the pass door, and with a squeezing hand gesture added, "Great tits."

Max beamed with delight for the first time that day and headed towards the stage ready to walk on and greet his public again.

***

The kitchen wall clock showed nine thirty. Time to leave.

Struggling into the driver's seat, Russell operated the remote control for the garage door. It opened with a whirring, monotone hum that filled the night air. He backed his car out of the garage and followed the route taken by his wife earlier that evening, only this time at the top of the road he turned right.

The clock on the dashboard showed nine forty-five. He drove along the promenade and approached the lights at the junction with Northbrook Road. They changed to green and he turned the car and drove past the King's Hotel and then the theatre. Curling his lip and sneering at the building, he continued up the road and a few seconds later, pulled into the car park at the side of the Dog and Trumpet.

He could see no sign of Barrie's car. "I hope he doesn't chicken out at the last minute," he muttered.

Five minutes later a familiar powder blue Jaguar drove in and parked in a far corner of the car park. Russell flashed his headlights a couple of times and a figure dressed in black ran across and got in beside him.

"Look at this, I'm shaking like a leaf," said Barrie, holding out his hand.

"Don't worry," Russell assured him, "everything will be fine."

"I wish I had your confidence." Barrie could feel his stomach performing somersaults and silently wished he would soon wake up from this nightmare.

Both of them looked across at the theatre's stage door. Russell started grinding his back teeth together in a growing frenzy of impatience.

Nine fifty-five.

They now had to wait for everyone to leave the theatre.

***

The dark blue house tabs fell after the third curtain call and an enthusiastic audience began to file out into the night air. Brad left his seat and joined Trevor and Amelia at the back of the stalls.

"It really is a beautiful theatre," he enthused, looking around the auditorium.

"And one that deserves to survive," said Amelia.

"I have every confidence it will after the publicity we've been getting," said Trevor. "Another great article in tonight's paper."

Reggie Dumont, who had crept into a vacant seat on the end of a row, ambled up to join them.

"How's tricks?" he called to Trevor. "Heard you've got a fight on your hands for the flea pit."

"Everything is under control," Trevor replied, curtly.

"Reggie Dumont," he said introducing himself to Amelia and Brad.

"Amelia Fothergill."

"And I'm Brad Harman."

Hearing Brad's accent, Reggie asked if he was living in this part of the world or just visiting.

"I'm over here on business," said Brad. "And to trace some of my family."

"You have relatives in these parts?"

"Only one. My mother is Beverly Dufayne."

Trevor thought people would pay good money to witness Reggie's stunned expression, which he held for a good ten seconds. Finally, a glazed smile broke the frozen facial look.

"Beverly's son? It's nice to meet you," he stammered. "Well, I'd better be off. I'm meeting Max backstage."

"Via a telephone call to his wife," said Trevor, as Reggie scurried off through the pass door. "I'd better warn Beverly to expect the third degree from Aurelia Dumont tomorrow."

The three of them met up with Delphina, who was holding court in the foyer, before making their way out of the theatre.

As Trevor predicted, Reggie was backstage on the public phone to Aurelia. He was speaking in hushed tones as members of the company left for the Dog and Trumpet.

"I don't know any more than that," he whispered. "You'll have to ask her yourself." He finished his call and disappeared into Max's dressing room before Beverly emerged from hers.

Delphina took hold of Brad's arm as they came down the steps in front of the theatre. Trevor offered his arm to Amelia who took it graciously. All four crossed the Northbrook Road and walked towards the pub. None of them noticed the black Audi parked on the other side of the car park.

***

For the last half-hour Russell briefed Barrie on his plan and handed him the paper containing diagrams and layout of the backstage area copied from drawings in the office.

They were both watching the members of the public leaving after the performance when suddenly Russell's attention was caught by the four people crossing the road. He stared hard at the young man with the older woman.

"I know him," he said, staring at Brad. "He's the idiot who nearly crashed into me the other day."

If he had continued looking at the group, he would have recognised someone else. As it happened, a number of the cast were leaving by the stage door and the whole crowd merged into one as they entered the pub.

"Not long now," said Russell, as one by one the lights at

the front of the theatre were being turned out. A few minutes later the light over the stage door went out as Stan, the stage manager, appeared and locked the door before crossing the road to join his colleagues.

"Right here we go." With a quick movement Russell started the engine.

The traffic had been very light all night and at that moment the road was deserted. Looking both ways to make sure they weren't observed, he pulled out of the car park and drove further up Northbrook Road.

The unmarked road to the old fish paste factory was near the top and Russell turned into it. Pot holes and rough, broken tarmac shook the car as they proceeded along a route and past the derelict buildings.

Russell's eyes suddenly widened as the back wall of the theatre came into view. He continued driving the car down the service road, passing more crumbling buildings, and coming to a stop by a barbed wire perimeter fence. Pushing the button to wind down the electric windows, they both listened for any sound of movement. All was quiet except for the odd vehicle travelling along Northbrook Road.

"Come on," commanded Russell, opening his door. They cautiously got out of the car and moved to the boot. Russell took out the carrier bag and removed a hammer and chisel from the toolbox.

The adrenaline was now pumping through Barrie's veins as he took the bag from Russell. "It's quite exciting," he said with a smirk. "All this cloak and dagger stuff."

"Just concentrate on the job in hand," warned Russell, and pointed to a small window in the back wall of the building. "That's your best point of entry. It's out of sight of the main road and you could make it look as though vandals had broken in."

Barrie pulled something out of his pocket. It was a dark ski mask from a holiday in Austria the previous year. He pulled it over his head completing his breaking and entering outfit.

"How do I look?"

"Terrific," said Russell, rather unconvincingly. "You look as though you're about to descend the piste at St Moritz!"

Ignoring Russell's jibe, Barrie picked up the hammer and chisel and put them in his bag.

"Now when you have finished," continued Russell. "Leave by the stage door. If anyone sees you, they'll think you're a stagehand. But for God's sake take that mask off first. I'll drive back to the far end of the car park and keep watch." He got back in his car and slowly reversed before heading back to the main road.

With the instructions safely in his pocket and clinging tightly to the bag of pyrotechnic objects, Barrie made his way to the fence. It was in a desperate state of repair and easily breached.

Taking care not to snag his clothing on the barbed wire, he moved quickly to the back of the theatre. Constantly checking to make sure he hadn't been observed, he took out the torch and shone the beam onto the wall, illuminating the window.

"Bugger it." he said under his breath. The window was a toilet one and about six feet off the ground. He had to find something to stand on, so he returned to the factory buildings in search of a box or crate. He shone his torch around the deserted area, but nothing of any use could be found. He was just about to give up when he noticed an old wooden ladder clamped to one of the walls. On closer inspection he saw that the clamp was padlocked. Another obstacle, but one that Barrie was now committed to overcome.

Swiftly taking out the chisel and positioning it next to the padlock, he hit it hard with the hammer. The sound of steel on steel echoed around the empty building, disturbing the sleep of some birds nesting in the rafters. The noise subsided, but the padlock stayed in place.

Barrie moved the torch nearer to the clamp and saw that it was held in place by bolts going into the masonry. He jabbed at it with the chisel and chunks of it, weakened by time and weather, fell away. Soon quite a large part of one of the bolts was exposed. With one final dig, it sprang lose from the wall and the whole ladder fell to the ground with a resounding clatter.

Again, the birds complained. Taking no notice, Barrie quickly retrieved the ladder and carried it back to below the window.

"Perfect," he said smiling to himself, and began to climb. Half way up a rotten rung broke in half almost sending Barrie to the ground. He held on and managed to get a foothold on the next one up.

Pausing for a second, then carefully continuing his climb, he reached the window and noticed it had a partly decaying wooden frame. The chisel again came in handy and he easily prized the frame from the catch.

Now came the difficult part — climbing through.

The window was big enough for Barrie to put one leg through and sit astride of the ledge. This he managed with a lot of huffing and puffing. Below him on the inside were a couple of wash basins. He dropped the carrier bag into one of them and began to manoeuvre his other leg over the ledge. It was then that his heart almost stopped as he heard footsteps approaching from the corridor beyond the toilet.

***

Max and Reggie had already consumed a good three quarters of a bottle of whisky before Reggie felt the need to empty his bladder.

They had turned out the dressing room lights and kept quiet while Stan locked up the theatre, thinking everyone had left.

"We'll stay here," said Max. "I don't want to be bothered with that lot tonight."

"Will we be able to get out?" asked Reggie, thinking about his last bus home.

"No problem. It's only a Yale lock. We'll pull the door shut behind us, unless you fancy kipping down here for the night. That couch is quite comfy."

Max moaned on to Reggie about the way he had been treated by the company, especially the younger members. "And Trevor ought to have more consideration, but all he's worried about is the closing of the theatre."

"What about Beverly, then?" said Reggie, hoping to get some more information about her illegitimate son.

"Quite a revelation," said Max, topping up the glasses.

They continued talking and drinking until Reggie excused himself.

"It's at the end of the corridor on the left," Max informed him, as his friend lurched across the dressing room.

The corridor was dark with only the faint glow from the

emergency light. Reggie weaved his way, clutching the wall for stability, until he came to the door to the men's toilet. At least he thought it was. Through an alcoholic haze, the figure on the sign was blurred to Reggie.

"What the hell, there's no one else here," he said to himself, and pushed open the door. His hand groped around until it found the light switch and flicking it, lit up the white tiled room.

It was the ladies. Reggie tottered to a cubicle and found the door locked. That's odd, he thought, must be out of order. He moved on to the next door that opened and enabled him to find relief.

Swaying slightly as he tried to keep his aim steady, he felt a chill all around him and shivered.

"Someone's left a bloody window open," he muttered. "And in this weather."

Zipping up his flies, he turned and began to make his way back to the warmth of Max's dressing room, unaware that in the next cubicle someone else was shivering.

The shivering was more on account of nerves rather than cold. How Barrie had managed to clamber down from the windowsill and hide in a cubicle before Reggie's untimely entrance, he would never know. He hadn't expected anyone to still be in the building after seeing the stage manager lock up. Desperately trying not to pant out loud after his mad dash, he waited until the sound of footsteps had receded before his fingers slowly slid back the door catch.

Reggie had obliged him by leaving the light on which, through a glass skylight above the door, lit up part of the corridor. Carefully inching open the toilet door so as to not make a sound, Barrie tiptoed out and stood for a moment. He quickly checked the piece of paper to get his bearings.

Straight ahead led to the dressing rooms from where he could hear voices and a lot of chuckling. To his right he could make out a sign that stated "To Stage Left".

Realising that time was of the essence and that he could be discovered any minute, Barrie moved swiftly in the direction of the sign. He remembered from Russell's diagram that the trap door to under the stage was located on the left-hand side. Turning on his torch he swept the beam across the floor until he saw a brass ring embedded in the lid of the trap.

With one almighty pull, Barrie yanked it open until it rested on its hinges at an angle of just over ninety degrees. The light from his torch yielded a set of stone steps leading down into the depths of the theatre. Tentatively he walked down them and on reaching the bottom, looked around at the various items of costumes, props and scenery that were stored there.

An amazing revelation suddenly came over him. He was actually enjoying this. An evil smile crept across his lips as he thought to himself how quickly a fire would take hold amongst all this stuff.

Taking out the barbecue lighter fuel, he sprayed some all over an old mannequin wearing a rather moth-eaten gown from the Victorian period. Next, he moved his attention to a stack of books used as props and gave them a soaking. His final action was to open a skip containing an assortment of shirts, coats and dresses and douse them with the remainder of the fluid. He then dragged the skip to the bottom of the steps, positioning it right under the entrance to the trap.

His intention was to return to the stage level and drop a lighted match into the skip that would ignite and start the demise of this historic building.

It was five to eleven and the two old performers had just drained the last drop.

"Shall we crack open this one?" said Max, holding up another bottle.

"I really ought to be getting back," said Reggie, slurring his words. "The last bus to Brighton is eleven thirty."

"I've told you, you can kip on that couch if you like."

"Thanks, old man, but I prefer my own bed."

"Just as you please. Been a good night though, hasn't it," chuckled Max. "We must do it again."

Clutching each other for support, they left the dressing room. It was now Max who needed the loo and, propping Reggie against the wall in a path of light coming from the ladies, he went inside. As his capacity for alcohol was greater than Reggie's, he wasn't as inebriated, and whilst in the toilet he became aware of a scraping noise.

"If that's mice they're having a hell of a party," he observed, and then laughed at his joke. As he left the toilet, he heard it again.

"Did you hear that? It's coming from the stage," he whispered to Reggie.

"Don't tell me there's a theatre ghost." Reggie hiccupped, and Max shushed him.

"Listen."

Now the sound was of footsteps on stone.

"Come on," he whispered, and they both crept along the corridor and onto the side of the stage.

Barrie, who was almost at the top of the steps, heard them coming and in a panic to go back down and hide, had dropped his torch. It clattered down the stone steps, crashed onto the basement floor and went out. The whole of backstage was pitch black.

"Who's there?" called out Max.

Barrie cursed under his breath and decided the only thing to do was stay perfectly still until he could make a run for it.

Max knew there was a switch for the working light by the stage managers desk and started to grope his way along with his drinking companion beside him.

Suddenly Reggie let out a yell as he came into contact with the edge of the open trap door. He, in turn, bumped into Max who staggered and fell against a large object in front of him. This was followed by a blood-curdling scream piercing the dark, and seconds later a rather ominous thud.

For a moment there was total silence.

"What the bloody hell was that?"

"Wait there, Reggie. I'll find the light," shouted Max, and headed for the switch. The working light lit up the wings of the theatre and Max moved back to Reggie.

Now able to see, the two men slowly peered down the open trap. There at the bottom lay the crumpled figure of Barrie Stone.

The weight of Max falling against him had plunged Barrie down the steps. The last thing the builder detected before departing this world was the smell of barbecue lighter fuel as he bounced off the skip and cracked his head open on the stone floor.

***

The King's Theatre company had enjoyed a pleasant hour in the Dog and Trumpet and said their temporary farewells to Beverly's son who was leaving for London the next day.

Beverly had walked down to the Hotel with Brad to say a private goodbye. Trevor, Amelia, Delphina, Gavin and Robert were talking outside the pub when suddenly the stage door across the road burst open and Max staggered out.

"What the hell's going on?" exclaimed Trevor.

"He's dead! I've killed him."

They all stared at Max who was holding his head and moaning.

"The man's pissed," said Delphina.

"What's he doing in the theatre?" said Gavin.

Max lurched towards them and repeated his words. "He's dead, I tell you."

"Who's dead?" said Trevor.

"The bloke in the basement."

"We'd better see what he's talking about," advised Robert, and pushing past Max, they all trooped into the theatre.

"What the fuck..." Russell, whose eyes had been glued to the stage door from his secluded spot on the car park, sat up so suddenly he almost banged his head on the windscreen. He watched the commotion going on and wound down the window just in time to hear Max's outburst.

The bloke in the basement — dead? Russell mouthed the words incredulously.

Now what should he do? If Barrie had been found, dead or alive, the police would be called. He needed to be at home concocting an alibi. Barrie's car was still in the car park so if he did manage to get out, he had the means to get away.

His hand moved to the ignition key at the same time his eyes picked out a face in the crowd that he knew well.

"Amelia Fothergill," Russell spoke out loud as he stared across at the group of people. Surely, he was seeing things?

But as the street light lit the faces of the people running towards the stage door, his suspicions were confirmed. It was his secretary — consorting with the enemy.

Russell was apoplectic. His knuckles were turning white as he gripped the steering wheel. She must know everything. What Curtis-Smyth was planning and who was helping him.

"But what about her?" Russell spoke his thoughts aloud. "Did she know in advance about the new development? No, how could she? She'd never been party to any meetings or had access to any of my files." His voice, rising in a crescendo, developed into a scream.

If anyone had witnessed this outburst, they would have thought a madman was behind the wheel. Russell was rocking with fury in his seat. His breathing was strong and intense. As he drove away from Northbrook Road, for the umpteenth time in the last few days his mind was turning over and over with numerous questions. It was all getting too much and on top of everything, the pains were raging again in his chest.

Arriving at the side of the stage they found Reggie slumped beside the open trap. He looked at them with a vacant expression and pointed down into the depths.

Five faces looked into the shadows at the body that was lying in a crumpled position. Amelia whimpered at the sight of the blood oozing through the woollen ski mask and buried her head on Delphina's shoulder. Trevor quickly pulled a switch on the side wall and the basement was instantly bathed in light. Gavin ran down the steps followed by Robert and crouched by the lifeless form.

"Call an ambulance," he shouted to Robert, who took out his mobile phone.

"You shouldn't move him," said Trevor.

"I don't think he's breathing. I can't tell with this ski mask on."

Robert had called the emergency services and was now beside the body, attempting to detect a pulse.

"I can't feel anything," he said. "Perhaps we should remove the mask and try resuscitation."

"There should be a pair of scissors on the work table down there," said Trevor, slowly walking down the steps.

Gavin found them and handed them to Robert who cut along one side of the mask and carefully pulled it away from the face revealing the enormity of the wound.

"Oh my God," he uttered, falling backwards and dropping the scissors. The blood was still pouring from the large crack in the skull, creating a deep red circle around the head.

From above the two women looked down and this time Amelia let out a gasp.

"I know him," she said, almost fainting. "It's Barrie Stone. He's the one who wants this land for the new development."

The ambulance and police arrived within minutes and took charge of the situation. The others waited in the green room where Delphina made them all tea, and Max unscrewed his second bottle of scotch.

Detective Sergeant Randall had already taken brief statements from each of them by the time his superior, Detective Chief Inspector Carlyle arrived. After conducting an initial investigation of the scene, he joined them all in the green room, and bit by bit pieced together the events of the evening.

"Was that man trying to burn the theatre down?" Trevor's question was the same on everyone's lips.

"I'm afraid I can't comment on anything at this stage in

the proceedings," Carlyle said, gravely.

"We could have been roasted alive," said Max.

Reggie, who had sobered up considerably, added, "We'd have been trapped in here and no one would have known."

"You shouldn't have been in the theatre," said Delphina, scolding Reggie as though he was a naughty schoolboy.

"What were you both doing here, sir?" asked the Detective Chief Inspector.

"Just having a quiet drink and a chat," said Max, innocently.

"But the company had gathered in the pub opposite, hadn't they?" Carlyle looked at his assistant.

"Yes sir," said D S Randall, checking his notes. "Except for Mr Pendleton and Mr Dumont.

"I was in dispute with some of them and didn't wish to partake of their company," stated Max, full of self-importance.

"What he means," said Gavin. "Is that because he missed out on some publicity shots, we got the blame for it."

"It was all planned..." began Max, pointing an accusing finger at Gavin.

"If we could just stick to the matter in hand." Carlyle's authoritative voice stopped any further argument.

Max sat back on one of the sofas, irritated at being silenced. The Chief Inspector continued.

"Now, you were here in your dressing room with Mr Dumont."

Max nodded.

"I'd just called in to say hello," said Reggie, quite obligingly. "Didn't expect all this carry on."

"And you heard nothing until you were about to leave?"

"Not a thing," said Max. "I went to pay a visit and heard

this scraping. Then it sounded like someone walking about, so Reggie and I went to investigate."

"Thought it was a theatre ghost," grinned Reggie.

"The scraping was probably the costume skip being dragged to the bottom of the steps," said Carlyle.

"I thought I could smell lighter fuel," added Robert.

"It was certainly all over a lot of the costumes," said Gavin. "And there was a discarded can by the skip."

Trevor looked across at Max and Reggie. "If you hadn't disturbed him, this place would have been a raging inferno by now."

Max thought for a moment before rising and assuming an air of superiority.

"So, what you are saying is that I, Max Pendleton, single-handedly saved the King's Theatre from utter devastation?"

Max stood before the assembled group, his head held high as though accepting a standing ovation.

"Me too," offered Reggie, and was totally ignored.

"You also caused the death of a prominent business man," said Carlyle, once again taking the wind out of Max's sails.

All of them sat quietly for a moment before a police constable entered. Gavin and Robert immediately recognised him as the one who had helped them in the traffic jam on Boxing Day.

"Hello," said the constable. "Fancy seeing you again."

Gavin and Robert smiled at him, but any further pleasantries were cut short by Carlyle.

"Yes Monkton, what is it?"

"We found where he got in, sir. Round the back there's a ladder under the window of the Ladies."

"Right. Anything else?"

"Yes, sir. We think he may have come through the fence from the old factory. There are fresh tyre tracks and footprints."

"Any sign of a vehicle?"

"No sir."

"Thank you. You'd better seal off the area until our boys have finished."

"Very good, sir." And, with another smile in the direction of Gavin and Robert, he left.

"Did any of you know Barrie Stone?" asked Carlyle.

Everyone shook their heads except Amelia.

"I did. Indirectly."

Carlyle looked at her and waited for her to elaborate. She glanced at Trevor who was sitting next to her and he gave her a reassuring smile and nod.

"Detective Chief Inspector," she said, after taking a deep breath. "I think I'd better tell you what I know about this matter."

Amelia told her story to Carlyle, who at times thought he was hearing the synopsis of the latest TV crime series.

"Quite a tale," he said. "I take it you don't think much of your boss?"

"He's despicable if you want my considered opinion," replied Amelia, with contempt.

"I can second that," said Robert.

Carlyle looked at Robert. "Would you care to elaborate, Mr…"

"Andrews," advised D S Randall, with a quick glance at his notes.

"Russell Craddick, I'm sorry to say, is my stepfather."

The plot was sounding more and more bizarre to Carlyle.

"What is your connection to the company?"

Robert looked at Gavin, who winked at him.

"I'm Mr Embury's partner," said Robert, in a very straightforward manner that made Gavin tremendously proud of him.

D S Randall shuffled his feet and made a quick note, but the DCI didn't seem at all fazed by Robert's answer.

"And you don't get on with your stepfather?"

"Not at all. We have nothing in common, and he has treated my mother appallingly over the years."

"I shall have a few questions for Mr Craddick in the morning. He could well be implicated in this case. Meanwhile, I would appreciate it if none of you said anything about the events of this evening, especially you two".

Catching the steely gaze from the Chief Inspector, Robert and Amelia both heartily agreed. The thought of Russell getting his just desserts was something beyond their wildest dreams.

"You will be required to make and sign official statements, so if you could all call into the police station at your convenience sometime tomorrow. That will be all for tonight."

As the group broke up, Trevor approached the Detective Chief Inspector.

"It will be all right for us to perform tomorrow, won't it? We have two shows."

"From what I can see, I'm pretty sure everything will be fairly straightforward. Our scene of crime boys will work on through the night and should finish up in the morning. They will seal off the basement and the area around the trap door, so as long as everyone keeps clear, you should be able to carry on

313

as normal." Carlyle's words helped to reassure Trevor.

"It's a miracle we've got a theatre to carry on in after the machinations of those two miscreants," said Delphina, making sure she had the last word before sweeping out.

***

Driving with one hand on the wheel and the other clutching his chest, Russell put as much distance between him and the crime scene before he was forced to pull into the kerb and stop. The pains were still shooting through his chest and he knew it was another angina attack. The third in two days. He reached for a spare prescription spray kept in the glove compartment.

Flinging various items on to the floor he found the bottle and squirted some of the contents under his tongue. After a short time, the attack seemed to ease and he prepared to continue his journey home. It was then that he heard sirens. An ambulance and two police cars came racing towards him from the town centre and turned down Northbrook Road.

Russell now looked like a zombie. He had no feeling — he was numb all over.

Slowly, his sense of reason started to return and he knew he had to get home. If Amelia Fothergill recognised Barrie and told the police of the connection with him, he had to have an alibi. He would have been at home all night with a sprained ankle. Hazel could vouch for the fact she had left him there and it would be his word against anyone else's that he hadn't moved all night.

The dashboard clock showed eleven fifty-five as he arrived outside his house. Hazel's car was nowhere to be seen.

"Good. She's not home yet," he surmised.

He put the car away, and went into the house. Checking the answer machine, he found no messages.

Again, good.

He turned off all the downstairs lights and got himself ready for bed. Under the duvet he started to put the evening's events into some sort of order.

Barrie must be dead, or in police custody. If they came asking questions, he would deny everything. Say it must have been Barrie's idea because of the development being suspended by English Heritage.

One thing he must do the next morning is to get rid of any incriminating evidence in his desk. He would have to be up early and in the office before anyone else.

Eventually, the stress of the evening began to take its toll as his body demanded sleep. He was just beginning to drop off when he became aware of someone else entering the room.

Hazel was home. Lying perfectly still and feigning a deep sleep, Russell squinted at the bedside clock.

Twelve twenty-five.

SCENE SIX
THURSDAY, JANUARY 6TH

"I hope you have enjoyed your brief stay with us, Mr Harman," the assistant manager of the King's Hotel said to Brad.

"Very much," replied Brad, handing over his American Express card to settle his bill. "I hope to be back for a few days around the fourteenth — for the last night of the pantomime."

"How splendid. I hope we can be of service to you again."

"I'll phone when I know a definite date." Brad retrieved his card and receipt and made his way to the car park.

He was still oblivious to the events of the previous night, as he and Beverly had gone back to the hotel for a few private mother and son moments together.

"I'll call you every day and I promise to be here for your last night," he said as Beverly wiped away a tear. They were sitting together in a corner of the lounge.

"I swore I wouldn't do this," she said. "I should blame it on the gin for making me maudlin, but I know that's not true."

Brad laughed and she joined in, albeit through a fresh set of tears.

"I got you this," he said, taking out the gift-wrapped perfume he had bought in the duty free at Kennedy Airport. "It's meant to be a Christmas, New Year and 'Hello, I'm your long-lost son' present all rolled into one."

Beverly took the gift and sat bleary-eyed, looking at him.

"Oh, you shouldn't have," was all she could find to say.

"It's nothing much. I really didn't know what to get. I was going to give it to you on New Year's Day, but I thought now would be more appropriate."

"There really wasn't any need," she started and then gasped when she saw the bottle. "Brad. This is one of the most expensive lines. I couldn't even get Greg to buy me this."

"I hope you like it."

"Like it!" she exclaimed and gave him a big hug. They spent another half an hour together before saying a final farewell.

Beverly had told Greg to take the car home and she would get a taxi from the hotel. This meant she didn't pass the theatre on her way home, so was oblivious to the drama that was unfolding up the road.

Brad took his hire car back to the station where he was catching the ten thirty-five express to London. As the train pulled into platform one, he couldn't help overhearing a conversation between a station porter and the duty policeman.

"Yes, it seems they disturbed a burglar," said the policeman. "I don't know all the facts yet, but I think someone's dead."

"Really?" said the inquisitive porter.

Brad lifted his case into the first-class carriage as the porter continued his question. "And this was last night at the King's Theatre?"

Brad stopped in his tracks. Had he heard correctly? He turned to speak to the policeman, but the carriage door was already sliding closed.

A shrill whistle instructed the train to start for London.

"Is Mr Russell Craddick at home, madam?"

"I'm afraid not," said Hazel, rather taken aback at the sight of two official looking men on her doorstep at eight thirty in the morning.

"Detective Chief Inspector Carlyle and Detective Sergeant Randall." Both men produced their warrant cards for Hazel's inspection. "Where is your husband?"

"At the office. He went in early this morning." Hazel noticed the two police officers' glance at each other. "What's this all about?"

"We're investigating a death."

"Death?" There was more than a touch of anxiety in her voice.

"Perhaps if we could come in…"

"Of course, of course." She showed them into the lounge while nervously blurting out, "It's not one of the family, oh please don't let it be…"

"We don't think so," said Randall, trying to calm her.

"Does the name Barrie Stone mean anything to you?" asked Carlyle.

Hazel stared at him and slowly sank into an armchair.

"Yes. He's a builder. His company has done some work for the Council. Russell knows him very well."

"Do you know if they are involved in any business at the moment?"

"I've no idea. Russell hardly ever discusses his work with me." She answered Carlyle quickly before returning to the subject of the death. "It's not him, is it? It's not Barrie?"

In a solemn policeman's voice, Carlyle gave an

affirmative reply.

Hazel sat quite still. Relief that it wasn't one of her family showed visibly on her face and Carlyle proceeded with another question. "Is your husband in the habit of leaving for the office so early, Mrs Craddick?"

"No," Hazel replied tentatively. "Only he's been suffering with a sprained ankle for the past couple of days, so not spent much time at work. I expect things have piled up."

"Did you see your husband this morning?" Randall had taken over the questioning.

"No, he left before I got up. I was late home last night — a supper at my bridge club."

"And where was Mr Craddick last night?"

"Here. I left him nursing his ankle and when I got home, he was already asleep in bed."

"How long were you away from the house?" Carlyle resumed.

"I left at about a quarter to eight and was home around twelve thirty."

D S Randall, who had been making copious notes asked a final question. "And you've no idea whether your husband left the house during that time?"

"No," Hazel said. "I've not spoken to him since yesterday evening. He just left me a note this morning to say he was going to the office."

"Thank you, Mrs Craddick, you've been very helpful," said Carlyle, rising and moving to the door.

"Surely you don't think Russell had anything to do with Barrie's death?" Hazel now wanted answers.

Carlyle played the evasive investigators game. "We're just at the beginning of our enquiries. We need to talk to everyone connected with Mr Stone."

The two detectives said their goodbyes to an anxious Hazel and got into the car.

"To the Council offices, Randall," said Carlyle. "And make it quick."

***

Amelia had hardly slept. The evening's traumatic end had been a shock to her system and she had lain in bed tossing and turning, reliving the horror of seeing the blooded body and recalling the revelations that followed.

At around three thirty she finally drifted off into a disturbed sleep, only to wake up a few hours later with a start. It was still dark and she felt very disorientated.

In a dream, she had seen an image of Russell Craddick coming towards her with a depraved leer on his face and wielding a drainpipe. As he got closer, she observed there was something sticking out of the top of the drainpipe. A miniature head with a hideous expression, as though the rest of the body had been squeezed down the pipe.

Closer and closer Russell got, and then she heard his voice.

"You're going to get the same as Barrie. So is he…"

A crooked finger pointed to the miniature head and Amelia could plainly see it was Trevor. Now she was cowering under a large desk as the pipe came nearer and nearer. She tried to scream, but nothing came out. Her throat felt as though it was on fire and she pushed herself further and further back under the desk.

It was at that point that she woke herself up. Her heart was beating fast and she felt perspiration on her forehead. The bedside clock showed six fifteen.

The nightmare had left her with the sensation of being exhausted. But she was wide-awake, so decided to get up and make a strong cup of tea.

Sipping the hot beverage, Amelia carefully thought everything through. Detective Chief Inspector Carlyle had said he would be interviewing Craddick the next morning, but if her boss was party to the break in and knew about Barrie, he would try to destroy any evidence that linked himself with Barrie and the King's Theatre.

And that evidence was in the top left-hand drawer of Craddick's desk.

She shuddered as she recalled her nightmare.

I've got to get to the office early, she thought. Finishing her tea, she quickly made her way up stairs to shower and dress.

***

Russell was indeed intending to get rid of anything that could incriminate him. At seven fifty-five he was outside the Council House ringing the night security guard's bell.

"You're an eager beaver this morning, Mr Craddick," quipped the guard, as Russell pushed past him with an excuse of needing papers for an important meeting. He made his way as quickly as he could to his office and went straight to his desk.

Unlocking the top left-hand drawer, he extracted an armful of papers and files. Laying them on the table he sifted through them putting to one side all the ones he needed to destroy. He replaced what was safe to keep, locked the drawer and picked up the rest.

Moving swiftly out of the office he hurried along the corridor to the stairs and down to the floor below. A large room next to the stairs housed a number of printing machines, computers, faxes and most importantly for Russell, a shredder.

Switching on the power, he glanced at his watch. Ten past eight. People would be arriving anytime and he didn't want to be caught doing a job that his secretary would normally do.

The machine took in each page through the top and spewed out confetti sized pieces into a container.

Quarter past eight and still a lot of paper to get rid of.

Finally, the last page. Russell picked up the container of shredded paper and emptied it into a black disposal bag. He knew there was a shoot the cleaners used for waste paper that went straight to the incinerator. It was at the other end of the corridor.

Emerging from the print room, he listened for any sound from the ground floor below. The receptionist had just arrived and was flirting shamelessly with the security guard.

Russell lifted the black bag and started to hurry towards the disposal shoot. It was then that he felt another twinge in his chest. All this stress and strain was taking its toll and he promised himself, a few quiet days, as soon as he could possibly get away.

Pulling the metal hinged flap in the wall open, he flung the black bag into the shoot and listened as it rattled down to the basement.

Now there were more voices and someone was coming up the stairs. Russell darted into the first available room with a door that was unlocked and found himself surrounded by mops and cleaning equipment. In the small, dark room, the overpowering smell of floor polish made him gasp and almost choke.

He inched the door open and squinted at the figure climbing the stairs. Amelia Fothergill. That snake in the grass. That treacherous Mata Hari.

She hurried on up the second flight of stairs as he emerged from his hiding place.

More Council workers were now arriving as Russell casually walked along the corridor saying the occasional good morning to people that he recognised. He paused outside the men's toilet and then went inside, deciding to wait a few minutes before going back to his office.

Amelia flung open the door expecting to see Russell already there. She had been informed he was in by the receptionist and knew there was only one reason for his early arrival. Expecting to find him emptying his desk drawer, she took a deep breath and calmly began to go through the mail. But there was only one thought in her head. Where was the man?

***

"Bev, it's Trevor for you," Greg called to his wife who was still slumbering in bed.

"At this time?" She roused herself and sat up as her husband handed her the phone. "What's happened, has the theatre burned down?"

"Very nearly," said Trevor, on the other end of the line.

By the time he had finished telling her what happened after she and Brad had left them the previous night, Beverly was wide awake.

"How maddening to have missed it," she said. Trevor was a little taken aback at her taste for the macabre.

"Believe me you were well out of it. We all found the whole experience ghastly. Poor Amelia was very distraught."

"I'm sure you were there with a comforting word or two."

"Don't be flippant," snapped Trevor.

"I'm sorry." Beverly realised she had hit a nerve. "It must have been awful."

"The police have more investigating to do. Forensics closed the place last night, and have cordoned off the area around the trap door. but I've just been told we can continue with today's performances."

"Is there anything you want me to do?"

"No, just turn up and give a great performance."

"I'll do my best," said Beverly, pushing the bed sheets back. "What are you doing now?"

"I'm getting onto the press of course. Don't want to miss a publicity opportunity like this."

***

A game of cat and mouse was being played out in Russell's office. After washing his hands and face in cold water and taking a few minutes to calm down following his hasty visit to the shredder, Russell casually strolled in and said his usual curt "good morning" to Amelia.

She forced a smile, returned the greeting and prepared to follow him into his office to deal with the morning mail.

"We'll leave it for a few minutes, Miss Fothergill," he said. "I have some urgent calls to make."

"I'll bet you do," thought Amelia, as she sat back down at her desk. She too had a call to make, to her friend Elaine.

Russell sat at his desk and thought for a full two minutes. Had he covered his tracks? Was there anything left that could link him with Barrie and the proposed land deal?

No. He was sure the only documents remaining in his drawer were the original proposals for redeveloping the old fish paste factory site. Nothing about the King's Theatre.

The one thing he had to do now was find out what he could about Barrie. He lifted the receiver and dialled the Stone house.

"Hello?" An unfamiliar female voice answered.

"May I speak to Mr Stone?" said Russell, in as light a tone as he could muster.

"Oh!" Russell detected a slight catch in the voice. "You haven't heard the news then?"

At that point Russell knew that his worst fears were about to be realised. "News?" he asked.

"Mr Stone died last night. A terrible accident."

Russell was silent as the full impact of the words hit home. At length he spoke.

"Accident? How awful. Was it in his car?"

"Oh no," the voice sounded a little gossipier. "It was at the King's Theatre, of all places."

"The King's?" repeated Russell, innocently.

"Yes." The voice went on to graphically describe what she had heard about the events of the previous night.

Everything Russell had feared was true. Barrie had obviously been caught in the act of trying to set fire to the place and met an untimely end.

"Is Ann — Er, Mrs Stone there?"

"Yes, but she's asleep. I'm her sister, Pat. She called me late last night after the police arrived to break the news. They need her to go and identify the body later. It's all been terribly distressing for her. She nearly passed out, poor dear. I called the emergency doctor and he gave her a sedative. Said she would be out for a good twelve hours. They're coming back later to ask her some questions; the police that is. Of course, I shall be here for as long as Ann needs me."

She was chatting away non-stop when Russell tried to interrupt. "I wonder ..." But the sister ploughed on.

"We're very close, you know. Always have been. We tell each other everything; no secrets. Well, there shouldn't be secrets between sisters, should there?"

Russell tried again, more forcefully this time. "I wonder if I could leave a message for Mrs Stone?"

"Of course. I'll just get a pen."

The voice mercifully ceased for a few seconds while sister Patricia looked for something to write with. Russell needed to know if Barrie had said anything before he died. Anything that could incriminate him. His head was hurting through lack of sleep and constantly churning things over. Then the gossipy voice came back.

"Here I am. You can never find a pen when you want one, can you? Anyway, I've got one now, so who shall I say called?"

"Russell Craddick," he said, gritting his teeth. "I'll give you my mobile number in case I'm out of the office. Please ask her to call me the moment she wakes."

He gave her the number and before she could start another stream of verbal inanities, quickly said goodbye and put the phone down.

In the outer office, Amelia had just finished informing Elaine of the previous night's adventure.

"What an exciting life you lead," enthused her friend.

"Believe me, I could have done without last night," said Amelia, shuddering again at the thought of seeing Barrie Stone lying motionless at the bottom of the steps.

"How is Trevor taking all this?"

"Well of course he was shocked at the thought of someone trying to burn the theatre down, but he's got that old 'show must go on' spirit, so hopefully he'll get through it all. I'm going to call in at lunchtime. The police should have finished up by then."

"Now tell me," said Elaine. "Is this thing with Trevor getting serious?"

"I've only known him a few days."

"Yes, but in those few days you've practically lived in each other's company."

The internal call light on Amelia's phone began to flash, which gave her the perfect opportunity to cut short the probing questions from her inquisitive friend. "Elaine, I've got another call, so I shall have to go. I'll call you later. Bye." She pushed a button and the voice of the front desk receptionist came through.

"Miss Fothergill, there's a Detective Chief Inspector Carlyle in reception. He needs to talk to Mr Craddick."

"Please send him straight up," said Amelia. In anticipation of her boss being put through the third degree, she clasped her hands triumphantly above her head and spun herself round in her swivel chair.

A few moments later the door opened and in walked Carlyle, accompanied by the faithful D S Randall.

"Good morning, Miss Fothergill. I take it your boss is in."

"He is indeed, Detective Inspector. Shall I announce you?"

"Please. And while I'm in with him, Detective Sergeant Randall has a couple more questions to ask you."

"By all means. Anything to help." She lifted the receiver and buzzed Russell.

"I thought I said I didn't want to be disturbed," snapped the frustrated voice on the other end.

On hearing it, the two Detectives glanced at each other. Amelia noticed the glance, and with relish continued talking to her boss. "I have a Detective Chief Inspector Carlyle here who would like to speak to you on a matter of some urgency, Mr Craddick."

"Oh," said Russell, and in a much quieter voice added, "Very well, ask him to come in."

Amelia smiled at Carlyle and indicated he should proceed into Russell's office.

"Good morning, Inspector, what can I do for you?" said Russell, as Carlyle closed the door.

"It's Detective Chief Inspector," corrected Carlyle. "And I'm afraid I have some very bad news for you."

"If it's about Barrie Stone, I already know," said Russell, forcing a pained look on his face.

"Oh? How did you find out?"

"I've just phoned his house. Mrs Stone's sister informed me of last night's unfortunate incident. Barrie was due to meet me here early this morning. He rang yesterday and said he needed to speak to me as soon as possible. That's when we made the arrangement. When he didn't turn up, I rang to see what had happened to him."

Russell's carefully concocted story sounded as though he had learned a script by heart.

"I see," said Carlyle. "And you've no idea what he wanted to see you about?"

"No. Not at all."

"What was your relationship with Mr Stone?"

"He was both a friend and a business associate. I've known him for years, and his father before him."

"Ah yes, Victor Stone. I understand he met with rather an unfortunate end as well."

"Yes. I wonder if it runs in the family?" Russell's feeble attempt at a joke met with a granite like stare from the Chief Inspector.

"Were you and Mr Stone involved professionally at the present?"

"Only in so much as he was going to tender for the redevelopment of the old fish factory."

"What about the King's Theatre?"

Russell avoided the policeman's steely gaze and idly pushed a paper clip around his desk.

"Well, that's a long way off in the future," he said.

"And maybe not at all if the recent articles in the paper are anything to go by."

"Well, you know what they say — don't believe everything you read—"

"Isn't it true that you recently received a letter from the Department of Culture, Media and Sport, putting a halt on any development of the King's Theatre for the foreseeable future?"

Russell felt the first pang of a pain starting again in his chest.

"Well, yes… But…"

"And isn't it true that you had already drawn up plans with Barrie Stone to redevelop that site?"

"Now wait a minute," Russell demanded, rising from his seat. "Are you insinuating that I'm in any way involved with what's happened to him?"

D S Randall came into the office and silently showed a page of his notebook to his superior.

Carlyle continued with another question. "Mr Craddick, where were you last night between the hours of eight thirty and midnight?"

"At home. I had sprained my ankle and was resting it."

"Was anyone with you?"

"My wife until she went to her bridge club. I took a sleeping pill and went to bed before she got home. My foot was hurting me."

"And yet you managed to get up and get yourself to the office this morning before she woke."

"It was a lot better this morning, after a good night's rest."

Russell was aware of the two policemen scrutinising his every move and began to moderate his responses.

"What kind of a car do you drive, sir?" asked Randall.

"An Audi," said Russell, and confirmed the registration number.

"And are you sure you didn't drive it anywhere after eight o'clock last night?"

"I've already told you, I was at home all night." His breath was starting to come in shorter gasps and he clutched briefly at his chest.

"Only we've found fresh tyre tracks on land immediately behind the King's Theatre that match the tyres on your car," said Randall, deliberately.

"So what? There are plenty of other Audi cars in Seahaven."

"We can get forensics to check for any traces of the same type of earth embedded in the tread. And I believe there are CCTV cameras in that area."

Russell was now feeling the use of his legs beginning to desert him and held onto the desk.

"Also, sir, have you ever seen this before?"

D S Randall took out a small plastic forensics bag. It contained a piece of folded paper on which was drawn a crude diagram and some scribbled words. He laid it on the desk in front of Russell.

Russell dropped back into his chair staring at the paper. Pains were continually pounding his chest.

"It was found in the pocket of Mr Stone's trousers," said Carlyle. "It's a diagram of the backstage area of the King's Theatre — where we found Mr Stone."

"I've never seen it before in my life," said Russell, and pulled out a white handkerchief to mop his face with.

"Are you sure, sir?" asked Carlyle. "I have good reason to believe that is your handwriting."

"It's not. It's not," screamed Russell, as D S Randall opened the door.

"Oh, but it is, Mr Craddick." Amelia stood in the doorway with an air of impending victory surrounding her. "I have transcribed numerous memos in your handwriting and I would recognise it anywhere."

Russell hauled himself out of his chair for a second time. "What are you talking about? What's this all about?"

"Mr Craddick, would you please open your desk drawer and show me the contents?"

"Look here, I've had just about enough of this," protested Russell, swaying to and fro with perspiration now cascading down his face.

"I can get a warrant to have your desk and files searched if you don't co-operate."

"Go ahead then," said Russell, attempting a very cavalier manner. And, with keys shaking in his hand, he unlocked the drawer. "You'll find nothing out of the ordinary in there." He lifted out the contents and slammed them down onto the desk in front of Carlyle.

The pain was now raging and Russell plunged his hand into his coat pocket trying to locate his spray.

As DCI Carlyle looked through the pile of papers, Detective Sergeant Randall noticed Russell's condition.

"Are you all right, sir?" he asked, as Russell tried another pocket without success.

"Yes, yes," shouted Russell, waving a dismissive hand towards him.

It was then that Amelia delivered her trump card. Her coup de theatre.

"There were a lot more files than that, Detective Chief Inspector. Letters, drawings, projected costings. Everything connected with the redevelopment of the land on which the King's Theatre stands." She looked Russell square in the eye. "I saw them with my own eyes."

"How could you have seen them? I always keep that drawer locked," yelled Russell, with what little breath he had left.

Carlyle gradually stopped leafing through the contents of the drawer looked up at Russell. "Then you admit there were more files than this in the drawer?"

Russell's whole body shook from head to foot and again he clutched at his chest. He had failed to locate his spray, which, in his haste to leave home that morning, he had left in his other suit coat pocket.

"I... I..." The pains soared, stifling his words.

"Russell Craddick, I am arresting you on suspicion of conspiring to commit arson. Anything you say—" but Carlyle's official warning was cut short. Russell moved around his desk in a foolish attempt to get away, only to find D S Randall blocking his exit. He looked at each one of them and then made a lunge at Amelia who stood her ground, a triumphant look of defiance on her face.

"You meddling busybody. You frustrated old harpy," he screamed with all the energy he could muster. "I'll kill you!"

In one quick move Carlyle and Randall grabbed each of Russell's arms and thrust him onto a chair beside the desk. Still he continued ranting, spitting venomous words in his secretary's direction. "You bitch, you clapped out old whore..." He suddenly stopped as a gigantic pain surged through his body, snatching eagerly at his penultimate breath.

Russell Craddick slumped back in the chair, his eyes wide open and a hideously contorted expression on his face. He was staring through the large office window at the outline of the King's Theatre, still standing proud and defiant in the distance.

It was the last thing he saw before joining his partner in crime in Paradise — or possibly Purgatory.

SCENE SEVEN
THURSDAY, JANUARY 6TH (CONTINUED) – FRIDAY, JANUARY 14TH

A good portion of that evening's Seahaven Courier carried the story of what had happened over the previous forty-eight hours.

Russell finally achieved front-page notoriety as his nefarious dealings were dramatically emblazoned in large headlines. Numerous pictures of him and Barrie Stone covered a centre spread, and any opportunity to condemn and denounce his unethical practices were seized on and reported in meticulous detail by Jack Shepperton.

Detective Chief Inspector Carlyle and Detective Sergeant Randall paid a second visit to Hazel to break the news. They informed her they would need to return at some time to go over Russell's papers. To their surprise she gave them permission to start straight away.

"Are you sure, Mrs Craddick?" said Carlyle. "We can easily come back tomorrow.

"I'd rather you took everything away that you need," Hazel said, showing them into Russell's study. "I'm sure what you want is in that desk."

She pointed to a large polished writing desk, which Carlyle found to be locked.

"Don't worry, I've got a spare key," Hazel told them.

Carlyle was sure he detected a wry smile on her lips. "Not exactly the grieving widow, is she, Randall?" he said, when Hazel had left the room.

"It'll probably hit her later," replied Randall. "Delayed shock and all that."

Hazel returned with a little key that fitted the roll top and all the drawers of the desk. "Help yourself Detective Inspector. I shall be in the lounge, my son has just arrived."

The two policemen spent the next half hour sifting through the contents of the desk. Many more incriminating pieces of evidence were found confirming nearly everything Amelia had told them the previous night.

Robert had dashed to his mother's house as soon as he received a call from her.

"I just don't know what to say."

"What is there to say? I always knew Russell played a dangerous game, getting back handers on contracts and doing deals with some very unsavoury characters. I expected his dealings to catch up with him one day. It's just a bit of a shock that it's happened so soon."

They talked about funeral arrangements and Robert offered to break the news to his stepsister.

"No, I ought to do it. It will hit her very hard. She was very fond of her father."

Holding on to Robert's hand, Hazel rang Lisa. It was then that she broke down. Not as a result of losing her husband, but of the devastating effect it had on her unsuspecting daughter.

After the phone call, during which arrangements were made for Lisa to drive over the next day, Carlyle and Randall returned.

"Thank you for your help, Mrs Craddick," said Carlyle,

and then saw Robert. "Hello again, sir."

"Do you two know each other?" said Hazel.

"It's a long story mother, I'll tell you later."

Robert saw the policemen out.

"Thank you for not saying anything about last night," he said to Carlyle. "I've yet to tell my mother about my connection with the King's."

"I quite understand," replied Carlyle, and added, "I thought she was holding up pretty well, but it seems to have finally hit her. It's a good thing you're around, sir."

Robert watched the unmarked police car drive away before returning to the house.

***

Large screens and yellow police tape surrounded the upstage area, shielding the trap door. The police forensic team had completed their initial investigation and given permission for the production to continue.

Hardly anyone's mind was on the impending matinee performance, either backstage or front of house. The entire company and staff had assembled quite early, eager to acquaint themselves with the facts of the audacious break in. Giving a blow-by-blow account of the whole proceedings in the most graphic and theatrical manner, was Max Pendleton. Realising full well that the press would be swarming all over the place, he had arrived at the theatre in plenty of time to make sure he featured prominently in any picture.

"You would all be standing in a mass of smouldering rubble if I hadn't acted with speed and dexterity in apprehending the monstrous villain." he boasted.

"I thought you bumped into him in the dark?" queried Willie Waters.

"Yes, and he fell down the steps," said Carl.

"Cracking his head open," Alex finished off the description of the fatal scene.

"Well, yes," mumbled Max, before his voice rose again to majestic heights. "But it was my presence that foiled his dastardly plan."

"And we'll all be eternally grateful, Max," said Trevor, who witnessed the tail end of the old actor's oration. "But we do have a show to perform for an eager audience. So, come along, let us focus on comedy and not tragedy this afternoon."

Everyone reluctantly dispersed and went to their respective dressing rooms or back to their posts at the front of the house.

Beverly told Gavin that Brad had called her from London having overheard the conversation at the station. Gavin in return revealed the connection between Robert and Russell.

"The plot gets wilder," she exclaimed.

"There was no love lost between them," said Gavin. "Craddick was a right rotten egg by all accounts. Robert's mother is well rid of the bastard."

"And she knew nothing of Craddick's involvement with Barrie Stone's wife?"

"I don't think so. Robert's with her now, so no doubt I'll hear more later. He couldn't say too much on the phone, but apparently the police have taken quite a lot of papers from the house."

Any more gossip about the case was cut short by Stan announcing over the PA, that beginners were requested to stand by, for Act One.

***

The newspaper headlines continued to report more of the story over the next few days. The demand for pantomime tickets was steadily growing due to the extra publicity, and someone even suggested they do backstage tours of the grisly scene.

Two funerals were hastily arranged by the Town Council in order to quell the continual damaging headlines and hopefully "bury" the story. Barrie Stone's funeral took place the following Thursday with a short service and cremation afterwards. Russell's was the next morning.

It was held at St Barnabas Church of England, located a mile from the Council offices, and was the third time Russell had been through the doors. The previous two were his first wedding and his daughter's Christening.

The day dawned a miserable grey with a few flurries of snow that disintegrated in the salt sea air. Considering the adverse publicity there was quite a reasonable turn out in the congregation, mainly from the Council and the golf club.

Robert escorted Hazel into the church, with Lisa and her husband following. Amelia felt she ought to attend out of duty and Trevor insisted on accompanying her.

"I don't know why you want to waste your time," Delphina had said. "Unless it's to make sure the evil sod isn't going to jump out of the coffin and wreak more havoc."

Gavin joined them in a pew near the rear of the church.

"I feel a bit of a hypocrite," he whispered, as the service started. "I'm driving Robert's car, as he had to go in the hearse with his mother. He asked me to take it to the house afterwards, but I don't think I'm ready to meet the family just yet."

The vicar started to speak about Russell from prompt cards compiled by Lisa and Hazel. As he only knew the deceased by reputation, his eulogy was nothing if not bland in tone — and mercifully for all concerned, short.

Rain started to fall quite heavily as they all left the church. About half of the congregation gathered around the family plot to watch the coffin lowered into the ground; and less than that accepted an invitation back to the Craddick house for tea and a light buffet.

Only two people were weeping as the proceedings came to an end. Russell's daughter and his mistress. Ann Stone stood slightly apart from the others, half-hidden under a large umbrella.

Hazel crossed the churchyard to thank Ann Stone for coming and apologise for not attending Barrie's funeral.

"I understand perfectly," Ann said, and politely declined an invitation back to the house.

"To lose a husband is bad enough, but a lover as well," said Gavin, as Ann Stone hurried out of the graveyard.

Back at the house, the few people who had turned up sat in twos and threes drinking tea and speaking in hushed tones. Finally, Hazel walked into the lounge and flashed a smile at the assembled group of family and friends.

"I'm sure we could all do with something a little stronger than tea," she announced, and pulled open the drinks" cabinet. "Who's going to join me in a large sherry?"

Robert and Lisa were slightly taken aback at her light hearted attitude, but after glasses were filled and people saw how well Hazel was coping, the atmosphere took on the feel of a party more than a wake.

After the last guest had offered their condolences and left,

Lisa turned to her mother.

"Are you sure you're going to be all right on your own?"

"Of course, darling. Anyway, I won't be on my own."

"What do you mean?"

"Well, Robert's only down the road; and I've still got the bridge club."

"I think you are bearing up remarkably well," said Lisa, near to tears again.

"Life has to go on, you know, said Hazel. "Besides, it's only what your father would have wanted. He lived life to the full and I'm sure he'd expect me to do the same." If there was more than a little irony in her voice, Lisa hadn't detected it.

"You are wonderful," said her daughter, giving her a big hug. "I'll ring you when we get home."

"Come and stay for a few days any time you want to," called Tim through the open car window.

"Thank you. Perhaps when I've sorted things out here. I'd like to spend some time with my grandchildren."

Robert joined his mother in waving them off and then, putting an arm around her, escorted her back into the house.

Gavin had kept himself out of the way whilst the post funeral gathering had taken place. He busied himself clearing up the glasses, cups and plates, and was in the kitchen when Robert and Hazel returned to the lounge.

"Who is that washing up?" said Hazel, as she heard crockery being moved about.

"Just a friend of mine who kindly drove my car."

"He doesn't need to do all that." She made a move towards the kitchen.

"He's all right," said Robert. "Come and sit down, there's something I've got to tell you."

Hazel turned and joined her son on the couch.

"I couldn't say anything while my stepfather..." The word stuck in his throat. "Was still alive. You know what I thought of him and what he thought of me. He would have been impossible to live with if I'd told you both what I'm going to tell you now."

Usually, Robert was completely articulate and fluent when giving professional advice or explaining a business plan, but now his tongue was in a hundred knots.

"It's just that — well, my life has been a bit different."

The tiniest hint of a smile began to appear on Hazel's lips as she gently laid a hand on top of her son's.

"What you are trying to tell me is that you're gay."

Robert was momentarily stunned. Stuttering slightly as he regained the power of speech, he answered, "Well, er... yes."

"And I assume that industrious young man in the kitchen is more than just a *"friend"*."

"Erm, yes. But... Well, how did you..."

Hazel's face now had a radiant smile as she looked at her beloved son. "Darling, a mother knows."

Robert flopped back into the plush cushions staring at her. "I can't believe this. I've wanted to talk to you for so long."

"You were quite right about Russell. He would never have coped with you coming out. You did the right thing."

"I didn't care about me. It was you. I was so afraid he would give you a hard time." He sat back up straight and took her hands. "My timing hasn't been the best. Today of all days."

"You're timing is perfect. Now, hadn't you better get that young man out of that kitchen sink and introduce me?"

Mother and son embraced. Their close bond was now even stronger. Still holding each other's hand, their emotionally tear-stained faces were smiling. The kitchen door opened slightly and Gavin saw two people in anything but a funereal mood.

"Is everything all right?" he asked tentatively.

"Could be better," said Hazel, standing up and holding a hand out to Gavin. "Hello, I'm Hazel."

***

"You'll never believe what happened," said Gavin to Beverly as they sat together in her dressing room before the evening performance.

"At the funeral?"

"No, afterwards."

Gavin related how indifferent Hazel had seemed over her husband's passing and how genuinely warm she had been about his and Robert's relationship.

"She really is a lovely woman. We got on like a house on fire."

"Don't mention fire around here," giggled Beverly.

The half-hour call came over the PA and she turned to the mirror and continued putting on her make-up. "Have you decided what you are going to do when the run ends on Saturday?" she asked him.

"We've not had much time to talk about it," said Gavin, with a little hesitation creeping into his voice. "These past few weeks have been so wonderful, certain other things excepted. I'm dreading it all coming to an abrupt end."

"I'm sure if you sit quietly and discuss it, something can be worked out."

"I do hope so."

Beverly looked at his reflection in her mirror. Such a ferocious looking make-up hiding such a puppy dog expression.

***

Robert had dropped Gavin off at the theatre and, at his mother's request, returned to the house.

"Thank you for coming back," Hazel said, pouring them both a drink. "You may have thought it a little odd today that I didn't react with as much emotion as people might have expected."

"How anyone could weep over him, I don't know."

"Your sister did," said Hazel. "She will miss Russell very much."

"Yes, I'm sorry. I shouldn't have said that."

"I know you didn't get on with him, but Lisa loved him and he adored her. And I have to say he always looked after me."

"But mother, you don't know what he got up to. What he did behind your back."

"You mean the affairs?"

Robert looked at her with surprise.

"I knew all right. I've known about him carrying on with Ann Stone for years."

For the second time that day Robert stared open mouthed at his mother.

"I'm amazed," he said. "I only found out recently. But why didn't you do something about it?"

"For a number of reasons. One, as I said Russell always looked after me very comfortably. And two, if all sorts of sordid details came out, Lisa would have been devastated. I didn't want that. She has such a happy normal life with Tim and the children, I didn't want anything to upset that."

"But you shouldn't have had to put up with his philandering."

"It was better than having a scandal with all the lurid facts reported in the paper. And I don't want you telling Lisa. What she doesn't know won't hurt her. Let her remember her father with dignity and love. Promise me, Robert."

"Of course. I promise. But I still don't know why you stayed with him."

"I had my reasons." Hazel opened her handbag and took out what looked like a bank statement. "Take a look at that," she said, handing Robert the paper.

He studied it with incredulity written all over his face. It was indeed a bank statement from Unity Trust Bank, Douglas, Isle of Man. The account was in the name of Delancey Holdings and the balance stood at £682,000. It was something the police had somehow overlooked.

"What does all this mean?" he finally asked his mother.

"It's no secret that Russell operated some very shady deals over the years with contractors and developers. He would secure contracts for buildings — usually apartments or houses — on land the Council was selling off. Of course, there would be generous back handers and he needed somewhere to deposit the money where it couldn't be found by the Inland Revenue."

"But that's virtually impossible," said Robert. "I should know."

"Nowadays yes," replied Hazel. "But fifteen years ago, it was much easier"

"Fifteen years?"

"It was old man Stone who set the whole thing up. He already had a similar offshore account in Cayman Islands and gave Russell all the contacts he needed. Stone's back-handers were a big contributor to Delancey Holdings in the early years. After he died, Barrie, and a number of other contractors, continued with the rather disreputable tradition."

"But how come he told you about it?"

"Because, as an added precaution, he thought it best to put the account in my name. Actually, my maiden name. Delancey. I, of course, didn't know where the money was coming from originally. Russell told me it was an investment for us when he retired. If anything happened to him, it would come to me with no questions asked. Little did he think his words would come true so soon."

"But you must have suspected something was wrong."

"Not at first. He blinded me with all sorts of talk about savings and pension funds, and I believed him. Why not? It was only some years later when I found by accident a statement with Delancey Holdings on, that I became suspicious. Over a period of time, and with the aid of a key to his study desk that I'd had copied, I found out what Russell was up to. I also found a small pocket book with names, addresses and telephone numbers in. That's when I discovered about the other women."

"So, you've known what he's been up to all along?"

"And continued to play the loving, devoted wife, because I knew that seventy miles across the Irish Sea there was a considerable reward waiting."

"Six hundred and eighty-two thousand. But why didn't you get out before?"

"I've told you why. Besides, why cut off the supply

prematurely?"

"Mother." Robert looked at Hazel with amazement and more than a little admiration. "I still don't know how you could live with him for all these years knowing he was sleeping around."

There was a look of smug satisfaction on his mother's face.

"He wasn't the only one."

"What?"

"I knew the love had gone out of our marriage years ago. I was hurt and angry at first, then I discovered bridge."

"Bridge? How did that help?"

"When I joined the club, I was partnered with a very nice man who just happened to be a bachelor. By a strange coincidence his name was Bridge, Marcus Bridge. Well, darling, to cut a long story short, we've remained partners ever since — in more than one sense of the word. So, you see I never lied to your stepfather. When I said I was going to Bridge, that's exactly where I was going."

Robert was flabbergasted. "Mother I can't believe today. I thought I was the one with the secret, but you've trumped my hand."

They both started to laugh again, and neither of them felt guilty for doing so.

"Are you happy with this Marcus Bridge? He certainly seems good for you."

Hazel got up from the couch to replenish their glasses and said quiet casually to her son. "I believe the modern phrase is 'he's a good fuck'."

FINALE
SATURDAY, JANUARY 15TH – TUESDAY, DECEMBER 19TH

The final performance of the King's Theatre pantomime had all the trappings of a gala occasion.

Because of the notoriety surrounding the stories of the theatre, the Seahaven Council and the foiled arson attack, the Nation's press was out in force. TV camera crews from all major stations were also covering the events unfolding in the South Coast town and Brad had made sure his company got a full U S exclusive.

The last week's performances were practically sold out. Demand for tickets was so great that the usually deserted upper circle was hastily cleaned and opened.

Delphina, dressed to the nines, was in her box, this time sharing it with Trevor and Amelia. Robert escorted his mother, Greg and Brad, who had returned from London the day before, to the house seats in the front row of the Grand Circle.

The performance went like a dream; the atmosphere charged with enough electricity to light up the whole town. Whoops and cheers greeted the numerous curtain-calls at the end, and Trevor was coerced into joining the company on stage and received a standing ovation.

He gave a brief curtain speech thanking everyone for their whole-hearted support, and announced that the King's Theatre had received a long overdue preservation order, and that the Council had generously offered to fund further improvements to the building.

The final curtain fell after which a party was held in the lounge bar of the Grand Circle.

Elaine, who had been personally invited by Trevor in recognition of her assistance in helping save the theatre, rushed up to Amelia as she entered the lounge.

"You looked like royalty up there in the box," she said, giving Amelia a kiss on the cheek. "And I must say, Trevor cuts a very dashing figure sitting beside you."

"I thought so, too," said Amelia, who was looking particularly radiant in a new evening gown bought especially for the occasion.

Usually after the last night of a production everyone in the cast leaves for their various homes, but not this time. The entire company stayed to enjoy the celebrations, which continued in full swing well into the early hours of the next morning.

***

The months following that momentous milestone in the chequered history of the King's Theatre were packed with excitement for everyone concerned.

Robert got to meet Hazel's mysterious Mr Marcus Bridge, who turned out to be a most charming man.

"He's obviously besotted with mother," he told Gavin. "And dotes on her. They've decided to go on a world cruise, and mother's paying for it all."

Gavin registered a look of surprise. "Your stepfather must

have left her well off."

"Oh, she'll be able to manage," said Robert, thinking of a certain bank account.

They were sitting on the balcony of Robert's apartment overlooking the Marina. It was the first warm day of the year and the sun glinted off the calm green ocean. Its gentle motion effortlessly rocked the numerous small crafts moored at the quayside.

Gavin had just arrived from filming the first three episodes of the aborted TV series. A week off meant that he could drive down from Manchester for a few days by the sea. Robert had spent a couple of weekends with him in the northern city, but this was their first time alone without interruptions since the panto finished.

Knowing that their relationship would always have to cope with the irregularities of Gavin's profession, they had done as Beverly had suggested and talked the situation through at great length. Realising that what they had was worth preserving, they saw no reason to change a thing.

"Have you seen anything of Beverly or our esteemed director?" Gavin asked, as he sipped a perfectly prepared gin and tonic.

"As a matter of fact, I have. Brad was over from the States again last week and we all had dinner at Beverly and Greg's. Trevor was there — with Amelia."

"So, it's still on then?"

"Very much so. And I have some further news on that subject," said Robert, tantalisingly.

Gavin put down his glass and turned his attention from the sunbathers on the beach below. "Don't tell me…"

"They have announced their engagement."

"That was sudden. Mind you, neither of them can afford

to wait much longer."

"Now who's being a bitch?" said Robert, smiling and waving an accusing finger in Gavin's direction.

***

Amelia was at her desk in the Council offices. Her new boss — an extremely likeable man by the name of Daniel Norris — had insisted she remain as his personal secretary and had found her knowledge and efficiency invaluable during his first few months in the job.

Clearing up the mess left by Russell's abrupt departure hadn't been easy, but things were moving smoothly now, both at work and in Amelia's private life.

The phone rang.

"Good morning, Daniel Norris's office."

"Good morning, Miss Fothergill, I wish to book an appointment with you on August 26th at 11.30."

"Trevor," she said, laughing at the sound of his very official sounding voice. "What are you talking about?"

"I've just had a call from the vicar of St. Barnabas and he has a cancellation on that day, so how would you like to become Mrs Trevor Curtis-Smyth in church instead of a registry office?"

"Oh, yes, Trevor," she shouted. Her hand flew to her chest as she gulped a breath in excitement. The response to Trevor's suggestion was so loud that her new boss opened his door to check if everything was all right.

"Congratulations," Daniel Norris said, on hearing the news. "I'm very happy for you." And he headed across to her desk and gave her a kiss on the cheek. Something her previous boss would never have done. Nor would she have wanted him to.

***

The King's Theatre was rarely out of the news during the first year of the new century.

As well as a further refurbishment programme with Local and Arts Council funding, the theatre had been attracting a number of touring companies, eager to cash in on the publicity generated over the Christmas period.

This had attracted much larger audiences who wanted to see TV personalities live on stage. Interest was also heightened all over Great Britain by an announcement that in the spring of the following year, the King's Theatre would host an annual drama festival. This would bring in the much-needed tourists to the town — ironically, something Russell had hoped to achieve by demolishing the building.

Brad's next return to his homeland shores was to bring the news that an idea of his had been taken up by International Television and Films Incorporated. It was to make a documentary on various listed buildings by known architects in the British Isles and the United States. It was to be a joint venture by his company and a British one, and would receive worldwide distribution. The King's Theatre would be the first programme of the series.

On that occasion he stayed with Beverly and Greg who hosted yet another of their famous parties to celebrate the news. A few days later they were all at another celebration.

The August wedding of Trevor and Amelia was a production in itself. Delphina had taken it upon herself to act as wedding planner and director of the entire day. The guest list included as many of the cast from the pantomime who were "resting", as well as friends and relations.

Amelia was a radiant bride and Trevor suffered more nerves than he had done on any opening night. Greg was his best man and Beverly and Elaine were Amelia's Matrons of Honour. The reception was held — where else? — at the King's Theatre.

Gavin, who had just finished filming his TV series, returned to Seahaven for the wedding. The next day he and Robert left with Brad for their promised holiday in New York. The newlyweds were also on the flight, as were Beverly and Greg.

Trevor and Amelia intended to do a whistle stop tour of the Eastern Seaboard, while Brad arranged a long overdue meeting between his adoptive parents and his mother.

*****

The year ended as it had begun, with the King's Theatre annual pantomime. This time it was "Cinderella", with no flimsy scenery, precarious cave scenes or flying carpets. Instead, there was a sparkling, brand-new set and a stunning array of costumes.

Beverly had decided to hang up her tights and tunic, but after a tremendous amount of cajoling from Trevor and even some letters to the paper, she agreed to do just one more season. No thigh-slapping this time. She took on the role of the Fairy Godmother, a part she felt very at home in.

Gavin also agreed to return, much to the delight of everyone, especially Robert. He was given the role of Prince Charming which involved him singing most of the songs. His lyrical tenor voice came to the attention of a number of West End producers; giving him the hope that future career prospects looked very promising.

The threat of an early evening snowfall had receded as the opening night audience made its way into the theatre. Backstage there was the usual last-minute panic going on as Stan gave the half-hour call. Delphina had done her "break a leg" rounds and taken up her usual position in the box, gazing regally down at the audience.

Across the road, Trevor stood with his arms round his wife. They were looking at the lights illuminating the brand-new sign over the entrance to the King's Theatre.

"Who would have thought a year ago we'd be standing here like this?" he said, giving her a squeeze.

"Come on, we don't want to be late for your opening night," Amelia said, beaming up at him. They entered the foyer and were greeted by a bevy of well-wishers as the three-minute bell rang out requesting everyone to take their seats.

Trevor pulled one of the plush double doors that opened into the stalls. "After you, Mrs Curtis-Smyth," he said.

Amelia walked through and was momentarily separated from Trevor as more friends gathered around him. Anxiously looking across at her, he received a smile and a nod, indicating she was fine.

For a moment, before taking their seats, Amelia stood against the back wall and looked around the packed auditorium. Taking in the sights and sounds of excitement and anticipation, her mind flashed back to that time in her childhood when she had stood in the same place with her Grandfather, all those years ago.

CURTAIN

Printed in Great Britain
by Amazon